Within The Precincts

Vol. I

by

Oliphant

Double9 BOOKS

Within The Precincts
Vol. I
by Oliphant

ISBN: 978-93-71130-11-0

Published by

DOUBLE 9 BOOKS
2/13-B, Ansari Road
Daryaganj, New Delhi – 110002
info@double9books.com
www.double9books.com
Tel. 011-40042856

ABOUT THE AUTHOR

Margaret Oliphant was a Scottish author and historical writer who usually wrote under the name Mrs. Oliphant. She was born Margaret Oliphant Wilson on April 4, 1828, and died on June 20, 1897. She writes "domestic realism, the historical novel, and tales of the supernatural" as her short stories. Margaret Oliphant was born in Wallyford, near Musselburgh, East Lothian. She was the only daughter and youngest child still living of Margaret Oliphant (c. 1789–17 September 1854) and Francis W. Wilson, a clerk. We lived in Lasswade, Glasgow, and Liverpool when she was a child. In Wallyford, a street called Oliphant Gardens is named after her. As a girl, she was always trying new things with writing. Passages in the Life of Mrs. Margaret Maitland, her first book, came out in 1849. This was about the mostly successful Scottish Free Church movement, which was something her folks agreed with. Next came Caleb Field in 1851, the same year she met publisher William Blackwood in Edinburgh and was asked to write for Blackwood's Magazine. She did so for the rest of her life and wrote over 100 articles, including one that criticized Arthur Dimmesdale in Nathaniel Hawthorne's "The Scarlet Letter".

CONTENTS

CHAPTER I
ST. MICHAEL'S

The Abbey Church of St. Michael's stands on a low hill in a flat and fertile country. The holy places which are sacred to the great archangel seem to settle naturally upon a mount; and this, one of the noblest structures consecrated under his name, had all the effect of a very high elevation—so wide-spreading was the landscape round, so vast the sweep of plain, fields, and woods, great parks and commons, and gleaming white villages like ships at sea, which could be seen from its walls and terraces. Though the settlement was ecclesiastical, the place had been walled and defensible in the days when danger threatened wealth whatever form it assumed. Danger, however, had long been far from the thoughts of the dignified corporation which held its reverend court upon the hill. The Abbey was as splendid as any cathedral, and possessed a dean and chapter, though no bishop. It was of Late Gothic, perpendicular and magnificent; and the walls and towers which still surrounded it, and even the old houses within the precincts, were older still than the Abbey, and could have furnished many "bits" to make the heart of a mediæval architect glad. The very turf which filled the quadrangle and clothed the slope of the Dean's Walk was a production of centuries; the Chapter House was full of historical documents, and the library of rare books; and there were antiquarian fanatics who protested that the wealthy livings belonging to the Abbey, and its old endowments, were the least of its riches. Nor was this establishment on the hill confined to ecclesiastical interests only. The beautiful church was the chapel of an order of knighthood, and opposite to it—forming an integral part of the pile of buildings—was a line of small ancient houses, forming a kind of screen and inner wall of defence to the sacred citadel, which were the lodges of a supplementary order of pensioners—Chevaliers of St. Michael—which at the time of the foundation had given such a balance, as the Middle Ages loved, of Christian charity and help, to the splendour and braggadocio of the more glorious knights. Thus the little community which inhabited this noble old pile of buildings was varied and composite. The highest official in it was the costly and aristocratic Dean, the lowest the lay clerks, who were housed humbly in the shadow of the church in a little cloister of their own, and who daily filled the Abbey with the noblest music. The Deanery was close to the Abbey, and embraced in its irregular group of roofs the great tower, which showed for miles round, with its lighted windows, rising up into the night. The canons' houses, if not equally fine, were still great old houses, standing on the edge of the hill, their walls rising straight from the green slopes dotted with trees, round the foot of which a little red-roofed town had gathered; and the Abbey itself stood between those stately habitations and the humbler lodges of the Chevaliers, which shut off the lower level of sloping bank on the other side. The Dean himself was of a great family, and belonged not only to the nobility, but, higher still, to the most select circles of fashion, and had a noble wife and such a position in society as many a bishop envied; and among his canons were men not only of family, but possessed of some mild links of connection with the worlds of learning and scholarship,—even it was said that one had writ a book in days when books were not so common. The minor canons were of humbler degree; they formed the link between gods and men, so to speak—between the Olympus of the Chapter and the common secular sphere below. We will not deceive the reader nor buoy him up with hopes that this history concerns the lofty fortunes of the members of that sacred and superior class. To no such distinction can these humble pages aspire; our office is of a lowlier kind. On Olympus the doings are all splendid, if not, as old chronicles tell, much wiser than beneath, amid the humbler haunts of men. All that we can do is to tell how these higher circles looked, to eyes gazing keenly upon them from the mullioned windows which gave a subdued light to the little rooms of the Chevaliers' lodges on the southern side of St. Michael's Hill.

These lodges were two storeys in height, with small rooms and very solid masonry, little gardens in front of them, and a tower at each end. Many creeping plants clung about the old walls, and especially there were clouds of Virginia creeper which made them glorious in autumn. It was, however, on a summer afternoon, at the time this history begins, that Lottie Despard—the only daughter of Captain Despard, a Chevalier not very long appointed to that office—sat, with her head out through the open window, framed between the mullions, watching the broad slope of the Dean's Walk which lay between her and the church, and led to the Deanery and the heights beyond. The Deanery was at this moment the most important place in the world, not only to Lottie, but to many other spectators who thronged the slope beneath her window. For this day a great event had happened in St. Michael's. The Dean's only daughter, Augusta Huntington, had been married that morning with all the pomp imaginable. It had been like a royal wedding, sumptuous in ritual, in music, and fine company; and now, after taking a little repose during the time which the wedding-party spent at breakfast, the Abbey precincts were beginning to fill again with gazing groups, and all the people within were coming to their windows to see the bride and bridegroom go away.

Lottie Despard was beyond all comparison the prettiest, and she was also the youngest, of all the ladies in the lodges. She was of Irish descent, and she had the whiteness of skin, the blackness of abundant hair, the deep blue eyes that so often go with Milesian blood. Such eyelashes had never been seen at St. Michael's; indeed, they had never been seen anywhere "out of Mrs. Jarley's waxworks!" some ill-natured critics said. Sometimes, when Lottie was specially pale or weary, they seemed to overshadow her face; but she was neither weary nor pale at this particular moment. She was in great excitement, on the contrary, and flushed with expectation. Though she was only the daughter of a poor Chevalier, Lottie had advantages which separated her from the rest of that little company. Her father was of good family, a point on which she insisted strenuously; and she herself was the possessor of a beautiful voice. The former particular would not have been of much advantage to her, for what was the Despards' old and faded quality to the great people at St. Michael's? But a voice is a different matter; and there had arisen between Miss Huntington and the Chevalier's daughter a kind of intimacy very flattering (the neighbours thought) to Lottie. They had sung together so much and seen so much of each other, that the lodges expected nothing less than that Lottie would have been asked to the wedding, or even—greater honour still!—to be a bridesmaid; and Lottie herself had been wounded and disappointed beyond measure when she found herself left entirely out. But there was still the possibility that the bride might show she had not forgotten her humble friend altogether; and it was for this that Lottie was waiting so anxiously as the time of departure approached. A word, a sign, a wave of the hand surely would be vouchsafed to her as the carriage passed. Her heart was beating loudly as she leant out—a pretty sight to see from without, for the window was framed in luxuriant wreaths of green, with trailing tendrils of the young delicate leaves which in autumn flamed like scarlet flowers against the wall. The people who were gathering on the road below gave many a look at her. And, though the young ladies from the shops, who had got half-an-hour's leave to see how their handiwork looked in the bride's travelling-dress, were deeply sensible of the fact that a poor Chevalier's daughter was not much richer than themselves, yet they could not help looking and envying Lottie, if only for the window at which she could sit in comfort and see everything that went on, instead of standing in the sun as they had to do. They forgot her, however, and everything else as the carriage drove up to the Deanery to take the bridal pair away. The Dean's daughter was so much the princess of the community that a compromise had been made between popularity and decorum; and it was in a carriage partially open, that an admiring people might behold her as she passed, that she was to drive away. There was the usual long waiting at the door while the farewells were made, during which time the outside world looked on respectfully; and then, with a crowd of "good-byes" thrown after her, and a few—but only a very few, for the Deanery was nothing if not decorous—white satin slippers, and a prance and dash of the impatient horses, and a flourish of the coachman's whip, and a parting gleam of the wedding favour on his breast, the bridal pair rolled rapidly past, and all was over. How quickly they went, everybody said, and how well she looked; and how well that brown dress looked, though it had been thought rather dowdy for such an occasion; and the feather in the hat, how well it matched, about which there had been so much trouble! Some, who had the time, paused to see the wedding guests disperse, and catch other beatific glimpses of fine bonnets and gay dresses; but most of the spectators, after this last and crowning point of the performance, streamed down the slope and out at the great gateway, and were seen no more.

Lottie drew in her head from the window the moment the carriage passed. She grew red when other people grew pale, being pale by nature; and her face was crimson as she withdrew it from the opening, and came in again to the little room in which most of her life was spent. Her lips were closed very tight, her soft forehead contracted; the fire in her blue eyes, gleaming with anger and disappointment, was (most unwillingly) quenched in tears. She clasped her hands together with a vehement clasp. "It would have cost so little to give a look!" she cried; then bit her lips and clenched her hands and stamped her foot upon the floor, in a forlorn but vigorous effort to restrain her tears.

"What does it matter to you?" said a tall young fellow, sufficiently like Lottie to prove himself her brother, who had looked out lazily over her head while the carriage was passing. He had his hands in his pockets and a slouching gait generally, and looked too big for the little room. She had almost pushed against him in her rapid movement, for his movements were never rapid; and he had not had time to take one hand out of his pocket before she flashed round upon him with two red spots on her cheeks and fury in her heart.

"What does it matter? Oh, nothing! nothing!" cried Lottie. "Why should anything matter? It only shows me a little more, a very little more, how cold the world is, and that nobody has a heart!"

"Few people have very much, I suppose," said the young man; "at least, so the governor says. But what good or harm could it do you to have a parting sign from *her*? I knew she would never give it you. I knew she would be thinking of nobody but herself—"

"What did you know about it?" cried the girl. "You were never a friend of hers! you were never begged and prayed to go and sing at the Deanery! she never came down the Abbey Hill to look for you! But me she has done all that for; and when I thought just for once she would let everybody see that Lottie Despard was a friend—Oh, Law, for the love of Heaven, go and work at something, and don't stand there staring at me!"

"What am I to work at?" said the young man, with a yawn. "It's past working hours; besides, in summer how can anyone work? I can't make head nor tail of that Euclid when the sun is shining."

"But when the sun is not shining, Law?"

"Oh! then," said the youth, with a smile breaking over his somewhat cloudy face, "I can make out the head, but not the tail, and the sting is in the tail, you know! Good-bye, Lottie, and never mind any mother's daughter of them. They cannot make us anything but what we are, whatever they may do."

"And what are we?" said Lottie to herself, as her brother strolled lazily out. There was more air to breathe when he was gone, which was something. She sat down upon the little old faded sofa, and shed a few more bitter tears of disappointment and mortification. We all like to think well of ourselves when that is possible; to think well of our belongings, our people, our position in the world—all that makes up that external idea of us which we make acquaintance with years before we know our own real being. No one can tell what the atmosphere of well-being, of external credit, and public esteem is to a child; and this Lottie had never known. They had been poor, but poverty is no hindrance to that feeling of harmony with the world around which is the higher soul of respectability. But there had not been much about the Despards to respect. The father had been a good officer in his day, and, if he had not been without money and interest, and everything that could help him on, might have been distinguished in his profession. But those were the days of "purchase," and Captain Despard had remained Captain Despard, and had bitterly resented the fact. His wife, too, though she was Lottie's mother, had not been of a kind to reclaim for her husband the failing credit of his life. They had lived as most poor officers on half pay, with pretensions to gentility and hankerings after pleasure, do live. They were in debt all round, as need not be said; and Mrs. Despard's life would have been rendered miserable by it if she had not escaped from the contemplation by means of every cheap merry-making or possible extravagance she could attain to. All had been huggermugger in Lottie's early life; a life not destitute of amusements, indeed, but full of bitterness, small mortifications, snubs, and the cold shoulder of social contempt. Lottie herself had heard in childish quarrels, through the frank recriminations of her childish companions, the frankest statements of what other people thought of her parents; and this had opened her baby eyes prematurely to the facts of the case. It must be supposed that there was some respectable grandpapa, some precise and orderly aunt in the Despard kindred, who had given to Lottie a nature so different from that of her immediate progenitors. As she grew older everything about her had looked to Lottie as the fairy splendour looked in the eyes of the disenchanted human spectator. Her mother's gay dresses, which she once thought so pretty, came to look like the miserable finery they were; her mother's gaiety had become noise and excitement. Her father's grand air grew the poorest false pretension; for must he not know, Lottie thought, how everybody spoke of him, how little anyone thought of his assumption? And the house was miserable, dirty, disorderly, mean, and gaudy, full of riot and waste and want and poverty—one day a feast, another nothing. Even careless Law—the big boy who was too much at home, who was scarcely ever at school, and who often had no clothes to go out in—even Law saw how wretched it was at home, though he was hopeless as well as careless, and asked his sister what was the good of minding, what could they do? But Lottie was not of the kind which can let ill alone, or well either, for that matter. She did mind; and as she grew older, every week, every day, added to the flame of impatience in her. Just, however, when ruin seemed coming beyond the possibility of further staving-off, Mrs. Despard fell ill and died; and Lottie at sixteen was left alone, miserable, with remorseful thoughts of having secretly blamed the mother who was now out of reach, and to whom she could never make amends for those injurious secret fault-findings; and full of anxieties unspeakable—forlorn wonderings what she was to do, and eagerness to do something. Her grief, however, was lightened by the feeling that now she had everything in her hands and could "make a change,"—even when it was made more heavy by the thought that she had found fault in her heart with the mother who was dead. It seemed to the girl that she must be able, by dint of devoting herself to it, to change everything—to keep the house in order if she did it with her own hands, to pay the bills, wherever the money came from. She was overflowing with life and energy and activity, and disapproved of all the ways of the past. She was like a new king coming to the throne, a new ministry of idealists bent upon undoing all their predecessors had done, and doing everything as it ought to be done. Alas, poor Lottie! the young king with all the stiff precedents of a hundred years against him, the young ministry confronted by a thousand problems, and finding their ideal pronounced impracticable on every side, were nothing to the heaven-born reformer of the household with a pleasure loving impecunious father to whom debt was second nature, and who had always preferred fun to respectability. And she dashed at her reforms too boldly, as was natural to her age, insisting upon brushings and sweepings till Betty threw up her situation, and asking for money till her father swore at her. "It is to pay the bills, papa! I want to pay the bills!" she had said, reduced to plead for that which she thought she had a right to demand. "D—— the bills!" was all Captain Despard replied.

And even Law, when Lottie tried to order him off to school, was unmanageable. He was no reformer like his sister, but on the whole preferred going just when it suited him and lounging at home between whiles. To be sure home was less amusing now that poor mammy, as they called her, was gone. Her laughter and her complaints, and her odd visitors, and all her slipshod ways, had kept noise and movement, if nothing more, about the house. The tawdry women and the shabby men who had been her friends were all afraid of the dulness which naturally follows a death in the family. Some of these women, indeed, had come to Lottie all tears and kisses, offering to stay with her, and asking what they could do; but their sympathy did not comfort the girl, who even in her deepest grief was all tingling with plans and desires to be doing, and an eager activity and impatience to make the changes she wished. But they fluttered away, every one, when the first excitement was over and the dulness that is inevitable fell upon the house. To do them justice there was not one among them who would not have come daily to "sit with" Lottie, to comfort her with all the news that was going, and tell her that she must not mope. But Lottie wanted none of their consolations, and did not miss her mother's friends when they abandoned her. She did not miss them, but Law did. Yet he would not go to school; he sat and made faces at her when she ordered and scolded him. "If I didn't do what *she* told me, do you think I will do what you tell me?" said Law; and then Lottie wept and prayed. "What will become of you, Law? what will you ever be good for? Papa has no money to leave us, and you will not be able to do anything."

"Who said I wanted to do anything?" said Law flippantly; and then, "who said I should not be able to do anything?" he added, with offence. "I can pick it up whenever I like." But Lottie, preternaturally, awfully wise, feeling the burden of the world upon her shoulders, knew that he could not pick it up when he pleased. She knew that education had to be acquired painfully, not sipped a little mouthful at a time. She had never had any education herself, but yet she knew this, as she knew so many things, by instinct, by constant critical observation of the habits which she disapproved. There are few more vigorously successful ways of finding out what is right, than by living among people whom we feel indignantly to be wrong.

"You may think what you like," she said, "Law—but I *know* that you cannot learn anything in that way. Three days at home and one at school! I wonder they let you go at all. I wonder they don't turn you out. I wonder they did not turn you out long ago!"

"And that is just what they are always threatening to do," said Law laughing; "but they have not the heart of a mouse, the fellows at the grammar-school. And they'll never do it, though I shouldn't mind. I should be free then, and never have to trouble my head about anything at all."

"You'll have to trouble your head when you have to work and don't know how," said Lottie. "Oh, if I was a boy! It's no use wishing, I am only a girl; and you are a great lump, neither one nor the other; but if I were only a boy, and could get something to do, and a little money to pay those bills— —"

"Oh, dash the bills, as papa says. He doesn't say 'dash,'" said Law, with provoking calm; "but, then, I mustn't swear."

"Oh, Law, I should like to beat you!" said Lottie, clenching her little fists in impotent anger and setting her teeth. But Law only laughed the more.

"You had better not," he said, when he had got over his laugh, "for I am a deal stronger than you."

And so he was, and so were they all, much stronger than poor Lottie; even Betty, who would not scrub, but who was too well used to all the ways of the family and aware of all their troubles, to be sent away. She fought for a time hard and bitterly, striving with all her might to clean, and to dust, and to keep things straight, to the infinite discontent of everybody concerned. But yet perhaps the girl's struggles were not utterly without use; for when the next astonishing change came in their lives, and their little income was suddenly increased by half, and a removal made necessary, Captain Despard, of his own accord, turned Lottie's despair in a moment into hope and joy. He said, "Now, Lottie, you shall have things your own way. Now you shall see what you can do. This is a new start for us all. If you can keep us respectable, by Jove, you shall, and nobody shall stop you. A man ought to be respectable when he's made a Chevalier of St. Michael." Lottie's heart leaped up, up from where it lay fathoms deep in unutterable depression and discouragement. "Oh, papa, papa, do you mean it? Will you keep your word?" she cried, happy yet dubious; and how he kept it, but with a difference, and how they set out upon this new chapter in their career, shall be told before we come back again to Lottie in her proper person, in the little drawing room in the Chevaliers' quarters within the Abbey precincts, on Miss Huntington's wedding-day.

CHAPTER II
THE CHEVALIERS' LODGES

The name of a Chevalier of St. Michael sounds very splendid to innocent and uninstructed ears. It is a title which stands alone in England at least. Poor Knights have been heard of both in flesh and blood and in confectionery, in other places; but the title Chevalier is preserved in St. Michael's, and there alone. Lottie thought it very imposing, and her heart leaped, partly with a sense of her own injustice all her life to her father, of whose merits, in youthful irreverence, she had hitherto thought but little. He must be, she thought involuntarily, a great deal braver, better, and altogether of more importance than she had supposed, when his qualities could win him such a distinction from his country; for that it was a distinction accorded by the country Lottie had no manner of doubt in those days. She was overawed and overjoyed: first of all on account of the people in Fairford, where they had hitherto lived, and who had shown but little respect for the family: but much more on her own account. She felt reconciled to herself, to her kind, to all her circumstances, when she reflected that she was the daughter of a Chevalier of St. Michael, and that Betty would never leave Fairford, and that Captain Despard had expressed himself in favour of respectability as a thing to be cultivated. Life suddenly took a new aspect to her. She thought they would be able to shake off every incumbrance when they went away. Her father would henceforward live a stately and dignified life as became his position. He would not haunt the place where billiards were played, and wear a number of shabby coats, each worse than the other, but every one with a flower in it. The flower, which most people would have thought a softening clause, was intolerable to Lottie; it looked like a piece of braggadocio, a wilful defiance of public opinion or declaration of independence. But henceforward if he must wear a flower it must be at least in a tolerable coat; henceforward he would be trim and smooth, and come in at a respectable hour; henceforward there should be no bills except weekly ones, and Law should go to school—nay, Law was too old for school now—but at least he would read with a tutor, and grow into a creature of whom his sister might be proud. Perhaps this was but another way of expressing the domestic tyranny of which Lottie's will was full. She was so anxious to be able to be proud of her father and brother; was not that another way of saying that she wanted to get them up, or down, to her feminine standard, and control and bind and keep them at her apron-string? So, perhaps, a cynic might have said. But Lottie was unconscious of any such intention. She was eager to have something which she had not, the opposite of what she had—and thus, too, it may be said, she fell into a commonplace.

But when the family got to St. Michael's, Lottie's hopes came to a melancholy conclusion. Not only did Captain Despard remain very much the same, which was a thing that most people anticipated—and Law decline the tutor, upon whom Lottie had set her heart, but St. Michael's itself and the Chevaliership turned out something very different from the girl's exalted expectations. She found that this office was not looked upon on the spot as a reward of distinguished merit bestowed by the country, but only as a sort of retiring pension for a number of old soldiers whose friends had interest enough to have them thus provided for. She found a hierarchy of a totally different kind constituted and reigning, in which the Chevaliers had no place. And she found herself—she whose chief inspiration was this proud and eager desire to be somebody—in a place where she could never be other than nobody, and where no nobler self-denial on the part of her father, no virtue in Law, could call forth the acclamation of the world. In Fairford there were people as poor as themselves whom all the world thought well of, and of whom Lottie was envious; but here she was one of a class who were poor among the rich, and did not get the social honours which many of them deserved; while at the same time, close before her eyes, daily visible, appeared another class which seemed to fulfil all Lottie's requirements: refined people with beautiful houses, living serene in an atmosphere of universal respect. But alas, these were ecclesiastical people, not the Chevaliers: and showed little disposition to notice Lottie. Lottie did not like this. She had expected something so different. Society, she thought, and a brighter world were going to open upon her; and lo! nothing at all opened upon her that was new. It is very hard, especially when you feel yourself to be, as the proverb says, as good a gentleman as the king, to find yourself in contact with a higher class which ignores you. Most of us have to bear something of the kind, and learn to take it with philosophy. But Lottie was very young and sadly disappointed. Nobody took any notice of her save the other Chevaliers, their wives and daughters, and these were not very much more splendid people than the society she had been used to. Lottie was sore, and disappointed, and humbled in her own conceit.

And there was another way in which the word of promise was kept to her ear, with far other meaning than she had hoped. Captain Despard had a very serious interview with his daughter when they arrived in their little house. He called her out of the little box which was her drawing-room to the other little box where he had established himself, and deigned to enter upon the question of income.

"Now, Lottie," he said, "you have chosen to bother me lately about money, and expressed views which I could not sanction about weekly bills."

"Only to save you trouble, papa," said Lottie; "if we do it every week, we may hope to keep within our income; but how can you ever do that when you leave butchers and bakers for a year?"

"My child," said Captain Despard, with his grand air, "circumstances have enabled me to yield to your wishes. I don't say if it's a system I approve or don't approve. I say to myself, Lottie is my only girl, and she is like her dear mother; she shall have her way. From this day, my dear, the new income which I receive from my country will go straight into your hands. It is but a pittance. A poor soldier stands a poor chance in these times, but such as it is, my love, it shows your father's trust in you. Take it, Lottie, and pay your bills according to your pleasure. I will ask no questions; weekly, monthly, or once a quarter, as long as I have a bit of dinner and a cup of coffee when I want it. Your father's confidence in you is perfect, Lottie, and I leave it all to you."

"Papa!" said the girl, trembling, half delighted, half frightened, half taken in by that grand air. But he would hear no more. He kissed her forehead with the favourite action of the *père noble,* and hurried away. "No thanks, my child; no thanks," he said.

It *was* a pittance. Lottie stood where he left her gazing after him, her veins tingling with mingled disappointment and pleasure. To the inexperienced it seems always possible to do a great deal with a little, and the power of paying bills at all seemed a heavenly power. But Captain Despard chuckled to himself as he went away. He had purchased by that fine address the right to be disagreeable ever after, to wave his hand loftily, and to decline all knowledge of details. "Keep to your bargain, my dear, and I'll keep to mine," he had the right to say; and whereas some of his former income always had to be wasted upon the household, let him make what resistance he would, at least that would be the case no longer. Thus Lottie had her way, but in such a changed form that it no longer seemed her way. With the addition of the St. Michael's allowance she had hoped that there would be plenty for all needs; but what was she to do with the St. Michael's allowance and no more? Nevertheless, Lottie plucked up a heart. To feel that she had something was always exhilarating, and inexperience has wild hopes which knowledge does not venture to share. Her little room was full for a week after of little bits of paper scribbled over with calculations. She was determined to do it. If the dinner was not good enough for papa, he must just go and dine elsewhere. And there was no Betty to make herself disagreeable, but only a young girl, whom Lottie, heaven save her! meant to train. Once a week or so Law and she could very well do without a dinner. They were both still great on bread and butter, and capable, not knowing anything about digestion, of swallowing innumerable cups of tea. Her fond hopes of furniture and "picking up things" to make the little old house pretty, must be relinquished, it was true; but, still, at nineteen one can put up with a great deal in the present. There is always the future, so much of the future, like the sky and the plain from St. Michael's Hill, spreading above, below, everywhere, without limit or bound, save in the eyes which can only reach a certain distance. So Lottie comforted herself for "just now," and marched on into her life, colours flying and drums beating, taking as little heed as she could of those stragglers who would always fall out of the ranks—her father always shuffling off to some new haunt or other, the places which such men find out by instinct in the least-known locality, and large loose-limbed Law, whose vague career was always dubious, and who could not keep step. Never mind! Lottie herself set out, brave, head erect, eyes straight, all her faculties in fullest attention to the roll of her own cheerful drum.

The earliest part of her career here, however, was brightened yet disturbed by a discovery which considerably confused her mind in her outset, and seemed to open better prospects before her. Lottie found out that she had a voice. She had known that she could sing long before, and had performed many a time in the little parlour at Fairford to the admiration of all hearers, singing every new comic song that burst upon the little provincial world from the music-halls in London, and knowing no better, so long as she was a child. There was no harm in the songs she sang, nothing but absolute silliness and flippancy, such as are natural to that kind of production; but as Lottie grew into womanhood, and began by instinct to know better, she gave them up, and knowing no others except some ancient sentimental ditties of her mother's, gave up singing so far as a musical creature can give up what is another kind of breathing to her. But when she heard the choir in the Abbey church, Lottie woke up, with such a delightful discovery of what music was, and such an ecstatic finding out of her own powers, as words cannot express. She had an old jingling worn-out piano, and had "learned to play" from her mother, who knew nothing about it, except as much as could be taught to a school-girl twenty years before; but this meagre instruction, and the bad instrument, and the half-dozen "pieces" which were all Mrs. Despard's musical library, had not attracted the pupil, and it was not till she heard the organ pealing through St. Michael's, and the choristers singing like angels—though they were not like angels out of doors—that Lottie awoke to a real consciousness of her own gift. She had never had any education herself. Though she was so anxious for school for Law, it had not occurred to her that she wanted any schooling. Lottie was narrow-minded and practical. She did not understand self-culture. She wanted Law to learn, because without education he could not do anything worth speaking of, could not earn any money, could not get on in the world. Perhaps it is true that women have a natural inclination to calculate in this poor way. She did not care a straw for the cultivation of Law as Law—but that he should be made good for something, get a good situation, have some hopes of comfort and prosperity. For herself, what did it matter? She never could know enough to teach, and Captain Despard would not let his daughter teach; besides, she had plenty to do at home, and could not be spared. She could read and write, and do her accounts, the latter very well indeed; and she had learned to "play" from her mother, and she could sew, rather badly at first, rather well now by dint of practice. What did a girl want more? But Lottie discovered now that a girl might want more.

"Is there any place where they will teach you to sing without money?" she said one day to old Mrs. O'Shaughnessy, her next-door neighbour, the old lady of all her neighbours whom Lottie liked best.

"Me jewel!" cried the old lady; "is it without paying youre meaning? They send an account if you do but look at them here, me dear."

"All of them?" said Lottie; "for I can sing, and I should like to learn to sing; but, you know, I can't pay—much——"

"I know; nothing at all, if you're like us, me honey. But maybe you're better off. O'Shaughnessy, we don't make a secret of it, rose from the ranks, and we've never had a penny—I don't care who knows it—barring our pay."

"We are not like that," said Lottie, drawing herself up. "Papa was always a gentleman" ("Then I don't give much for such gentlemen," murmured the other Chevalier's lady, under her breath), "and we have a little. That is—I mean, that he has a little—papa has a little"—the girl said on the edge of a confidence; and then stopped suddenly short.

"It don't do much for the children, I'll go bail," said the old lady. "That's the worst of fine gentlemen, me dear. O'Shaughnessy he asks me for a shillin' when he wants it, bless him—and that's the only way when there's small pay. Singing, is it? If you're always to make such a stand on being a lady, me friend Lottie, I don't see how I can help you; but if you will come in free and comfortable, and take a dish of tay when Rowley's there—oh, to be sure, puff! my lady's off—but there's no harm in him; and he'll make you die with laughin' at him, him and his airs—but they tell me he has the best voice and the best method of any of the lay clerks."

"A singing man!"

"Well, and that was what ye wanted!" said the old woman. "You know as well as me, Miss Lottie, there's no singin' woman here."

Lottie protested that she could not consent to appear in such company—that papa would not allow it—that it was impossible. But she ended by promising to "run in" before old Major O'Shaughnessy began his rubber, and see this singing man. And the result was that, half out of friendship for his Irish hosts who did not pretend to be above him, and half out of pride to be interrogated so graciously about his invalid daughter by a young lady who gave herself such airs, Rowley, the first tenor, agreed for so low a rate as had never been heard of before to train Miss Despard's beautiful voice. "If the young lady had been a little boy, and if the Signor could but ha' gotten hold on it!" Rowley said, in enthusiasm. It was the voice, which is impersonal, of which he spoke, and the Signor was the organist. But good fortune had not as yet thrown him in Lottie's way. Soon, however, Rowley began to whisper it about that he had got a pupil who was quite good enough for Exeter Hall, if not for the Italian Opera, and the whole community was interested. Lottie herself, and her pretty looks, had not attracted any notice—but a voice was a very different matter. And then it was that steps were taken to make, for Lottie's behalf, a practicable gap in the hedge of prickles which surrounded the Cloisters and kept intruders out. Miss Despard was invited to join the St. Michael's Choral Society, in which the Divinities on the hill did not disdain to mingle their voices even with the lower-born outside the Abbey walls. And when it became known what a voice Lottie's was, a remarkable thing happened. The Dean *called!* It was not Lady Caroline, but the Dean; and a gentleman's visit, as is well known, is not the same thing as a lady's. But Lottie, who knew nothing of the laws of society, was flattered and happy, and saw a hundred lovely visions unfolding before her when the Dean invited her to go to a private practice, which was then going on in the Deanery drawing-room. "My daughter bade me fetch you, Miss Despard, if you would be good enough to come," he said, gravely; but waited very impatiently till she was ready, in great terror lest "the father" should make his appearance, and his visit be construed into a call upon Captain Despard. Lottie put on her hat with her heart leaping and bounding. At last she had done it! At last Paradise was opening before the Peri! At last the wrongs of fate were to be set right, and herself conveyed back into her natural sphere. She went by the Dean's side demurely, with downcast eyes, across the slope to the Deanery garden. The very stones felt elastic under her feet, there was a ringing of excitement and delight in the air and in her ears. She arrived breathless at the door, though they had not walked fast. So absorbed was she by all that was about to happen that Lottie never thought of the sensation that ran through the Abbey when the Dean was seen walking to his own dignified door in company with Captain Despard's daughter. Miss Despard? Lottie? The Chevaliers, and their wives and daughters, could not believe their eyes.

Lottie held her head as high as usual when she came back. It no longer drooped with diffidence and delight. Once more she had come down with a jar into the realms of reality from those of hope. She was not received with open arms in that higher celestial world. Miss Augusta Huntington said, "How do you do, Miss Despard?" very sweetly, but Lady Caroline only bowed with her eyelids—a new mode of salutation which Lottie did not understand—and kept aloof; and no one else said anything to Lottie, except about the music. They gave her a cup of tea when all was over, but Lottie had to drink it in silence, while the others laughed and chatted. She was not of them, though they had brought her among them for the sake of her voice. "Are you going, Miss Despard?" said the Dean's daughter, putting on the same sweet smile. "We are so much obliged to you for coming. The next practice is next Tuesday. Will you come as early as possible, please?" It was on Lottie's lips to say "No"—to tell them that she was a lady too, a better gentlewoman than they were, since she would not have treated any stranger so. But she was fortunately too shy to say anything, and made her exit hastily, and not so gracefully as the others, who were at home. But she would not allow, even to herself, that she had come down again in that painful tussle with reality, which is so much different from dreams. She kept very quiet and said nothing, which seemed the wisest way. And as she walked home with a much more stately gravity than was her wont—a state put on to console herself for humiliation and disappointment, and to vindicate, so to speak, her own dignity to herself, but which the lookers-on gave a very different interpretation of—Mrs. O'Shaughnessy, nodding and smiling, and in a state of great excitement, threw up the window and called to her, as she was going past. "Come up, come up, and tell me all about it," the old lady said, so audibly that some of the ladies and gentlemen who had been in the Deanery turned round to look, and smiled at each other, making Lottie furious. As she could not stand there and explain before all the world, Lottie obeyed the call, and rushing upstairs to the kind old Irishwoman's little bit of a drawing-room, appeared, crimson with shame and wrath at the door.

"How could you call out so loud and make them laugh?" she said, with a strong inclination to burst into hot tears.

"Laugh, was it? and sure I'm ready to laugh too. To see you and his Reverence the Dean, Miss Lottie—no less would serve you!—arm in arm like a pair of young——"

"We were not arm in arm," said Lottie, stamping her foot. Then she had the sense to perceive that the wicked old Irishwoman would but laugh the more at her petulance. She put her music on the table with a recovery of her dignified manners, and sat down.

"What did he say to ye? and what did me Lady Caroline say to ye? and were they all wild over yer beautiful voice, me honey?" said the old lady. "Come, take off your hat, me pet, and ye shall have the best cup o' tea in the Abbey. And tell me all about it," she said.

"I have had a cup of tea, thank you," said Lottie. "Oh, yes, they are all nice enough. Nobody talked to me—but then, I didn't expect them to talk to me. They wanted me to sing—and I sang; and that was all."

"And what more would you have, me jewel?" said Mrs. O'Shaughnessy. "Now, you take my advice, Lottie. I'm old, and I know the world. Take what you can get, me dear, and wait till your time comes. Don't go and take offence and throw up the cards, and lose all you've got for a tantrum. Tantrums pass off, but life goes on. If they don't speak to you, it's their loss, for you have a clever little tongue o' your own. And you'll not be long there till they find out that. Don't say a word, me honey. I'll not bother you; but never take offence with the gentry——"

"The gentry!" cried the girl furious, starting to her feet. "I am as much a lady as any of them—and more, for I would not be such—— I would not be unkind——"

"Well—well—well! There, I have put my foot in it!" said the old lady. "I was thinking of meself, me dear, as if ye were a girl of my own. But you *are* a lady, honey; one has but to look at you," said the astute old woman; "and just you wait a bit, and all will come as it ought—sure, I know it will."

Lottie did not much trust the assurance, but she took the advice, feeling a quick admonition within herself as to the absurdity of her complaint, and the horrible possibility of anybody supposing that she felt herself not to be of the gentry, as good as any Dean's daughter. So she went to the next practice, taking no notice of any want of courtesy: and the result was that there arose a kind of intimacy, as has been indicated, between Miss Huntington at the Deanery and the daughter of the Chevalier—an intimacy, indeed, of a peculiar kind, in which all that was given came from the side of the poorer and more insignificant, and the great young lady was content with taking all that poor Lottie was so willing to give. She sang the solos in their private little concerts, and though her science was less perfect than her voice, her ear was so good that Lottie was able to be of a great deal of use. They sent for her when they had parties, when there was anyone who wanted entertaining, and put Lottie to the only unnecessary personal expense she had ever gone into—a white muslin frock to make her presentable among that fine company. And thus she had gone and come, and had been called upon on all occasions, but without making any nearer advance than at first. Lady Caroline still made her a little inclination of her eyelids, though now and then she went so far as to say, "How do you do, Miss Despard?" All of this, however, Lottie would have pardoned, if the bride, when she went away, had but at least remembered her, and made her some little sign of farewell.

CHAPTER III
THE ABBEY PRECINCTS

The bells began to ring for evensong soon after the bridal party dispersed. Some of them, indeed, stayed for the beautiful service, which was a thing that visitors from a distance thought a great deal of, and there were a number of fine bonnets and dresses in the stalls when Lottie went in. The daily service was part of the daily life of the dwellers in the Abbey. There were those who went for devotion, and those who went for the music, and those who went because they had nothing else to do. It was an occupation and an amusement at the same time, and some people thought it a duty. To listen to the service more or less critically, to note if any of the boys' voices were breaking, and whether Rowley sniffed as usual, or Bowler, the great bass, was hoarse; to observe how the minor canons sang, if they were in too great a hurry to get through the service, and who it was that read the lessons; to look at any notable persons that might be there; visitors to the Deanery, or other persons of distinction; to walk in the nave while the Signor played the voluntary; and finally to pause and talk to one's friends before going home to tea, was the established rule of St. Michael's. The old Chevaliers mixed with the ladies, here and there one. They were obliged to go in the morning, and they seldom repeated their church going in the afternoon; but still there were always two or three, and very interesting to strangers were the old soldiers, with their old moustaches and upright bearing. Some of them might have been veteran generals well entitled to command an army, and, indeed, there was valour enough among them, and such achievement as personal bravery is still capable of—enough to equip a dozen generals; but fortune had not been on the side of these noble old soldiers; and you may be sure there were no prosperous commanders among them. They stood about on the terrace in front of the Lodges and talked for five minutes or so before they went in to tea. But Lottie, when she came out of chapel and saw the last of the fine people streaming away in their light dresses through the aisle, did not feel much disposed to go indoors to Law and the bread and butter. They could wait. She went and leaned on the low wall close to the library and gazed out upon the landscape below. At the foot of the slope was the street of the little old town, a sweep of steep masonry, with old-fashioned red houses, like trees in autumn, on the other side; and beyond these the river meandered between its leafy banks in endless windings, and the great breadth of champaign swept away towards the horizon. At this time of the year it was rich and cloudy with foliage: the trees arranging themselves in every kind of way, singly and in clumps, and groves, and long hedgerows, and surrounding every house and every village and every church spire as far as you could see. The billowy greenness thus spreading far into the silvery-grey of the distance; the sky of a pale blue, faint with summer heat and long drought: stretched out like a map before the gazer from that mount of vision. The mottled clouds were floating together and rolling into masses as if with the intention of putting a stop to this long reign of brightness, and the level lines of the landscape and the great vault of the sky dropped together into a haze which also spoke of rain. Lottie leaned disconsolately over the wall, spreading abroad her thoughts over this vast breadth of space and silence. She let them go like a flock of birds flying to all the winds. Thoughts! they were not thoughts but feelings, vague movements of the mind, half sentiment, half-personal sensation. Why she should have been so deeply affected by this marriage she could not have told anyone. She did not herself know. It seemed to penetrate through and through her system of life, unsettling everything. After the disappointments of her beginning at St. Michael's, this connection with the Deanery had seemed a thread of promise, a clue to something better; not a very splendid promise indeed, but still something; a little link of ambition which looked finer and more noble after it was snapped than it had ever done before. It was not very noble in itself. Lottie felt vaguely that to have so strong a desire for admission within that charmed circle was not a very lofty thing. The people she had seen within it had not satisfied her ideal. Except that they dressed better (some of them at least), they had been very much like the humbler classes with which she was acquainted; and to wish for a footing among them only because they were better off and more highly thought of than her own neighbours, was not an elevating sentiment. In the perpetual disappointments to which she had been subject, the slights she had been obliged to put up with, Lottie had felt a great many pangs of shame mingled with the stings of humiliation. She had felt that it was the poorest of ambitions which had taken possession of her. And now that it was over, this sense of unworthiness still mingled with her consciousness of failure and exclusion. But though it might not be a door into heaven, still to feel that it was shut, to be obliged to turn away, and to see no other door at which she could enter, was hard. Her heart sank down into painful depths of abandonment, and tears came to her eyes in spite of herself. She had nothing to cry about, but her lips quivered and two big tears rose and hung suspended under her long eyelashes, so filling up the whole space before her, that Lottie saw nothing but a waving greenness and blueness, a blurred shadow of earth and sky.

It was just at this moment, while she was still uncertain whether she could get these tears swallowed or whether they must fall, betraying her, that she was aware of some one at her elbow. "I think we shall have rain, Miss Despard," said a deliberate voice; "do you not think we shall have rain? The summer has been so fine that we have no right to grumble. You were the one lady in all St. Michael's whom I most wanted to see."

"I, Signor? I do not know what you should want with me," said Lottie, forced by circumstances into rudeness. She did not want to be rude, but the shock of his sudden address had brought down that shower, falling like drops of a thunderstorm, and she would not turn round to show him her wet eyes. He smiled a little to himself at this petulance, and that was all. He was used to waywardness in young ladies. He was a spare, olive-coloured man, not tall, but wiry and close-knit. He had all the aspect of an Italian and the name; but he was not really an Italian, being an Englishman born, a good Tory and a good Churchman, and all that the organist of St. Michael's ought to be. But he was not disinclined to keep up a mystery on this score, having a little love of mystery by nature, and feeling, musically, that his foreign name and looks were in his favour. How far back the Signor had to go for his claim to be considered an Italian, nobody knew, but everybody (except the perverse and disagreeable, who would occasionally say Mr. Rossinetti to annoy him) called the musician the Signor. His complexion, his moustache, the wonderful dark eyes, which were the chief feature in his face, were all of Southern origin; and he spoke with a curious deliberation and clear pronunciation of every syllable, which almost looked as if, at one time, there had been difficulties about the language, and as if he had not courage even yet to take any liberties with it. But his accent was as good English as could be desired; and in respect to this as well as to all other questions about his origin the community of St. Michael's were entirely in the dark, as he intended them to be.

"This event," said the Signor, in his clear slow voice, "will bring our little societies, our practisings, to an end, Miss Despard. We were getting on very well. I am sorry to come to an end of anything, and of these above all."

"Yes, I suppose so," said Lottie, drearily. "Will it, do you think? She had not very much of a voice."

"No; but there are other things besides voice. You have a very beautiful voice, Miss Despard."

"But I have nothing else," said Lottie, forgetting her precautions and turning quickly upon him; "that is what you mean to say? And you never even allowed before that I had a voice."

"No, not much else," said the deliberate organist; "you have no science, no method. You don't know how to manage what you have got. It is a fine organ by nature, but you cannot produce it as you ought, because you do not know how. To have so much and to do so little is a great pity. It is a waste of a great gift, it is— —"

"How dare you tell me all this to my face?" said Lottie, transported with vivid anger. She would have taken it more quietly if she had not been weakened in spirit by the discouragement into which she had fallen before. Her fierce, sudden glance was even still unwillingly softened by the wetness of her eyes. But the Signor did not flinch. There was a kind of smile in his own as he met her look. He was not afraid of her. He looked, indeed, amiably, genially at Lottie—as she had never seen him look before—and as she turned round she became aware that he was not alone. Over his shoulder, with an alarmed, indignant aspect, which half amused while it consoled her, was another face with which Lottie was very well acquainted. It was the face of his favourite pupil, a young man who followed the Signor about like his shadow, always a few steps behind him, always in devout contemplation of him. But young Purcell was not of this mind to-day; he was looking at his beloved master with a mixture of rage and pathos very droll in their combination. Lottie was easily moved, and almost before the words of defiance had left her lips a laugh forced itself after them. She had to turn round again to conceal the conflict of sudden mirth in her face.

"Would you rather I said it to others than to you? No, because that would do you no good— —"

"And do you really think that I—I— —" Why should she laugh? Young Purcell's face brightened slightly, but took a still more curious look of bewildered inquiry. As for the Signor, he thought she had become hysterical, which he believed was a common weakness with womankind in general, and he was alarmed.

"I beg you a thousand pardons if I have seemed rude," he said. "All that I wanted was to begin the conversation; for I have—a little proposal to make."

"Do you call that beginning a conversation to tell me I am quite ignorant, and cannot sing, and waste my voice?" said Lottie, recovering her indignation. "It is not a very civil way."

"Miss Despard, I think you will miss the society's singing, and I want to tell you it was not good for you. These people were dazzled by your voice," said the organist, with unintentional confusion of metaphor, "and they made use of it. All these fine people, they make use of us, and often forget to say 'thank you.' I was sorry that you should suffer, *too*; so was Purcell; he knows what it is—a little. And you have had no teaching, you have not had a thorough professional training as he has— —"

Lottie turned upon him with flashing eyes; and this time she did not laugh at the young man who, over the Signor's shoulder, followed every movement of hers with such eager attention. His look of wonder and fear was not less comic than the other changes which had come over his countenance, but she took no notice of it. "I don't know what you mean," she said, "by professional training. What do I want with professional training? What has Mr. Purcell to do with it? What do you mean, or how should I suffer? If they thank me, or if they don't thank me, what is that to me?"

The Signor cast a glance round at young Purcell, who answered with a look of despair. "If you would but confide in us, we thought we could help you. Indeed, Miss Despard, it is no presumption on Purcell's part, only a fellow-feeling— —"

"Only a feeling—of respect!" This Purcell timidly gasped out, with alarm painted on every feature. Lottie, turning her back to the wall and confronting the two musicians, solemnly made them a very awful curtsey. It was an art she had learned (though the teacher was unaware of the fact) from Lady Caroline; and therefore it was of the very finest and most imposing kind.

"The puzzle is," she said grandly, in a voice not unlike Lady Caroline's, "what the link between us may be."

They were both silenced by this speech, and by her imposing aspect generally; for Lottie was very handsome, and this defiant grandeur suited her. Purcell felt disposed to sink into the earth, and showed it; but as for the Signor, he was less alarmed, and, indeed, a little amused—he had seen a great number of heroines, both in public and private life.

"It is always wrong to beat about the bush," he said. "Perhaps I have made a mistake; I thought you probably intended to sing, Miss Despard, as a profession."

"I!" Lottie's voice broke into a half shriek. "I!" The suggestion gave her a shock which it was hard to get over. She felt a trembling of giddiness and insecurity, as if the ground had suddenly been cut from under her; she could have cried for mortification, injured pride, horrible humbling and downfall. She who had been mourning this change as taking from her all chance of ascent into the society she had a right to, the society she really belonged to, and they thought it was professional work, a profession that she was thinking of! She drew back unconsciously to the support of the wall, and propped herself by it. She could have cried, but pride would not let her. "You are mistaken, altogether mistaken," she said. "I don't suppose that you mean to insult me; but you forget that I am a gentleman's daughter."

Here the ghost of a smile flitted across the Signor's olive-coloured face. It was as momentary as the passing of a shadow, but yet Lottie saw it, and it stung her as nothing else could have done; she was angry before, but this excited her to passion. She could have flown at him and strangled him for this smile; she understood it well enough. "You smile!" she said. "You think, perhaps, that a poor Chevalier, a soldier who is not rich, is not a gentleman. You think it is only money that makes a gentleman. There are many people who are of that opinion; but," said Lottie with a smile, "you will perhaps not be surprised if I think differently. I will bid you good evening, please, now."

"One moment," said the Signor; "you must not go away with a wrong impression. Forgive me the mistake, if it is a mistake. You are mistaken, too, Miss Despard, if you think a gentleman's daughter may not sing—to the great generous public as well as to poor little coteries that never say thank you. You mistake, too; but never mind. I meant to have offered, if you would let me, to help you— —"

"Thank you, very much!" said Lottie with great state, "it is not necessary. When I want lessons, I can—ask for them, M. Rossinetti." She had been about to say *pay*, but Lottie was honest, and though she longed to inflict the insult, would not say what was not true. She did not even see young Purcell's pathetic looks as he gazed at her, with the air of a suppliant on his knees, over his master's shoulder; but she saw the half shrug of the Signor's shoulders as he stood aside to let her pass. And perhaps had she but known it there was something comic, too, in the dignity with which she swept past with a little wave of her hand. It was like Lady Caroline, though Lottie did not intend it to be so. The two musicians stood looking after her as she walked majestically homewards, with so many commotions in her bosom. She had to pass through the little square in which the lay clerks lived, on her way, and as if to accomplish Lottie's humiliation, Rowley the tenor—who was her teacher—was standing at his door as she passed. The Chevaliers of St. Michael's took little notice of the lay clerks as, may be supposed (except the O'Shaughnessys, who were not particular); and though Lottie was his pupil, Rowley had never transgressed the due limits of respectfulness or pretended to any friendship with the young lady. But the wedding had affected the morals of St. Michael's generally, and made a revolution for the day; and as Lottie passed, the tenor took advantage of the opportunity. "How are you, Miss?" he said, with a sniff and a lurch which showed the source of his boldness; "won't you come in and have a chat? won't you come in and have some tea with my little girl, Miss Lottie?" Good heavens! what had Lottie done to be addressed in this way? and she knew that the two others would hear this demonstration of intimacy. She rushed past, stumbling over her dress, wild with resentment and mortification. This was what it was to be poor, to be in a false position, to be a poor gentlewoman among the rich! One mortification had followed another, so that she did not know how to bear it. Augusta's neglect, the Signor's insulting suggestion, and Rowley's familiarity! Lottie did not know which was the most hard to bear. She never drew breath until she had reached her own door.

"Is that you, Lottie? and where have you been?" said Law. "Let's have tea now; I've been waiting and waiting, wanting to go out, and wondering what had become of you." He had begun his bread and butter on the spot.

"Where is papa, Law?"

"Papa? How should I know? You didn't expect him, did you? I say, I'm going out—do make haste. And look here! I wish you'd speak to him, Lottie. I wish you'd tell him he oughtn't to; I'd give twenty pounds (if I had it) not to have such an uncommon name!"

"It is a very good name—better than anyone else's I know. The Despards never were anything but gentlemen."

"Oh! it's a great deal you know about it," said Law, with a groan. "Perhaps once upon a time we were somebody when everybody else was nobody! But when it turns the other way, when we are nobody and everybody else somebody, and when it's known where-ever you go whose son you are— —"

"You don't need to continue nobody," she said; "you are a boy, you can do what you like. If we are down now, *you* need not stay down, Law. But then you must not hang about and lose your time any longer. If you will work, you can soon change that."

"Can I!" said the youth; "that shows how much you know. I have never been taught to do anything. If I had been put apprentice to a butcher or a baker when I was young—but you never did anything but bully me to work and go to school. What good is school? If you are to do anything, you ought to be taught when you are young. I have been mismanaged. I doubt if I will ever be good for much now."

"Oh—h!" cried Lottie, with a deep breath of aspiration from the depths of her chest, "if it was only me! I should find something to do! I should not be long like this, lounging about a little bit of a place, following bad examples, doing no work. Oh, Law! if I could put some of me into you; if I could change places with you! Fancy what was said to me to-day: the Signor came up to me when we came out of church, and asked me if I was going to sing—for a profession."

"By Jove!" cried Law! he woke up even from his bread and butter, and looked at her with sparkling eyes.

"I had almost said, 'You may be very glad my brother is not with me to hear you ask such a question.' But on the whole I am glad you were not. I said all that was necessary," said Lottie with dignity. "He will never repeat such an insult again."

"By Jove!" Law repeated, taking no heed of what she said, but looking at her with visibly increased respect. "Do you mean to say that he thought you good enough for that?"

"Good enough!" she said, with severe contempt. "I always knew I could sing; even poor mamma knew. But I did not condescend to say much to them. I said, 'I am a gentleman's daughter,' and walked away."

"Well, girls are very funny," said Law. "How you bully me about working! morning, noon, and night, you are never done nagging; but the moment it comes to your own turn— —"

"To my own turn!" Lottie looked at him aghast.

"To be sure. Oh, that's all very fine about being a gentleman's daughter. We know pretty well what that means, and so does everybody. I wonder, Lottie, you that have some sense, how you could be so silly? He must have laughed."

"Oh, hold your tongue, Law! I suppose they think nothing counts but money. When you are poor you are always insulted. I should not care for money, not for itself, not for the gold and silver," said Lottie; "nor even so very much for the nice things that one could buy; but, oh, to be above people's remarks, to be known for what you are, not looked down upon, not insulted— —"

"It depends upon what you call being insulted," said Law; "if any man had said that to me, I should have thought him next to an angel. What is insulting about it? If you like money (and who doesn't like money?) why there's the easiest way in the world of getting it. Sing! I'd sing my head off," said Law, "if that was all that was wanted. And you sing *for pleasure*; you *like* singing! I can't tell what you are thinking of. If I had known you were so good as that—but one never thinks much of one's own sister, somehow," the youth added, with easy frankness. He was so much excited, however, that he left his tea, and strode up and down the room (three paces and a half, that was all the size of it) repeating "by Jove!" to himself. "If you mean not to do it, you had better not let *him* know you could do it," he announced, after an interval. Never in his life before had the easy-going young man been so moved. "It's untold the money they make," he said.

As for Lottie, her whole being was in a ferment. She looked at her brother with a gasp of pain. The bread and butter had no charms for her on that night of emotion. She took up her basket which was full of things to mend, and sat down in the window, speechless with vague passion, pain, discontentment. Lottie was not a wise or enlightened young woman. She had not even taken the stamp of her age as many people do who are not enlightened. She had never learned that it was desirable that women should have professions like men. Her thoughts ran entirely in the old-fashioned groove, and it seemed to her that for "a gentleman's daughter" to work for her living, to be known publicly to work for her living, was a social degradation beyond words to express. It implied—what did it not imply? That the family were reduced to the lowest level of poverty; but that was a small part of it—that the men were useless, worthless, without pride or honour; that they had no friends, no means of saving themselves from this betrayal of all the secrets of pride. These were the foolish feelings in her mind. Gentlemen's daughters were governesses sometimes she had heard, and Lottie pitied the poor girls (orphans—they were always orphans, and thus set aside from the general rule), with an ache of compassion in her heart; but it was her private impression that this was a stigma never to be wiped off, a stain, not upon the girl, but upon her family who could permit such a sacrifice. Lottie's view of sacrifice was one which is rarely expressed, but which exists not the less among women and all other persons from whom sacrifices are demanded. Could Alcestis have the same respect after for the man who could let her die for him? Could she go on living by his side and think just the same of him as if he had borne his own burden instead of shuffling it off upon her shoulders? The ancients did not trouble themselves with such questions, but it is a peculiarity of the modern mind that it does. And Lottie, though her point of view was very old-fashioned, still looked at it in this modern way. When Law, whom it was impossible to stir up to any interest in his own work, became so excited over the thought of a possible profession for her, she looked at him with something of the feeling with which Isabella contemplated the caitiff brother in his prison who would have bought his life by her shame. What! would he be "made a man" in such a way? would he buy idleness and ease for himself by exposing her to a life unworthy of "a gentleman's daughter"? She knew he was lazy, careless, and loved his own gratification; but it hurt her to her very heart to think so poorly of Law, who was the only being in the world whom she had ever been able to love heartily as belonging to herself.

Let it not be thought, however, that any unwillingness to work for Law, to make any sacrifice for him, was at the bottom of this disappointment in him. She was ready to have worked her fingers to the bone, indoors, in the privacy of the family, for her father and brother. She did not care what menial offices she did for them. Their "position" demanded the presence of a servant of some kind in the house, but Lottie was not afraid of work. She could sweep and dust; she could cook; she could mend with the most notable of housewives, and sang at her work, and liked her people all the better because of what she had to do for them in the course of nature. That was altogether different; there was no shame to a lady in doing this, no exposure of the family. And Lottie was not of the kind of woman who requires personal service from men. She was quite willing to serve them, to wait upon them if necessary, to take that as her share of the work of life;

but to work publicly for her living, what was that but to proclaim to all the world that they were incapable, that they were indifferent to their duties, that there was no faith to be put in them? If Law had leaped up in wrath, if he had said, "No, it is my place to work; I will work; no one shall say that my sister had to earn her living," how happy, how proud Lottie would have been! That was the ideal for a man. It was what she would do herself if she was in his place; and, oh, if she could but put herself in his place, and do what Law would not do! oh, if she could but put herself, a bit of herself, into him, to quicken the sluggish blood in his veins! When Law, having exhausted all that was to be said on the subject, went out (and where did he go when he went out?), Lottie sat at the window and darned and darned till the light failed her. She ploughed furrows with her needle in the forefinger of her left hand; but that did not hurt her. Oh, if she could but move them, inspire them, force them to do their duty, or at the worst do it for them, so that the world might suppose it was they who were doing it! That was the aspiration in her heart; and how hopeless it was! "Oh, if I could put some of me into him!" Lottie thought, as many a helpless soul has thought before her. But to move out from the shadow of the house, and betray its nakedness, and take the burden visibly on herself, that was what Lottie felt she would rather die than do.

Meanwhile, in the soft evening, various people were promenading up and down between the Abbey church and the lodges of the Chevaliers. Some of the old Chevaliers themselves were out, with their wives hanging on their arms. Either there would be two old gentlemen together, with the wife of one by his side, or two ladies with a white-haired old gallant walking along beside them, talking of various things, perhaps of politics when there were two men, and of any signs of war that might be on the horizon; and if two were women, of the wedding, and how Lady Caroline took the marriage of her only daughter. The Signor was practising in the Abbey, and the great tones of the organ came rolling forth in a splendour of softened sound over the slope with its slowly strolling groups. Some of the townspeople were there too, not mixing with the others, for the Signor's practising nights were known. The moon began to climb after a while behind the Chevaliers' lodges, and throw a soft whiteness of broad light upon all the pinnacles of the Abbey; and Lottie dropped her work on her knee, unable to see any longer. When the moon rose, she was thrown into shade, and could watch the people with the light in their faces at her ease. And by and by her attention was caught by two single figures which passed several times, coming from different directions, and quite distinct from each other. They both looked up at her window each time they passed, calling forth her curiosity, her scorn, her laughter, finally her interest. Watching them she forgot the immediate presence of her own annoyances. One was the young musician Purcell, at whom Lottie had secretly laughed for a long time past, at his longing looks and the way in which the vicissitudes of her countenance would reflect themselves in his face. But the other she could not for a long time make out. It was not till, seeing no one, he stood still for a full half-minute in the light of the moon, and looked up at her, that she recognised him—and then Lottie's heart gave a jump. It was young Rollo Ridsdale, Lady Caroline's nephew, the best man at the wedding; and what could he want here?

CHAPTER IV
LADY CAROLINE

Lady Caroline was in the drawing-room at the Deanery alone. Now that her daughter was married this was no unusual circumstance. It was late in the summer evening, after dinner, and she lay on a great square sofa so placed that the view from the large window was dimly visible from it, had she cared for the view. As a matter of fact, at no hour of the twenty-four, however bright or tempting it might be, did Lady Caroline care much for the view; but still, when a room is artistically arranged, such a possibility cannot be altogether kept out of consideration. This evening, however, there was no light to see anything by. The room was dark, nothing distinctly visible in it but the great broad Elizabethan window which filled one end. The upper part of this window was filled with old painted glass in silvery tinted quarries, soft greys and yellows, surrounding the golden and ruby glories of several blazons of arms, and drawing the eye irresistibly with the delight of radiant colour; underneath opened the great plain all dim and wide, a suggestion of boundless air and distance rather than a landscape, while in the room itself nothing was distinct but here and there a glimmer of reflection from a mirror breaking the long line of the walls. Nor was its only occupant very distinguishable as she reclined upon her sofa in absolute stillness and tranquillity. The lace on her head and about her throat showed faintly white in the corner, that was all. Perhaps if the mind could have been seen as well as the body, Lady Caroline's individual soul, such as it was, would have told for little more amid the still life around: a something vaguely different from the chairs and softly cushioned sofas, a little more than one of the dim mirrors, a little less than a picture, was this human creature to whom all the rest belonged. She had lived irreproachably on the earth for a number of years (though not for nearly so many years as the most of her furniture), and fulfilled all her functions very much as they did, honestly holding together, affording a temporary place of repose occasionally, convenient for household meals, and ordinary domestic necessities. Perhaps now and then Lady Caroline conferred something of the same kind of solace and support which is given to the weary by a nice warm soft easy-chair, comfortably cushioned and covered; but that was about the highest use of which she was capable. She was waiting now quite tranquilly till it pleased the servants to bring her lights. They were in no hurry, and she was in no hurry. She never did anything, so that it was immaterial whether her room was lighted early or late, and on the whole she liked this dim interval between the active daylight, when people were always in motion, and the lamps, which suggested work, or a book, or something of the sort. Lady Caroline, though she had not very much mind, had a conscience, and knew that it was not quite right for a responsible creature to be without employment; therefore she made certain efforts to fulfil the object of her existence by keeping a serious volume on the table beside her, and putting in a few stitches now and then in a piece of wool-work. But at this hour there was no possibility for the most anxious conscience to speak, and Lady Caroline's was not anxious, only correct, not troubling itself with any burden beyond what was necessary. It may be supposed, perhaps, that she was sad, passing this twilight quite alone, so soon after the marriage and departure of her only daughter; but this would have been a mistake, for Lady Caroline was not sad. Of course she missed Augusta. There was no one now to wake her up when she dozed, as now and then happened, in a warm afternoon after luncheon; and, as a matter of fact, one or two visitors had actually been ushered into the drawing-room while her head was drooping upon her right shoulder, and her cap a little awry. But at this tranquil hour in the dark, when nobody expected anything of her, neither without nor within—neither conscience, nor the Dean, nor society—it cannot be said that any distressful recollection of Augusta mingled with her thoughts. Nor, indeed, had she any thoughts to mingle it with, which was perhaps the reason. She was very comfortable in the corner of her sofa, with nothing to disturb her. Had Jarvis her maid been at hand to tell her what was going on in the precincts, or any bit of gossip that might have floated upward from the town, it would probably have added a little more flavour to her content; but even that flavour was not necessary to her, and she was quite happy as she was.

Some one came into the room as she lay in this pleasant quiet. She thought it was Jeremie coming to light the candles, and said nothing; but it was not so dignified a person as Mr. Jeremie, the Dean's butler, who was generally taken for one of the Canons by visitors unacquainted with the place. This was indeed a shirt-front as dazzling as Jeremie's which came into the soft gloom, but the owner of it was younger and taller, with a lighter step and less solemn demeanour. He gave a glance round the room to see if anyone was visible, then advanced steadily with the ease of an *habitue* among the sofas and tables. "Are you here, Aunt Caroline?" he said. "Oh, you are there! Shall I ring for lights? it must be dull sitting all by yourself in the dark."

"If you please, my dear," said Lady Caroline, who, having no will of her own to speak of, never set it in opposition to anybody else's; answering a question as she did thus promptly, there was no occasion at the same time to answer a mere remark.

"I am afraid you are moping," he said, "missing Augusta. To be sure, it does make a great difference in the house."

"No, my dear," said Lady Caroline, "I can't say I was thinking of Augusta. She is quite happy, you know."

"I hope so," he said, laughing. "If they are not happy now, when should they be happy? the honeymoon scarcely over, and all sorts of delights before them."

"Yes; that is just what I was going to say," said Lady Caroline; "so why should I mope?"

"Why, indeed?" He took his aunt's soft hand into his, and caressed it. Rollo was fond of his aunt, strange though it may appear. She had never scolded him, though this was the favourite exercise of all the rest of his family. When he came home in disgrace she had always received him just the same as if he had come in triumph. Whoever might find fault with him for wasting his talents, or disappointing the hopes of his friends, his Aunt Caroline had never done so. He could not help laughing a little as he spoke, but he caressed her soft white hand as he did so, compunctious, to make amends to her for the ridicule. Lady Caroline, it need not be said, attached no idea of ridicule to his laugh. "But I have come to tell you," said Rollo, "that I have been out again walking up and down the Dean's Walk, as I did the night of the wedding, and I have not been able to hear a note of your singer—the girl with the wonderful voice."

"Did I say there was a girl with a wonderful voice, my dear? I forget."

"Not you, but Augusta; don't you remember, Aunt Caroline, a girl in the Cloisters, in—in the Lodges, a Miss—I don't remember the name. Lottie something, Augusta called her."

"Ah! Augusta was too ready to make friends. It is Miss Despard, I suppose."

"Well; might we not have Miss Despard here some evening? If her voice is as fine as Augusta said, it might be the making of me, Aunt Caroline. An English *prima donna* would make all our fortunes. And unless I hear her, it is not possible, is it, I appeal to your candour, that I can judge?"

"But, my dear!" "But" was a word which scarcely existed in Lady Caroline's vocabulary. It meant an objection, and she rarely objected to anything. Still there was a limit to which instinct and experience alike bound her. She was not unkind by nature, but rather the reverse, and if there was anything that approached a passion—nay, not a passion, an emotion—in her nature, it was for the poor. She who was little moved by any relationship, even the closest, almost loved the poor, and would take trouble for them, petting them when they were sick, and pleased to hear of all their affairs when they were well—conscience and inclination supplementing each other in this point. But the poor, the real "poor," they who are so kind as to be destitute now and then, with nothing to eat and all their clothes at the pawnbroker's, and their existence dependent upon the clergyman's nod, or the visit of the district lady—these were very different from the Chevaliers in their Lodges. There even Lady Caroline drew the line. She did what was suggested to her in a great many cases, but here she felt that she could make a stand when necessity required. Not the people in the Lodges! people who though they lived in small houses on small incomes considered themselves to be ladies and gentlemen as good as the Royal Family themselves. The very mildest, the very gentlest, must pause somewhere, and this is where Lady Caroline made her stand. "My dear," she said, something like a flush coming to her sallow cheek, for Jeremie by this time had brought the lamps and lighted the candles and made her visible; "I have never visited the people in the Lodges. I have always made a stand there. There was one of them appointed through my brother Courtland, you know—your papa, my dear—but when Beatrice asked me to notice them I was obliged to decline. I really could not do it. I hope I never shrink from doing my duty to the poor; but these sort of people—you must really excuse me, Rollo; I could not, I do not think I could do it."

Mr. Ridsdale had never seen anything so near excitement in his aunt's manner before. She spoke with little movements of her hands and of her head, and a pink flush was on her usually colourless face. The sight of this little flutter and commotion which he had caused amused the young man. Jeremie was still moving noiselessly about, letting down a loop of curtain, kindling a distant corner into visibility by lighting one of the groups of candles upon the wall. The room was still very dim, just made visible, not much more, and Jeremie's noiseless presence did not check the expression of Lady Caroline's sentiments. She made her little explanation with a fervour such as, we have said, her nephew had never before seen in her. He was greatly astonished, but he was also, it must be allowed, somewhat disposed to laugh.

"You must pardon me," he said, "for suggesting anything you don't like, Aunt Caroline. But did not Augusta have Miss Despard here?"

"Oh, yes—with the rest of her people who sang. Augusta was always having her singing people—who were not in our set at all."

"I suppose that is all over now," said Rollo in a tone of regret.

"Oh, not quite over. Mrs. Long brought some of them the other day. She thought it would amuse me. But it never amused me much," said Lady Caroline. "Augusta was pleased, and that was all. I don't want them, Rollo;

they disturb me. They require to have tea made for them, and compliments. I am not so very fond of music, you are aware."

"I know; not fond enough to give up anything for it; but confess it is often a resource after dinner, when the people are dull?"

"The people are always just the same, Rollo. If they have a good dinner, that is all I have to do with them. They ought to amuse themselves."

"Yes, yes," he resumed, laughing. "I know you are never dull, Aunt Caroline. Your thoughts flow always in the same gentle current. You are never excited, and you are never bored."

A gentle smile came over Lady Caroline's face, no one understood her so well. She was astonished that so many people found fault with Rollo. He was, she thought, her favourite nephew, if it was right to have a favourite. "It is no credit to me," she said. "I was always brought up in that way. But girls do not have such a good training now."

"No, indeed—the very reverse, I think—they are either in a whirl of amusement or else they are bored. But, Aunt Caroline, people in general are not like you. And for us who have not had the advantage of your education, it is often very dull, especially after dinner. Now you are going to have a gathering to-morrow. Don't you think it would be a good thing to have a little music in the evening, and ask Miss Despard to come and sing? Have her to amuse the people, just as you might have Punch and Judy, you know, or some of the sleight-of-hand men?"

"I should never think of having either the one or the other, Rollo."

"But a great many people do. It was quite the right thing for a time. Come, Aunt Caroline! My uncle is often bored to death with these duty dinners. He will bless you if you have a little music afterwards and set him free."

"Do you really think so? I can't understand why you should all talk of being bored. I am never bored," said Lady Caroline.

"That is your superiority," said the courtier. "But we poor wretches often are. And I really must hear this voice. You would not like to stand in the way of my interests now when I seem really about to have a chance?"

"It is a very curious thing to me," said Lady Caroline, stimulated by so much argument to deliver herself of an original remark, "that such a clever young man as you are, Rollo, should require to connect yourself with singers and theatres. Such a thing was never heard of in my time."

"That is just it," he said, putting on a mournful look. "If I had not been a clever young man, things would have gone a great deal better with me.

There was nothing of that foolish description I am sure, Aunt Caroline, in your time."

"No," she said; then added, almost peevishly, "I do not know how to communicate with the girl, Rollo. She is so out of society."

"But only on the other side of the way," he said. "Come, write her a note, and I will take it myself, if Jeremie or Joseph are too grand to go."

"Must I write her a note? I never in my life sent a note to the Lodges," said Lady Caroline, looking at her hands as if the performance would soil them. Then she added, with a look of relief, "I very often see her when I am out for my drive. You can tell the coachman to stop if he sees her, and I will tell her to come—that will be much the better way."

"But if she should be engaged?"

Lady Caroline gave him a very faint smile of amiable scorn and superior knowledge. "You forget these people are not in society," she said.

To make head against this sublime of contempt was more than Rollo could do. Lady Caroline vanquished him as she had vanquished many people in her day, by that invincible might of simple dulness against which nothing can stand.

Mr. Rollo Ridsdale was one of the many very clever young men in society who are always on the eve of every kind of fame and fortune, but never manage to cross the border between hope and reality. He had been quite sure of success in a great many different ways: at the university, where he was certain of a first class, but only managed to "scrape through" the ordeal of honours in the lowest room;—in diplomacy, where he was expected to rise to the highest rank, but spoiled all his chances by a whisper of a state secret, of no importance to anybody, when only an unpaid attaché;—in the House of Commons, where he broke down in his maiden speech, after costing what his family described as a "fortune" to secure his election;—and finally, in commerce, where his honourable name was just secured from the *éclat* of a disgraceful bankruptcy by the sacrifice of a second "fortune" on the part of the family. It is but fair to add, however, that Rollo had nothing to do with the disgracefulness of the commercial downfall in which he was all but involved. And here he was at eight-and-twenty once more afloat, as the fashionable jackal and assistant of an enterprising *impresario*, indefatigable in his pursuit of the prima donna of the future, and talking of nothing but operas. This was why he had made that moonlight promenade under Lottie Despard's windows on the evening of his cousin's wedding-day. He did not know her, but Lottie knew him as the populace know all, even the most insignificant, members of the reigning family. Lady Caroline's nephew, Augusta's cousin, was of much more importance to the community than any of the community had been to him up to this moment, though the thoughts which passed through Lottie's mind, as, with extreme surprise, she recognised him gazing up at her window, suggested a very different hypothesis. What could Lottie imagine, as, with the most bewildering astonishment, she identified Mr. Ridsdale, but that he had seen her as she had seen him, and that it was admiration at least, if not a more definite sentiment, which brought him to wander in front of the window, as poor young Purcell did, whose delusion she regarded without either surprise or compassion? Rollo Ridsdale was a very different person; and Lottie had been too much bewildered by his appearance to found any theory upon it, except the vaguest natural thrill of flattered pleasure and wonder. Was it possible?—When a young man comes and stares at a lady's window, going and returning, waiting apparently for a glimpse of her—what is anyone to suppose?—There is but one natural and ordinary explanation of such an attitude and proceeding. And if Lottie's fancy jumped at this idea, how could she help it? It gave her a little shock of pleasure and exhilaration in her depressed state. Why should she have been exhilarated? It is difficult to say. She did not know anything of Mr. Ridsdale—whether his admiration was worth having or the reverse. But he was Lady Caroline's nephew, who had always been inaccessible to Lottie; he was Augusta's cousin, who had neglected her. And if it really could be possible that, notwithstanding this, he had conceived a romantic passion for Lottie, what could be more consolatory to the girl who had felt herself humiliated by the indifference and contempt with which these ladies had treated her? The idea brought the light back to her eyes, and her natural gay courage revived again. She would make reprisals, she would "be even with them," and pay them back in their coin; and where is the girl or boy to whom reprisals are not sweet?

This, however, is a digression from Lady Caroline, who went to her tranquil couch that night with a heavier heart than she had known for years. It was a revolution which had occurred in her life. During Augusta's reign she had been passively resistant always, protesting under her breath against the invasion of the singing people of all kinds into her sacred and exclusive world. She had supported it with heroic calm, entrenching herself behind the ladies who were really in society, and whom she could receive without derogation; but to Lottie and the other people who were outside of her world she had never shown any civility, as she was glad to think, on surveying the situation that night. She had not brought it on herself. She had never shown them any civility. A salutation with her eyelids, a cup of tea from her table, the privilege of breathing the same air with her—this had been all she had ever done for her daughter's *protégées*, and hitherto nobody, she was obliged to allow, had presumed upon it. But *that* Miss Despard was not like the timid and respectful singing ladies from the town. She was a bold young woman, who thought herself as good as anyone, and looked as if she ought to be talked to, and taken notice of, as much as anyone.

And it was not possible to get rid of her as the ladies in the town could be got rid of. Lady Caroline could not go out of her own door, could not go to Church, without meeting Miss Despard, and feeling what she called within herself, "the broad stare" of that dangerous girl. And now was it possible, was it conceivable, that she was herself to take the initiative and re-invite Miss Despard? Not for years, if indeed ever in her life, had Lady Caroline gone to bed with such a weight on her mind. She sighed as she laid down on that bed of down—nay, not of down, which is old-fashioned and not very wholesome either, now-a-days, people say—but on her mattress of delicately arranged springs, which moved with every movement. She sighed as she lay down upon it, and the springs swayed under her; and she sighed again in the morning as she woke, and all that had happened came back into her mind. Poor dear Rollo! She did not like to cross him, or to go against him, since he had made so great an object of it. Oh! that Augusta had but held her peace, and had not inflamed his mind about this girl's voice! After all, her voice was nothing wonderful; it was just a soprano, as most girl's voices were; and that she, Lady Caroline, should be compelled to exert herself—compelled to go against her principles, to come into personal contact with a person of a different class! She who had always been careful to keep herself aloof!—It was very hard upon Lady Caroline. She sighed at breakfast so that the Dean took notice of it.

"Is there anything the matter?" he said. "Rollo, do you know what is the matter? This is the third time I have heard your aunt sigh."

"I am sure she does not look as if anything was the matter," said Rollo, with that filial flattery which women like, at Lady Caroline's age.

She gave him a faint little smile, but shook her head and sighed again.

"Bless my soul!" said the Dean, "I must look in upon Enderby, and tell him to come and see you."

"Oh, there is nothing the matter with me," Lady Caroline said; but she had no objection to see Enderby, who was the doctor and always very kind. It even pleased her to think of confiding her troubles to him, for indeed she had the humbling consciousness upon her mind that she had never been a very interesting patient. She had never had anything but headaches and mere external ills to tell him about. She had never till now been able to reveal to him even a headache which had been caused by trouble of mind. Lady Caroline, though she was dull, had a faint wish to be interesting as well as other people, and it would be a relief to pour out this trouble to his sympathising ear.

The idea of meeting Lottie when she went out was a very happy one, Lady Caroline thought. She could not but feel that necessity was producing invention within her. Perhaps she might not meet Lottie, perhaps Lottie might be frightened and would decline to come. She drove out that afternoon with a little excitement, full of hope, if she felt also the palpitation of a little fear. These emotions made quite a pleasant and unusual stir in the dull fluid that filled her veins. She was half disturbed and half pleased when she found that Rollo proposed going with her, a very unusual compliment from a young man. He said it was because he had hurt his foot and could not walk. "Dear me!" Lady Caroline said, "I will send Jarvis to see if it is a sprain." "Oh no, it is not a sprain," he said; "a little rest is all it requires." "You will find carriage exercise very nice," Lady Caroline said; "a perfect rest—and much more amusement than walking, which tires one out directly." And thus they set out perfectly pleased with each other. But the coachman had got his instructions carefully from Rollo's own lips, and there was now no possibility of escape for the poor lady, over whom Rollo himself had mounted guard. They had not gone above a few yards from the Deanery door, when the carriage suddenly drew up with a jar, to the side of the high terrace pavement which lay in front of the Lodges. Rollo, who was on the alert, looked eagerly out, and saw a light erect figure, full of energy and life, coming up, in the plainest of morning frocks, one of those simple toilettes which fashion has lately approved. She looked perfectly fresh, and like the summer morning, as she came along, with a little basket in her hand; and suddenly it burst upon Rollo, as Lottie raised her eyes with a glance of astonished interest in them, wondering why it was that Lady Caroline's carriage should stop there, that this unknown girl was extremely handsome—a thing for which the young man had not been prepared. "Is this Miss Despard? but she will be gone unless you send to her. Shall I go and call her to you?" he said.

"Oh, she will come when she sees I want her," said Lady Caroline. But the only answer he made was to jump up and let himself out of the carriage before Joseph could get off from the box. He went up to Lottie with his hat in his hand, very much surprised in his turn by the vivid blush which covered her cheeks at sight of him. He was flattered, and he was surprised; was it a mere trick of unformed manners, the *gaucherie* of a girl who had never been in society, and did not know how to behave herself? or was it that she saw something unusually fascinating in himself, Rollo? To see so handsome a girl blush at his approach was a tribute to his attractions, which Rollo was not the man to be indifferent to. He almost forgot the business side of the transaction, and his hunt after a prima donna, in the pleasure of such an encounter. Could she have seen him somewhere before and been "struck" with him? Rollo wondered. It was an agreeable beginning. He went up to her with his hat in his hand as if she had been a princess. "I beg your pardon," he said, "my aunt, Lady Caroline Huntington, has sent me to beg that you would let her speak to you for a moment." Lottie looked at him bewildered, with eyes that could scarcely meet his. She could hardly make out what he said, in the sudden confusion and excitement of meeting thus, face to face, the man whom she had seen under her window. What was it? Lady Caroline asking to speak with her, awaiting her, in her carriage, in the sight of all St. Michael's! Lottie stood still for a moment, and gazed at this strange sight, unable to move or speak for wonder. What could Lady Caroline have to say? She could not be going, on the spot, out of that beautiful chariot with its prancing horses, to plead her nephew's suit with the girl who knew nothing of him except his lover-like watch under her window. Lottie could not trust herself to make him any reply—or rather she said idiotically, "Oh, thank you," and turned half reluctant, confused, and anxious, to obey the call. She went to the carriage door, and stood without a word, with her eyes full of wonder, to hear what the great lady had to say.

But it was not much at any time that Lady Caroline had to say. She greeted Lottie with the little movement of her eyelids. "How do you do, Miss Despard?" she said. "I wanted to ask if you would come to the Deanery this evening for a little music?" There was no excitement in that calmest of voices. Lottie felt so much ashamed of her wonderful vague absurd anticipations, that she blushed more hotly than ever.

"At half-past nine," said Lady Caroline.

"You have not presented me to Miss Despard, Aunt Caroline—so I have no right to say anything; but if I had any right to speak, I should say I hope—I hope—that Miss Despard is not engaged, and that she will come."

How earnest his voice was! and what a strange beginning of acquaintance! Lottie felt half disposed to laugh, and half to cry, and could not lift her eyes in her confusion to this man who—was it possible?—was in love with her, yet whom she did not know.

"Oh, I am not engaged—I—shall be very happy." What else could she say? She stood still, quite unaware what she was doing, and heard him thank her with enthusiasm, while Lady Caroline sat quite passive. And then the splendid vision rolled away, and Lottie stood alone wondering, like a creature in a dream, on the margin of the way.

CHAPTER V
AT THE DEANERY

Lottie stood as if in a dream, hearing the ringing of the horses' hoofs, the roll of the carriage, and nothing more; all the sounds in the world seemed to be summed up in these. She could scarcely tell what had happened to her. A great honour had happened to her, such as might have impressed the imagination of anyone in that little world of St. Michael's, but not so great a thing as she thought. Lady Caroline had asked her to tea. It was something, it was much; it was what Lady Caroline had never done to anyone in the Lodges before. Even Mrs. Seymour, whose husband was really *one of the Seymours*, people said, and whom Lady Courtland had begged Lady Caroline to be kind to, had not been so honoured. But for all that, it was not what Lottie thought. She stood there with her heart beating, feeling as if she had just fallen from the clouds, in a maze of bewildered excitement, scarcely able to realise what had befallen her—and yet that which had befallen her was not what she thought. Most things that happen to us are infinitely better in thought and in hope than they are in reality; but this was doubly, trebly the case with poor Lottie, who found the cause of this new happiness of hers in a delusion, a mistake, most innocently, most unwittingly occasioned. It was not a thing that anybody had intended. Rollo Ridsdale had meant no harm when he strolled along the Dean's Walk in the evening on two separate nights, looking up at Lottie's window and hoping to hear her sing in order that he might tell his partner of a new voice to be had for the asking. And neither had Lottie meant any harm; it was not vanity, it was the most natural conclusion from what she saw with her own eyes. How could she doubt it? He must have seen her when she was not aware of it, and fallen in love with her, as people say, at first sight! a romantic compliment that always goes to a girl's heart. There was no other interpretation to be put upon the fact of his lingering about looking up at her window. She had said to herself it was nonsense; but how could it be nonsense? What other explanation could anyone give of such a proceeding? And now he had managed to make Lady Caroline, she who was the queen of the place and unapproachable, take his cause in hand. For what other possible reason could Lady Caroline, who never noticed anyone out of her own sphere, have paid this special and public compliment to Lottie, and invited her to Paradise, as it were—to tea—not afternoon tea, which means little, but *in the evening*? But here

Lottie's fancies became so bewildering that she could not follow herself in her thoughts; much less would it be possible for us to follow her. For if Lady Caroline had thus interfered on her nephew's behalf, securing for him a personal introduction and an opportunity of making her acquaintance, what could this mean but that Lady Caroline was on his side and meant to help him and approved of his sentiments? This thought was too wonderful to be entertained seriously; it only glanced across the surface of Lottie's mind, making her laugh within herself with a bewildered sense that there was something absurd in it. Lady Caroline stoop from her high estate to lift her, Lottie, to a place upon that dazzling eminence! The girl felt as if she had been spun round and round like a teetotum, though it was an undignified comparison. She did not know where she might find herself when, dizzy and tottering, she should come to herself. All this time Mrs. O'Shaughnessy, at her window, where she always sat surveying everything that went on, had been knocking an impatient summons with her knuckles on the pane; and this it was at last which brought Lottie to herself. She obeyed it with some reluctance, yet at the same time she was glad to sit down somewhere till the giddiness should go off and the hurry of her thoughts subside. Mrs. O'Shaughnessy met her with a countenance full of interest and eagerness; a new incident was everything to her. She was as eager as if it was of vital importance to know every word that Lady Caroline said.

"Then what was she saying to ye, me dear?" cried the old lady, from whom excitement almost took away the breath.

"She did not say anything," said Lottie, relieving her feelings by a little laugh. "She never does say anything; she asked me to tea."

"And you call that nothing, ye thankless creature! It's spoilt ye are, Lottie, me darling, and I always said that was what would come of it. She asked you to tea? sure it'll be afternoon tea for one of the practisings, like it was in Miss Augusta's day?"

"No! I am to go in after dinner. It is not the first time, Mrs. O'Shaughnessy; Augusta has often asked me. What else did I get my white frock for?—for there are no parties here to go to. She used to say: 'Come in, and bring your music.' It is not me they want, it is my voice," said Lottie assuming a superiority of wisdom which she did not possess.

"All in good time, me dear," said Mrs. O'Shaughnessy. "And did my Lady Caroline bid you to bring your music, too? The daughter is one thing, and the mother is clean another. I hope you've got your frock in order me darlin'; clean and nice and like a lady? You should send it to Mrs. Jones to iron it out; she's the plague of my life, but she's a beautiful clear starcher—that I will say for her; and if you want a ribbon or so, me jewel, or anything I have that ye may take a fancy to—there's my brooch with O'Shaughnessy's miniature, sure ne'er a one of them would find out who it was. You might say it was your grandpapa, me honey, in his red coat, with his medals; and fine he'd look on your white frock— —"

"Thank you!" said Lottie in alarm; "but I never wear anything, you know, except poor mamma's little pearl locket."

"Sure I know," said the old woman, with a laugh; "a body can't wear what they haven't got! But you needn't turn up your little nose at my big brooch, for when it was made it was the height of the fashion, and now everything that's old is the height of the fashion. And so me Lady Caroline, that's too grand to say 'Good morning to ye, ma'am,' or 'Good evening to ye,' after ye've been her neighbour for a dozen years, stops her grand carriage to bid this bit of a girl to tea, and Miss Lottie takes it as cool as snowballs, if ye please. Well, well, honey! I don't envy ye, not I; but you're born to luck as sure as the rest of us are born to trouble, and that all the Abbey can see."

"I born to luck! I don't think there is much sign of it," said Lottie, though with a tumultuous leap of the heart which contradicted the words. "And what is there, I should like to know, that all the Abbey can see?"

"If you think I'm going to tell you the nonsense that is flying about, and put fancies in your little head!" said the old Irishwoman, "go your ways, and see that your frock's in order; and I'll run in and see you dressed, me pet, and I'll bring the brooch and the box with me best ribbons; may be at the last you'll change your mind."

Lottie went home with her head in the clouds; was she indeed "born to luck"? Was she going to be transplanted at once without the tedious probation which even in poetry, even in story-books, the good heroine has generally to go through, into that heaven of wealth and rank and luxurious surroundings which she felt to be her proper sphere? It was not that Lottie cared for luxury in its vulgarer forms; she liked what was beautiful and stately—the large noble rooms, the dignified aspect which life bore when unconnected with those small schemes and strugglings in which her existence was spent; but above all she liked, it must be allowed, to be uppermost, to feel herself on the highest round of the ladder—and hated and resisted with all her soul the idea of being inferior to anybody. This was the thing above all others which Lottie could not bear. She had been brought up with the idea that she belonged by right of nature to the upper classes, a caste entirely removed by immutable decree of Providence from shop-keepers and persons engaged in trade, and to whom it was comparatively immaterial whether they were poor or rich, nothing being able to alter the birthright which united them with all that was high and separated them from all that was low. But this right had not been acknowledged at St. Michael's. She and her family had been mixed up in the crowd along with the O'Shaughnessys, and other unexalted people; and nobody, not even the

O'Shaughnessys, had been impressed by the long descent of the Despard family and its unblemished gentility. Something else then evidently was requisite to raise her to her proper place, to the sphere to which she belonged. Lottie would not have minded poverty, or difficulty, or hard work, had she been secure of her "position"; but that was just the thing of which in present circumstances she was least secure. It was for this reason that Lady Caroline's notice was sweet to her—for this that she had been so deeply disappointed when no sign of amity was accorded to her on the wedding-day. And this was why her heart leapt with such bewildering hope and excitement at the new event in her career. She did not know Mr. Ridsdale; perhaps his admiration or even his love were little worth having; and nothing but what are called interested motives could have possibly moved Lottie to the thrill of pleasure with which she contemplated his supposed attachment. A girl whose head is turned by the mere idea of a lover who can elevate her above her neighbours, without any possibility of love on her part to excuse the bedazzlement, is not a very fine or noble image; yet Lottie's head was turned, not vulgarly, not meanly, but with an intoxication that was full of poetry and all that is most ethereal in romance. A tender, exquisite gratitude to the man who thus seemed to have chosen her, without any virtue of hers, filled her heart; and to the great lady who, though so lofty, and usually cold as marble to the claims of those beneath her, could thus forget her pride for Lottie. This feeling of gratitude softened all the other emotions in her mind. She was ready to be wooed, but then the very manner of the first step in this process, the lingering outside her window, which was a sign of the tenderest, most delicate, and reverential love-making (but she did not think it so in the case of poor young Purcell), showed what a respectful, ethereal, poetical wooing it would be. Thus Lottie's whole being was full of the most tremulous, delicious happiness, all made up of hope and anticipation, and grateful admiration of the fine generous sentiments of her supposed lover, even while it was founded, as you may say, on self-interest and ambition, and sentiments which were not generous at all.

And with what a flutter at her heart she put out her white muslin frock, which (not having any confidence in Mrs. Jones) she ironed herself most carefully and skilfully, with such interest in keeping it fresh as no Mrs. Jones in the world could have. For girls who have no ornaments to speak of, how kind summer is providing roses, which are always the most suitable of decorations! One knot of them in her hair and one at her breast—what could Lottie want more? Certainly not the big brooch with Major O'Shaughnessy in his red coat, which her old friend was so anxious to pin the roses with. Mrs. O'Shaughnessy thought it would be "such a finish," and prove satisfactorily that it was not poverty but fancy that made Lottie decorate herself with fresh flowers instead of the fine artificial wreath with a nice long trail down the back, which was what the old lady herself would have preferred. Mrs. O'Shaughnessy, however, was mollified by the girl's acceptance of the Indian shawl which she brought to wrap her in. "And you might just carry it into the room with you, me dear, as if ye thought ye might feel chilly," said the old lady, "for it's a beauty, and I should like me Lady Caroline to see it. I doubt if she's got one like it. Good-night and a pleasant evening to ye, me honey," she cried, as, under charge of Law, and with her dress carefully folded up, Lottie with her beating heart went across the broad gravel of the Dean's Walk to the Deanery door. It was a lovely summer night, not dark at all, and the Signor was practising in the Abbey, and the music rolling forth in harmonious thunders rose, now more, now less distinct, as the strain grew softer or louder. A great many people were strolling about, loitering, when Lottie came out, skimming over the road in her little white shoes, with the roses in her hair. All the rest of her modest splendours were hidden by the shawl, but these could not be hidden. The people about all turned their heads to look at her. She was going to the Deanery. It was the same in St. Michael's as visiting the Queen.

The Dean's dinner party had been of a slightly heavy description. There were several of the great people from the neighbourhood, county people whom it was necessary to ask periodically. It was so distinctly made a condition, at the beginning of this story, that we were not to be expected to describe the doings on Olympus, nor give the reader an insight into the behaviour of the gods and goddesses, that we feel ourselves happily free from any necessity of entering into the solemn grandeur of the dinner. It was like other dinners in that region above all the clouds. The ladies were fair and the gentlemen wise, and they talked about other ladies and gentlemen not always perhaps equally wise or fair. Mr. Rollo Ridsdale was the greatest addition to the party. He knew all the very last gossip of the clubs. He knew what Lord Sarum said to Knowsley, upbraiding him for the indiscretion of his last Guildhall speech. "But everybody knows that Knowsley is nothing if not indiscreet," Rollo said; and he knew that, after all, whatever anyone might say to the contrary, Lady Martingale *had* gone off with Charley Crowther, acknowledging that nothing in the world was of any consequence to her in comparison. "Such an infatuation!" for, as everybody knew, Charley was no Adonis. Lady Caroline shook her head over this, as she ate her chicken (or probably it was something much nicer than chicken that Lady Caroline ate). And thus the *menu* was worked through. There was but one young lady in the party, and even she was married. In Augusta's time the young people were always represented, but it did not matter so much now. When all these ladies rose at last in their heavy dresses that swept the carpet, and in their diamonds which made a flicker and gleam of light about their heads and throats, and swept out to the drawing-room: all, with that one exception, over middle age, all well acquainted with each other, knowing the pedigrees and the possessions each of each, and with society in general for their common ground, the reader will tremble to think of such a poor little thing as Lottie, in her white muslin, with the roses in her hair, standing trembling in a corner of the big drawing-room, and waiting for the solemn stream of silk and satin, and society, in which she would have been engulfed at once, swallowed up and seen no more. And what would have happened to Lottie, had she been alone, without anyone to stand by her in the midst of this overflowing, we shrink from contemplating; but happily she had already found a companion to hold head with her against the stream.

For when Lottie came in, she found some one before her in the drawing-room, a tall, very thin man, with stooping shoulders, who stood by the corner of the mantelpiece, on which there were candles, holding a book very close to his eyes. When Lottie went in, with her heart in her mouth, he turned round, thinking that the opening of the door meant the coming of the ladies. The entrance, instead, of the one young figure, white and slender, and of Lottie's eyes encountering him, full of fright and anxiety, yet with courage in them—the look that was intended for Lady Caroline, and which was half a prayer, "Be kind to me!" as well as perhaps the tenth part of a defiance—made a great impression upon the solitary inmate of the room. He was as much afraid of what he thought a beautiful young lady, as Lottie was of the mistress of the house.

After this first moment, however, when she perceived that there was nobody alarming, only a gentleman (an *old* gentleman, Lottie contemptuously, or rather carelessly concluded, though he was not more in reality than about five-and-thirty), she regained her composure, and her heart went back to its natural place. Lottie knew very well who the gentleman was, though he did not know her. It was Mr. Ashford, one of the minor canons, a very shy and scholarly person, rather out of his element in a community which did not pretend to much scholarship or any special devotion to books. Perhaps he was the only man in St. Michael's whom Lottie had ever really desired to make acquaintance with on his own account; but indeed it was scarcely on his own account, but on account of Law, about whom she was always so anxious. Mr. Ashford took pupils, with whom he was said to be very successful. He lived for his pupils, people said, and thought of nothing else but of how to get them into shape and push them on. It had been Lottie's dream ever since she came to St. Michael's to get Law under Mr. Ashford's care; and after she had recovered the shock of getting into the room, and the mingled thrill of relief and impatience at finding that there was nobody there as yet to be afraid of, Lottie, whose heart always rose to any emergency, began to speculate how she could make friends with Mr. Ashford. She was not afraid of him: he was short-sighted, and he was awkward and shy, and a great deal more embarrassed by her look than she was by his. And he was being badly used—so she thought. Why was not he asked to dinner like the others? Mr. Ashford did not himself feel the grievance, but Lottie felt it for him. She ranged herself instantly, instinctively, by his side. They were the two who were being condescended to, being taken notice of—they were the natural opponents consequently of the fine people, the people who condescended and patronised. Mr. Ashford, on his side, stood and looked at her, and did not know what to do. He did not know who she was. She was a beautiful young lady, and he knew he had seen her in the Abbey; but further than this Mr. Ashford knew nothing of Lottie. The signs which would have betrayed her lowly condition to an experienced eye said nothing to him. Her white muslin might have been satin for anything he could tell, her little pearl locket a priceless ornament. He did not know how to address such a dazzling creature; though to any ordinary person in society Lottie's attire would have suggested bread-and-butter, and nothing dazzling at all.

"It is a beautiful evening," said Lottie, a little breathless. "It is scarcely dark yet, though it is half-past nine o'clock."

To both these unquestionable statements Mr. Ashford said "Yes," and then he felt himself called upon to make a contribution in return. "I have just found a book which somebody must have been reading," he said, growing red with the effort.

"Oh, yes! is it a very interesting book? What is it about?" said Lottie, but this was something for which Mr. Ashford was not prepared. He got redder than ever and cleared his throat.

"It does not seem about anything in particular. I have not really had time to read it;" then he made a hasty dash at an abstract subject, and said, with a falter in his voice, "Are—are you fond of reading?" This question at once lit up Lottie's face.

"Oh, *very*, very fond! But I have not many books nor much time. I always envy people who can read everything they please. Mr. Ashford, I wonder if I might speak to you about something—before they come in," said Lottie, coming a step nearer, and looking eagerly at him with her dangerous blue eyes.

Mr. Ashford got the better of his shyness in a moment. It did not embarrass him when there was anything to be done. He smiled upon her with a most beautiful beaming smile which altogether changed the character of his face, and put a chair for her, which Lottie, however, did not take. "Surely," he said, in his melodious voice, suddenly thawed out of the dryness which always got into his throat when he spoke first to a stranger. It has not yet been said that Mr. Ashford's chief quality as respected the community at St. Michael's was an unusually beautiful mellow voice. "If there is any way in which I can be of use to you?" he said.

"Oh, yes; so much use! They say you think a great deal about your pupils, Mr. Ashford," said Lottie, "and I have a brother whom nobody thinks much about— —"

That was the moment Lady Caroline chose to return to the drawing-room. The door opened, the ladies swept in one by one, the first looking suspiciously at both Mr. Ashford and Lottie, the second, who knew Mr. Ashford, giving him a smile of recognition, and looking suspiciously only at Lottie, the rest following some one example, some the other. Lottie knew not one of them. She looked trembling for Lady Caroline, and hoped she would be kind, and save her from the utter desolation of standing alone in this smiling and magnificent company. But Lady Caroline coming in last of all, only made her usual salutation to the stranger. She said, "Good evening, Miss Despard," as she swept her long train of rustling silk over the carpet close to Lottie's trembling feet, but she put out her hand to Mr. Ashford. "It was so good of you to come," she said. Alas! Lottie was not even to have the comfort of feeling on the same footing with the minor canon. He was carried off from her just as he had begun to look on her with friendly eyes. The stream flowed towards the other side of the room, where Lady Caroline seated herself on her favourite square sofa. Lottie was left standing all alone against the soft grey of the wall, lighted up by the candles on the mantelpiece. When a person belonging to one class of society ventures to put a rash foot on the sacred confines of another, what has she to expect? It is an old story, and Lottie had gone through it before, and ought to have had more sense, you will say, than to encounter it again. But the silly girl felt it as much as if she had not quite known what would happen to her. She stood still, feeling unable to move, one wave of mortification and indignation going over her after another. How could they be so cruel? What did they ask her for, if they meant to leave her to stand there by herself? And Mr. Ashford, too, was cruel. She had made up her mind to stand by him; but he had been carried away by the first touch; he had not stood by her. Lottie could have torn off the roses with which she had decked herself so hopefully, and stamped her foot upon them. She almost wished she had the courage to do it, to cry out to those careless people and let them see what unkindness they were doing. Meantime she made a very pretty picture without knowing it. "Look at that pretty, sulky girl against the wall," said the young married lady to her mother. "Lady Caroline must have set her there on purpose to look handsome and ill-tempered. How handsome she is! I never saw such eyelashes in my life; but as sulky as a thundercloud."

"Go and talk to her and then she will not be sulky," said the mother, who, though by instinct she had looked suspiciously at Lottie, was not unkind; nay, was a kind woman when she saw any need for it. Neither were the others unkind—but they did not see any need for it. It was Lady Caroline's business, they thought, to entertain her own guests.

Lottie, however, had her triumph later when she sang, all the whispered conversation in the room stopping out of sheer astonishment. Her voice had developed even within the last month or two, during which there had been no singing in the Deanery, and as the Signor, who had come in after his practising, played her accompaniments for her, and did his very best to aid and heighten the effect of her songs, her success was complete. He had never accompanied her before, which was a fact Lottie did not remember. And she did not notice either in her preoccupation, thinking nothing of this but much of less important matters—that he knew everything she could sing best, and humoured, and flattered, and coaxed her voice to display itself to the very fullest advantage, as only a skilful accompanyist can. No doubt he had his motive. As for Rollo Ridsdale, he stood on the other side of the piano looking at Lottie with a gaze which seemed to go through and through her. It meant, in fact, at once the real enthusiasm of a man who knew exactly what such talent was worth, and the less practical but still genuine enthusiasm of the amateur who knew what the music was worth as well as the voice. In the one point of view he saw Lottie's defects, in the other he saw all that could be made of her. An English prima donna! a real native talent as good as anything that ever came out of Italy, and capable of producing any amount of national enthusiasm! Rollo's eyes shone, his face lighted up, he did not know how to express his delight. He said to himself that she would make "all our fortunes," with an exaggeration common to his kind. "I knew I was to be charmed, Miss Despard, but I did not know what delight was in store for me," he said, with eyes that said still more than his words. Lottie's eyes with their wonderful lashes sank before his. He thought it was perhaps a pretty trick to show that remarkable feature, and since he was sensible at all points to the beautiful, he did full justice to them. By Jove! how well she would look on the stage. Those eyelashes themselves! that pose! What a pensive Marguerite, what a Lucia she would make! He longed to rush up to town by the late train and rush upon his astonished partner, shouting, "I have found her!" "You will not deny me one more?" he said, turning to her with glowing eyes.

Poor silly Lottie! She grew crimson with pleasure and excitement, pale with excitement and feeling. What did she know about the young fellow's motives? She knew only that he had kept watch at her window, lounging about for a glimpse of her, a thing which to be sure explains itself; and that every note she sang seemed to make him happier and happier, and more and more adoring. The incense was delicious to her. She had never had it before (except perhaps from poor young Purcell—a nobody! what did he matter?), and the happiness of flattered vanity and soothed pride raised her to a pinnacle and climax of soft delight, such as she had never thought possible. It seemed almost more than Lottie could bear. Even Lady Caroline was so flattered by the plaudits addressed to her on the entertainment she had provided for her guests, that a sense of superior discrimination came over her placid mind, pleasantly exciting its tranquillity. "Yes, I knew that she was going to have a beautiful voice," she said. And she smiled, and accepted the thanks with an agreeable sense that she had deserved them. As for Rollo Ridsdale, it was he who got Miss Despard's shawl and wrapped her in it when the dreadful moment came, as he said, for her departure. "You have no carriage; you live on the other side of the way; then you must permit me to see you to your door," he said, "and to thank you once more for all the pleasure you have given me. This will be a white day in my recollection; I shall begin the dates in my history from the time when I first heard——"

"Mr. Ashford is going Miss Despard's way. And, Rollo, your aunt wants you, I think. We have all been so much delighted that we have forgotten the progress of time, and Lady Caroline is not very strong. Mr. Ashford," said the Dean, "I am sure we may leave to you the privilege of seeing Miss Despard to her own door."

"And I am here," said the Signor. Nevertheless, poor Lottie felt as if she had stepped suddenly out of heaven to earth again when she found herself between the musician and the minor canon outside the Deanery door.

CHAPTER VI
LAW

Law went with his sister dutifully to the door in the great cloister. He did not care much for the honour and glory of going to the Deanery, but he was pleased to walk with Lottie in her pretty evening dress, with the roses in her hair. This gave him a certain gratification and sense of family pride, though he scoffed at that sentiment in general. Law did not feel that on the whole he had much to be proud of. Still, he was proud of Lottie, who was a creature quite out of the common, and like nobody else he had ever seen. He waited till the Deanery door was opened to her. That was a world of which Law knew nothing, and did not want to know anything. How Lottie had managed to get among these fine people, and why she liked to get among them, were equally strange to him. He admired her for the first, and wondered at her for the last. She was, at the present moment, the only lady belonging to the Chevaliers who had got footing in the Deanery; and this was just like Lottie, just what he would have expected from her, he said to himself; but how she could stand those old fogies, with their pride and their finery, that was what he could not tell. All the same, it gave him a certain gratification to leave her there in her element among the great people. And when the door closed upon him Law went off about his own business. He went through the cloister, and a curious little back cloister beyond—for there were many intricacies about the Abbey, the different degrees of the hierarchy being very distinct, one cloister for the Chapter, another for the Minor people, and a third for the lay clerks. He went through the little square of the minor cloister, and came out upon a stone staircase which abridged the slopes of St. Michael's Hill, and led straight down into the town. The lights had begun to be lighted in the picturesque street which wound round the foot of the hill; they twinkled here and there in the shops opposite, and appeared in glimmers in the villages across the river. The dim misty plain lying doubly broad in the twilight, stretching out vaguely to the sky, was here and there defined by one of those twinkles which showed where a group of houses stood together. The town was all out in the streets, and on the river this lovely evening: boats floating dimly about the stream, people walking vaguely up and down the hill. And the air was filled with pleasant soft, uncertain sounds of talking, of footsteps, now and then the clocks chiming or striking, and a bugle sounding faint and far from where the soldiers were quartered, for there was a military depôt not far off. Law stopped at the head of the Steps, as they were called, and looked down over all this scene. The mere notion of being out in the *grand air*, as the French call it, with somehow a fuller sense of space and width than we can find a word for, was pleasant to Law; but if he paused, it was neither to enjoy the picture before him, nor was it because he had no definite place to go to. He knew very well where he was going. No vagueness on that point was in his mind; and he did not care a brass farthing for the landscape; but he paused at the head of the Steps and looked about, just as a child will pause before eating his cake, a pause of anticipation and spiritual enjoyment of the dainty before it goes to his lips. Then he ran down the Steps three at a time, skimming down the long flights, turning the corners like a bird. To take care of his sister had been duty, but Law was about his own business now.

What was Law's business? In all St. Michael's there was not a more idle boy. He was over eighteen, and he did nothing. Vague hopes that he would get some appointment—that something would turn up for him—that he would suddenly awake and find himself in an office somehow, doing something and making money—had been in his own mind and that of his family all his life. Law had no objection. Had some one taken him and set him down at once in any office, it was quite possible that he might have done the best he could in his place, and succeeded as well as most men; but in the meantime there were a great many preliminaries to go through, for which Law had never been required or encouraged to fit himself. In these days of examination, when the pitifullest little bit of an office builds up those prickly thorns, those red-hot ploughshares before its door, how was he to get into any office without education? He had spent all his earlier years, as has been seen, in eluding school as cleverly as possible, and doing as little as he could of his lessons; and now here he was on the verge of manhood, with nothing to do and no great wish to do anything;—a great, straight, powerful young fellow, without any absolute aim or tendency to evil, but good for nothing, not capable of anything, with neither purpose nor object in his life. He could row very well when anyone would give him an oar. He was not amiss at cricket when anyone asked him to play. He could walk with any man, and had won a race or two, and was quite capable of competing for a high jump, or for throwing a cricket-ball, or any of those useful accomplishments; but as for anything else he was not capable. He hated books with that sincere and earnest hatred which seems possible only to those who know books to be the preliminary of everything—a peculiarity of this examining age. Never before surely was such a candid and thorough detestation of the tools of knowledge possible. Law knew that no door could possibly open to him without them, and therefore he hated and despised them, illogically no doubt, but very cordially all the same; and so went drifting along upon the stream, not asking what was to become of him, never thinking much of the subject, though he suffered greatly from want of pocket-money, and would gladly have made some exertion from time to time to obtain that, had he known what to do.

This want of pocket-money is the grand drawback to the education or no education of the youths of the nineteenth century. So long as they can have enough of that, what a pleasant life is theirs! For it does you no particular harm to be supposed to be "working for an examination" so long as you don't work much for that, and are exempted, for the sake of it, from all other kinds of work. Boating and cricketing and running races, and every kind of exercise, are known now-a-days to be compatible with the hardest mental labour, and he is a stern parent indeed who interferes with his son's training in such essential points. But all these delights are more or less dependent upon pocket-money. Law, whose bread and cheese had never yet failed, and whose conscience was not active, would have found his life quite pleasant but for that; but it was hard upon him not to be able to pay his subscription to a cricket club, nor the hire of a boat, nor even the entry money for a race, though that was sure to repay itself abundantly if he won it. This was very hard upon him, and often stimulated him to the length of a resolution that he would work to-morrow and conquer all his subjects, and "scrape through" by sheer force of will, so as to have an income of his own. But the habit of idleness unfortunately overcame the resolution next morning, which was a pity, and Law "loafed," as he himself said, not being able to afford to "do anything." It is needless to inform the instructed who have to do with youths working for examinations, that it is cricket and boating and athletics these heroes mean when they talk of "having something to do."

Law, however, had a pleasure before him which had no connection with pocket-money. He went straight down with the directness of habit, till he came to a lane very tortuous and narrow, crowded with builders'-yards and coal-merchants, and affording glimpses of the little wharves where a little traffic was carried on, edging the river. Threading his way through them, he came to a red brick house, the front of which overhung the stream with its projecting gable. Law went in through a door which stood open always, and showed signs of much and constant use. There were lodgings upstairs, which were very pleasant in summer, and which were always let, and made a very comfortable item in the earnings of the family; but it was not upstairs that Law went, though that would have done him good. On the first floor, in the room with the square window, which overlooked and indeed overhung the river, the excellent curate was living with whom Law occasionally "read," and to whom no doubt he would have said he was going had Lottie seen him at this door. But Law had no intention of disturbing the curate, who for his part did not want his pupil. He passed the staircase altogether, and pushed open a green baize door, beyond which was a short passage leading into a room, all ablaze with gas. The door of the room was wide open, and so were the windows, to admit all the air that was possible, and round the large table between sat three or four young women working and talking. They were very busy; the great table was covered with silk and muslin, and all kinds of flimsy trimming, and though they chatted they were working as for bare life. As Law sauntered in they all looked up for a moment, and threw a smile or a nod or half-a-dozen words at him, but scarcely intermitted a stitch. "We're awful busy; we can't so much as look at you; we've got some wedding things to finish for to-morrow," said one fair-haired girl who seemed specially to appropriate his visit. She pushed her chair a little aside without pausing in her work, as if accustomed to make room for him; and Law took a chair and placed it sideways, so that he could lean his idle elbow on the table between this busy needlewoman and the rest. Perhaps as a stormy sea gives zest to the enjoyment of tranquillity on shore, so the extreme occupation of this workroom made him feel his own absolute leisure more delightful.

"Who is going to be married?" he said.

"Oh, you know just as well as I do. I am sure you have heard us talking of it for the last week. Polly, didn't you tell Mr. Despard all about it? It's a lady you know. It's Miss Hare at the Golden Eagle, who is one of your papa's great friends. I don't know what the Captain will do when she's gone. Polly, do you?"

"I don't know what the Captain has to do with her, nor me neither," said the young lady at the head of the table. The rest of the girls were sisters, with fair frizzy locks a little out of order after the long day's work, what with the warmth of the room, and the fluttering of the faint breeze from the river that ruffled the well-crimped tresses. But Polly was of a different stamp. She had a mountain of dark brown hair upon her head in plaits and curls and puffs innumerable, and though she was sallow in complexion, had commanding features, a grand aquiline nose, and brilliant eyes. "The Captain nor me, we hav'nt much to say to that sort," said Polly. "I don't go with them that has a word and a laugh for everybody. What I like is a young lady that respects herself. If you work for your living, that's not to say that you ain't as good as the best of them. Stick up for yourself, and other folks will think of you according, that's what I say."

"I am sure Miss Hare always sticks up for herself," said the girl by Law's side. "Going to be married in a veil, like one of the quality!"

"And so would I, if it was me," cried Polly. "The quality! What are they better than us, only they've got a pocketful of money. If I was the Queen, I'd do away with them all. I'd be the Queen, and all the rest should be the people. There shouldn't be one more than another, or one greater than another, only me. And then shouldn't I do whatever I pleased, and cut off their heads if they said a word!"

This instinctive perception of the secret of despotism made Law laugh, who thought he knew a great deal better. "It would be a funny world with Queen Polly over it," he said. "I hope you'd take me for your prime minister."

Polly gave him a look of saucy malice. "I'd take the Captain," she said.

"Has he been here to-night, Emma? I think he's always coming here," said Law, under his breath. It was a kind of growl which the young fellow gave out when he spoke low, in the voice which not very long ago had been treble, a soprano, as clear and pure as Lottie's—but it was extremely bass now.

"He wants to know," said Emma, with a glance at the others as she pinned her work straight, "if the Captain has been here;" upon which there was a chorus of laughter, making Law red and angry. He turned upon them with a furious look.

"I should like to know how you would all like it," said the boy, "if your governor were to come poking in the very same place where——"

"Oh, you may make yourself quite easy, Mr. Lawrence," said Polly, with a toss of her elaborately dressed head. "He don't meddle with you. The Captain is a man of taste, he ain't a boy, like some folks. He knows what's what, the Captain does. Other girls may have their fancies; I don't say anything against that, but give me a man as knows the world, and knows what he wants. That's the sort for me."

"She gets more insufferable than ever. I wonder how you can put up with her," said Law under his breath.

"Doesn't she," said Emma in a whisper. "I wish she had never come into our workroom; but she has taste, mother says, and we have to put up with it. Everything has to give way to the work," the girl added, threading her needle; and as she made a knot upon the end of the new thread, she shook her head with a sigh.

Everything has to give way to the work! Law could not but smile, feeling the superiority of his gentlemanhood. With him it was the work that gave way to everything. "Poor little Em!" he said, with a little laugh. She was only seventeen, a year younger than he was; her forefinger was seamed into furrows with her needle, and sometimes bled, which called forth no sympathy, but only scoldings, from the forewoman or her mother, when an unlucky red mark appeared on a hem. Emma did not very much mind the scoldings, which came natural to her, and she never made any comparison of herself with Law. He was a *gentleman*, that made all the difference. And it was a great deal nicer, and much more important, to have such a fine fellow to keep company with, than a young painter or carpenter, or even a tailor, which was what 'Liza had to be content with. Mr. Despard was a very different sort of person. As Law whispered to her, Emma felt her heart swell with pride. She went on with her work all the same, sometimes threatening to prick him with the needle which was at the end of that long thread. Emma was only "running a skirt," not trusted as yet with the more difficult parts of the work, and she pointed her needle at Law's nose when he came too close. But it was very sweet to her to have him there. Polly might brag as she pleased of the Captain—the Captain was old, and what was the good of him? He did nothing but puff Polly up with pride, the younger girls thought, and nothing would ever come of it. But Law was young, and there was no telling what might come of that. Emma threatened him with her needle, but in her heart was very proud of him. And there he sat and talked to her, while Lottie was having her little triumph among all the fine people at the Rectory. The Welting girls were all pleased to have Law there. They liked to talk of Mr. Despard, "from the Abbey," and how they "could not keep him out of their workroom." By and by they began to joke about his idleness, the only idle one among so busy a company. "Can't you give him something simple to do—a skirt to run up or a long hem?" "Oh, yes," said Emma. "Do, Polly, he bothers me so I can't get my skirt done." Polly opened her drawer, and drew out from it the current number of a distinguished periodical, which all these young women admired.

"I'll tell you what he can do," she said, "and make himself useful—for we've got to sit up all night a'most, and there's nothing makes work go like reading out loud. Mr. Lawrence, if you want to be as good as your professions, and help us young ladies on, as are far harder worked than the like of you knows of even, there's the last number of the *Family Herald*, and we're all that anxious, we don't know how to bear it, to hear how Lady Araminta got on——"

"Oh, give it me," said Emma, with her eyes sparkling. "Oh, give it me! Oh, you nasty cruel creature, to have it in your drawer all the time, and never to tell!"

"I'll give it to Mr. Despard," said Polly, "and we'll all be done half as soon again if he'll read it out loud."

"Give it here," said Law with lordly good-nature, and he began at once upon his task. How the needles flew as he read! Lady Araminta was a wonderful heroine. She wore nothing less than velvet and satin, and carried her diamonds about with her wherever she went, and the title deeds of her estate in the bosom of her dress. Law leaned his long arm on the table, sometimes pausing to take breath and playing with Emma's pins and cotton. He would thus tantalise them now and then when the story grew most exciting and his auditors most breathless. He was *bon prince* among them all, very good-natured and willing to please them, though Emma had his special vows. His head was not so much turned as was the head of virtuous Lottie, listening to the applause of Mr. Rollo Ridsdale, but he was very happy with this little court about him all the same.

CHAPTER VII
A NEW LIGHT

It was late before Law got home. In the first place he read the *Family Herald* through to his interested and busy auditors. Their needles flew like lightning along the lengthy seams; trimmings were as nothing to them, and even a hem became interesting as he read. When he had pursued Lady Araminta to the end of this little portion of her history, showing how she refused that wicked Duke who was at the bottom of all her troubles, and whose expedients to get her into his power were so manifold, he began the next story—and so on till all was finished. It took some time to get through the delightful pennyworth. What good it did to the poor girls at their work! They were not patient, superior, noble-minded needlewomen, pensively bearing up against the privations of their lot, but very commonplace girls, grumbling at their privations frankly, yet sitting up half the night over wedding finery or funeral robes, without any very clear idea that it was a hardship, or indeed more than an inevitable feature of "the dressmaking." It was under this simple matter-of-fact aspect that their vigil appeared to them now, and they did not feel it any very great grievance; but, such as it was, it was infinitely lightened by Law and the *Family Herald*. He was, to tell the truth, a little bit interested himself in the stories. He thought them very finely written. He liked the bits about Araminta's true, but alas! poor and unfortunate lover. This lover was tall and strong, interesting and clever beyond description. He could do whatever he tried to do, and managed to live comfortably upon nothing at all. Law had a half notion that this elegant and perfect being was like himself. He would not have breathed it to anyone, but yet he thought so. And when one story was finished he began another. He did not mind whether it was the beginning, or the middle, or the end of the tale; all was the same to Law; he went stoutly on, and read the whole number through—poetry, answers to correspondents, and all. It was not very fine literature perhaps, or, rather, it was very superfine literature, with nobody below the rank of a baronet in the leading stories; but what it did for these poor dressmaking girls! They followed Lady Araminta through every turn of her wonderful fortunes, with eyes that glowed and shone over their needlework. They identified themselves with her, exclaiming, "That's just what I'd have done!" and, "No, I wouldn't have had him, not I, if he'd been fifty dukes!" with true enthusiasm. Their needles flew, and the work got on as by magic; their excitement showing itself in the speed with which they worked. The wedding things were done an hour sooner than they would otherwise have been done, under this stimulus, and it was little more than twelve o'clock when Polly, after folding up the last dress, in readiness to be sent home first thing in the morning, said, "Now, Mr. Lawrence, you've been a deal of use. If you like, you can see me home!"

"As if it was a treat for him to see her home!" Emma cried, who owned the special allegiance of Law; but the youth for his part had no objection. It was a beautiful night, and a little additional walk was nothing but a pleasure to him; and he was quite good-natured, ready to exert himself in any way that was not legitimate and necessary. Emma, indeed, did not smile upon this undertaking. She (who had been obliged to do as much before now without anyone to take care of her) did not see what Polly wanted with an escort in a quiet place like St. Michael's. "You'll meet nobody worse than the policeman," she said.

"Policemen are bad enough, sometimes," said Polly.

"Mind you don't meet the Captain," said Emma's elder sister, "and get him into trouble with his papa."

At this Polly laughed, tossing her head with its innumerable plaits and puffs. "I hope I can manage the Captain," she said. And whoever had heard the style of Polly's conversation as she walked up the sweep of the steep street by Law's side, with the soft night air blowing in their faces, would have recognised at once the superiority of Polly to all the insinuations addressed to her. All was very quiet in the High Street of St. Michael's: they met nobody worse than the policeman, as Emma had suggested; and everything was still and dark, except the stars shining far away overhead; for the shop-windows had long been closed, and the lamps glimmered few and far between.

"You mustn't think anything of what these foolish things say about the Captain," said Polly; "because I'm a bit more reasonable than the rest, he likes to have a chat with me now and again. He's a very well-informed man is your papa; but you mustn't think nothing of what they say——"

"Oh, I don't!" said Law, with the serenest confidence; "I know the governor's way."

This, however, was not a reply which pleased Polly. "What do you mean by the governor's way?" she cried sharply. "You are not half respectful enough, if you would like to hear my opinion. You shouldn't talk of the Captain like that; he's a fine man, and he's one that many in this town thinks a deal of."

"Is he really?" said Law, in genuine surprise; "I did not know that. I wonder what kind of people they are? Is it far off where you live, Polly? I haven't got a latchkey, so I don't want to be very late."

"You never thought of being late so long as you were sitting by Emma; though what you can see in a little white-haired thing like that, like a white cat! You haven't got a latchkey? I should think not at your age. Mr. Lawrence, take my advice, and never be so late out of bed unless there is a very good reason for it."

"I like that!" cried Law, "when it was you that kept me there all the time."

"I thought it would do you good," said Polly. "I am almost sure you had not done a thing besides, or looked into a book for the whole day."

"Oh! I should not mind standing an examination in the *Family Herald,*" Law said with a laugh. He had occupied the post of reader in the workroom before, and knew a great deal about Lady Araminta. There could not be any doubt that he was very good-natured, and ready to make himself of use.

"I should like to know," said Polly—and though he could scarcely see her face, Law felt, with a mixture of amusement and indignation, by the sound of her voice, that Polly, too, meant to give him good advice—"I should like to know, Mr. Lawrence, what you intend to be? Are you going into the army, like the Captain? If I were a young gentleman, that's what I should choose above everything."

"I can't afford the army, worse luck," cried Law; "we haven't got any money, and a fellow can't live on his pay. And there's those dash'd examinations to pass everywhere before you can get into anything; it's enough to drive a man out of his senses. I sometimes think I shall emigrate—that's the only thing you can do without an examination."

"But you can't do that without money—a little money at least," said Polly. "If I were you, I should make a push and get in somewhere. I can't think how you can stay at home doing nothing, a great strong young man like you."

"Oh! as for being strong, that don't do much for an exam.," said Law. "The little fellows stand the best chance there."

"I wouldn't make jokes about it, if I were you. I wonder how you can go on living on the Captain, and such a burden on him—both you and your sister——"

"Hallo," said Law in extreme surprise. The mention of Lottie bewildered him. He was not even angry for the moment—he was so profoundly astonished.

"Yes, indeed, you and your sister too. You don't show any consideration for the Captain, and how can you expect that he's always to be thinking of you? The Captain is a young man still, and he is a fine man, and if he were to marry again, as would be very natural at his age, where would you and Miss Despard be?"

"Let my sister alone, if you please," said Law, with a momentary flash of anger; and then he relapsed into a laugh. "The governor should be much obliged to you, Polly, for taking his part."

"Somebody ought to take his part," said Polly. "I don't suppose he's much over fifty—what I call quite a young man still; and why should he deny himself and spend all he's got on two grown-up young people that ought to be making their own living? A man like the Captain, he wants his ease and his little comforts and a wife to look after him—that's what he wants. He ain't an old man to give in to his family. If I were to put upon my folks like that, do you think I'd be walking up St. Michael's Hill at this hour of the night, after slaving and stitching all day? Not a bit of it, Mr. Lawrence. If I were to do as you're doing, I might sit at home and make myself comfortable; but I was always one for being independent, and as for the Captain, poor dear! he oughtn't to be spending his money upon them that can do for themselves. It is himself he ought to be thinking of, to get all the pleasure he can as long as he's able to enjoy it. And if he were to marry again, as there's nothing more likely, where would you and Miss Lottie be? Oh, yes, I know your names quite well," said Polly. "We often talk about you. These sort of names for short are a mistake. For instance me, my name's Maria, that's a very lady-like name; but what does it matter when everybody calls me Polly? but, if my name's common, nobody can say of me that I don't behave handsome to my parents," Polly said with emphasis. As for Law, he had felt himself growing hot and cold all through this speech. It plunged him into an entirely new world of thought. He tried to laugh, but there was no laughter in his mind.

"It is very kind of you, Polly," he said, with scorn in his voice, "to take the trouble to give me so much good advice."

"Oh, I assure you it's not for your sake, but the Captain's," said Polly. "I told him if ever I had a chance with either of you, you should hear a bit of my mind—and I saw my opportunity to-night—that's why I asked you to come with me, Mr. Lawrence. Oh, it wasn't for the pleasure of your society! I told the Captain I'd give you a bit of my mind. This is my home, so I'll bid you good-night, and I hope you'll lay to heart what I say."

Law turned up the Abbey Hill when thus dismissed with much secret excitement in his mind. It was altogether a new idea to him that his father was as Polly said, quite a young man still, and that it was on himself, not on his grown-up children, that his money should be spent. Law had never looked upon the income of the family as belonging exclusively to his father. It *was* the family income, and it had seemed to him that he had just as good a right to have everything he wanted as his father had. As a matter of fact he did not get all he wanted, as Captain Despard managed to do; but that was because his father had the command of everything, not that he had a better right to it than Law. The idea that he had no right at all, as Polly seemed to think, and that his father might make the home untenable by marrying somebody, perhaps Polly herself, struck him as the most extraordinary of revelations. It was too extraordinary to be thought of calmly—his brain boiled and bubbled with the extraordinariness and novelty of the thought. The governor, who was only not an old fogey because he was so much less respectable, less orderly than old fogeys ought to be!—Law could not associate his father's image with the idea of, even, comparative youth. But he could not dismiss the suggestion from his mind. He tried to laugh, but something seemed to hang over him like a threat, like a cloud of evil omen. He walked quickly up the slope to the Abbey gate, trying to shake off the uneasy feeling in his mind—trying to postpone at least the new idea which he could not get rid of. When, however, Law had got into the Precincts he saw a passenger not much less active and considerably more jaunty than himself on the way before him, walking with a slight occasional lurch, up the pavement to the Lodges. The lurch was quite slight, and might not have been noticed by an indifferent eye, but Law noted it with the jealous observation of one whose own credit was at stake. It was hard upon a fellow, he thought, that his father should be seen going home night after night with a lurch in his walk, and that his name should be recognised in all the lowest quarters of the town as that of "the Captain's son." Why should he suffer for such a cause? Other old men were respectable, were no shame to their sons, but on the contrary furnished a margin of honour and reputation upon which to draw when there was occasion; but this was not the case with Captain Despard. Other old men—but there suddenly flashed across Law's mind as he instinctively placed his father in this class, a recollection of the words which had just been said to him—"He is what I call a young man still." Pricked by this thought, he looked at the figure before him with eyes suddenly cleared from the mists of habit and tradition, and saw it in an altogether new light. Captain Despard was straight and active: he carried his head high, and his step, though to-night slightly irregular, was both firm and light. To see him walking in front humming and whistling by turns, perhaps with a certain bravado to show how steady he was, gave Law the most uncomfortable sensation. It was true what Polly had said. This was no old fogey, no heavy father; though up to this moment Law had looked upon the Captain in no other light. He felt a shiver come over him, a sudden realisation of all the possibilities. Who should say that the governor ought not to do what he liked best, whatever that might be? Law felt conscious that he himself, who was so much younger, did what he liked in indifference to everybody's opinion, and he was under no affectionate delusion as to the superior virtue of his father. What if Polly were right? Polly perhaps had a better chance of knowing the Captain's wishes than either his son or his daughter, to whom he was not likely to talk on such subjects. A chill came over the lad though the night was so warm. Life had always seemed sure enough to him, though it had its privations. He had to put up with that chronic want of pocket-money—and with frequent "rows" from his father, and passionate remonstrances from Lottie. These were the drawbacks of existence; but Law was aware that, except in very favourable circumstances indeed, as when you were born a duke, or at least born to the possession of five thousand a year or so, existence was very seldom without drawbacks; this, however, was very much worse than the want of pocket-money; the governor with a new wife, perhaps Polly! The situation was too horrible to be realised, but for the moment the idea seemed to pour a current of ice into Law's veins.

He had no latchkey, but as soon as he saw his father he made up his mind to take advantage of Captain Despard's entrance in a way which he had found practicable before this. Light and swift as he was, when the Captain had fumbled and opened the door, Law stole close behind him and entered with him in the darkness. "What's that?" Captain Despard growled, feeling the movement of the air as his son passed. "I'll swear there's a ghost in this house," he added, grumbling to himself. Law, however, was safely out of the way before his father managed to strike a light, and went, swaying from side to side, up the narrow staircase which creaked under him. The young fellow, standing back in the darkness, saw Captain Despard's face illuminated by the light of the candle he carried, and gazed at it with eyes sharpened by anxiety. It was a handsome face—the contour still perfect, the hair crisp and curling, a heavy military moustache shadowing the well-formed lip. The Captain was flushed, his eyes were blinking, half-closed, and that unloveliest look that can be seen on a man's face, the look of partial intoxication approaching the sleepy stage, took all spirit and sentiment from him. Yet Law could not but acknowledge that his father was a handsome man. He stood quite still, watching that progress upstairs, half because he was unwilling to be seen, half because he was anxious to see. Captain Despard was "a fine man," as Polly had said. Law could see now, looking at him between the bars of the railing which guarded the little staircase, that there was nothing in common between him and the old white-haired Chevaliers, old men not strong enough to be warlike, but courteous and gentle as becomes old soldiers, who sunned themselves on the pavement before the Lodges. Captain Despard, middle-aged and self-assertive, was as different as possible from those old gentlemen with their honourable scars. He had none of their honours nor of the grace of old service; but he was strong in life and vigour, a kind of superiority which Law could appreciate. A grain of pride mingled in the exasperation with which he acknowledged this to himself—and yet he was not only exasperated but alarmed. He retired to bed very softly afterwards, creeping on tiptoe and in the dark up the stairs. There was still a gleam of light under Lottie's door, but Law preferred not to direct his sister's attention to the late hour of his own return by going straight to her room to relieve himself of his trouble. He did not want to be forced into confidences or to betray where he had himself been, and how he had heard the alarming prophecies which had so suddenly cleared his sight; and though the temptation was great he resisted it. Thus the lights were burning all at once in three of the little rooms in Captain Despard's house, each illuminating a separate world of excitement, unsuspected by the others. The Captain's share of the disturbance was less of the mind than the body. He had lost some money which he could not afford to lose, and was annoyed on this account; and he was excited, but more sleepy, on account of the potations which had accompanied his play. "By— —, I'll have it back to-morrow night—luck can't be so against me one night after another." This was the only burden of his simple and uncomplicated reflections. He thought nothing of his children one way or another. Both his children, however, though in different ways, were thinking of him. Lottie, though she dared not openly sit up for her father, remained up in her own room until he came in, and she had made sure that he did not want anything, and was not likely to set the house on fire. But Law's reflections were more serious than those of the other two. It seemed to the idle lad as if suddenly a real burden had got on to his shoulders. He was thoroughly frightened out of the pleasant calm of nature—the sense that everything must go on as everything had gone since he could remember. In later days, indeed, things had gone better for Law—Lottie had managed now and then to scrape a shilling or two off the housekeeping to give him, and of late she had not bullied him quite so much as usual. The current had been flowing more evenly—everything had conspired to make the happy-go-lucky of his life more smooth than before. He woke up with all the more fright and surprise to the sudden danger now.

CHAPTER VIII
TRIUMPH AND TERROR

Lottie had gone home that night, it need not be said, with her head full of excitement. Had she not good reason to look upon this evening as of importance in her life? She had met the man who, before he had ever spoken to her, had, according to all appearances, placed her on the highest pinnacle on which a girl can be placed—the throne of a romantic love. Though it had been a temporary downfall to her to be placed in the charge of Mr. Ashford and the Signor, instead of crossing the Dean's Walk in the company of this secret and poetical lover, yet she was almost glad to be thus let drop into quietness, to avert any word or look too much, which might have spoiled the visionary elevation on which she felt herself. Yes, she was glad that they had never been alone. Had he whispered an avowal of any kind into her ear, she was not, she knew, prepared for it; Lottie was honest even in her self-delusion, and she knew that, however profoundly to her advantage it might be, she could not make any response to a man whom she did not know, whom she was speaking to for the first time, notwithstanding her consciousness that he must have been thinking of her for a long time. She could not have made any fit reply. She must have said something which probably would have hurt him in the fervour of his romantic passion; for, though grateful to him and romantically touched by his evident devotion, Lottie could not have persuaded herself that he was anything to her except a delightful wonder and most flattering novelty. No, it was better, much better, that he did not come; she must have hurt his feelings, discouraged him, probably driven him away from her; and she was very far from wishing to drive him away. Lottie thought, with an innocent calculation, if she saw a little more of him, had a little time given her to make his acquaintance, that probably she would come to love him quite naturally and spontaneously; but at present it was not possible that she could do so, and she felt a natural shrinking from any premature disclosure of his feelings. Thus it was evidently most fortunate that the Dean had interposed, that Rollo had not been allowed to come home with her—fortunate, and yet a little disappointing too. There had been a very few words exchanged with her companions as they crossed the Dean's Walk. Mr. Ashford had most kindly and courteously reminded her that she had expressed a wish to speak to him about something. "It is too late now to ask what it was," he said; "I must not keep you out of doors at this hour; but if you will permit me, I will call and inquire in what way I can be of use to you?" "You know in what way *I* would like to be of use to you, Miss Despard," the Signor said on the other side. All this was very flattering, even though she might be displeased by the Signor's reiteration of his disagreeable offer. She made him a curtsey like Lady Caroline, while to the minor canon she gave her hand, which perhaps was quite sufficient to mark her different estimation of them. And indeed the Signor had been very kind about the accompaniments, which he had certainly played to perfection. This recollection came to her mind as he thanked her for her singing, undaunted by the stiffness of her leave-taking. "Indeed, I owe you more, a great deal more, than you can possibly owe me," Lottie said, with a burst of compunction; "I never sang so well before, because I never had such an accompaniment." "Then I hope I may accompany you very often again," he said, with a smile, as he went away. Thus even with the Signor, Lottie felt herself in perfect good-humour and charity. A man who paid such compliments to her voice, how could she be hard upon him, even if he made a little mistake in respect to her position? And she went in out of the summer night in a state of celestial satisfaction with all the people surrounding her—and herself. Even Lady Caroline had melted into something which was warmth for her. She had said, "I have enjoyed your singing very much, Miss Despard," and had touched Lottie's hand with two limp fingers—that was something, indeed it was much for Lady Caroline. And all the other great ladies had spoken, or at least had smiled upon Lottie, thanking her. What could she have wished for more? She went up into her little tiny room, which was not much bigger than Lady Caroline's grand piano, and throwing off the Indian shawl (if Mrs. O'Shaughnessy could but have seen it!) on the floor, sat down upon her little white bed and began to think. To think! nothing of the sort—to go over everything that had happened, with a dazzle of light and delight and triumph round her. She seemed to herself to have thrown down all the boundaries that had hitherto separated her from her lawful sphere. If a suitor should come from that higher and better world who could wonder now? Had she not been adopted into it—received to her just place at last?

And naturally it was upon Rollo that her recollections chiefly centred; he was the chief figure of the whole company to Lottie. She remembered minutely everything he had said and done, the expression of his face (though she put infinitely more meaning in it than was there), the tone of his voice. How the room had become at once full of interest, of excitement, when he came in, clearing away all the dimness! Lottie had scarcely time even to wonder how and where their next meeting would be, for thinking of this first meeting. How his face had lighted up when he saw that she was there; how he had been caught by some one on his way to her, and kept talking in spite of himself, with his eyes upon her all the time; how he had escaped and pressed through all the fine company to get to her side; how he had confessed that he had but a very visionary right to claim her acquaintance at all, but nevertheless meant to stand on that right as, for the time being, the son of the house! Lottie had scarcely forgotten a word of all he said. And, as a matter of fact, Rollo had been very careful to behave himself with due discretion, not to make it too apparent that her voice was the thing that most interested him. She thought that he admired her singing as a part of his enthusiasm for herself. She had not a suspicion of the real state of the case. It seemed to her that her voice was a delightful discovery to him, a something *pardessus le marché*, an added charm; that it was the sole foundation of his apparent enthusiasm never occurred to the girl; neither, though she knew that her general triumph was caused by her singing, did she solely set down to that cause the friendly looks and smiles and flattering compliments she had received. This was absurd, but we do not pretend that Lottie was beyond the reach of absurdity. She knew that it was her singing which had suddenly silenced all the conversation going on in the room, and called the attention of everybody; but yet it was surely something more; it was herself, not her voice, which brought that kindly look to their eyes as they smiled upon her. It is hard to acknowledge to ourselves that it is for some special, perhaps accidental, quality we may possess, that we are favoured and esteemed by our fellow-creatures. Human nature is humbled by the conviction that it is the possession of a gift worthy of popularity which makes an individual popular. We all prefer to be prized for nothing at all, for ourselves. And this, in the face of circumstances, and clean against all reason, was what Lottie hoped and determinedly believed. She could not consent to the other idea. To be praised and made friends with *for her voice* was intolerable. The only approbation which is really flattering and delightful is that which is given upon no ground at all.

She had been sitting thus for some time on her bed, musing, with eyes that sparkled and a heart that fluttered with happiness; and had taken off her evening gown, and loosed the roses from her hair, and wrapped her white shining satin shoulders in a white cotton dressing-gown; and had even brushed out those long dark locks, and twisted them up again close to her head for the night, with innumerable fancies twisted out and in of all she did, before Captain Despard, fumbling for the key-hole, opened his own door and came in, in the dark. It was Lottie's habit to sit up till he came in, but to-night she had been too much occupied by her own concerns to hear his approach, and it was only when he came upstairs that she woke up to think of him. Lottie's experienced ear caught the lurch in his step, just as Law's experienced eye had caught it. "Again!" she said to herself, with a momentary flash of anger; but it did not make her wretched as it might have done a more sensitive daughter. Lottie was accustomed to accept her father without question, not expecting much of him, and somewhat disposed, when he did not come up even to the little she expected, to satisfy herself that it was just like papa. But his entrance relieved her from her habitual vigil. She heard Law steal upstairs afterwards, and wondered how or when he had got in, and where he went at night, with more curiosity than she expended on her father; but even that did not much disturb Lottie, who had been used all her life to irregular entrances and exits. After a while all was still in the little house, notwithstanding the anxieties and excitements collected under its roof. Disquietude and trouble could not keep Law from sleeping any more than excitement and triumph could keep his sister; and, as for the Captain, the sleep of the just was never so profound as that which wrapped him in a not too lovely tranquillity. The air was all thrilling with emotion of one kind or another, but they slept as profoundly as if they had not a care in the world—as soundly as the good O'Shaughnessys next door, who had been asleep since eleven o'clock, and who had no cares but those of their neighbours to disquiet them; or old Colonel Dalrymple on the other side, who dozed through his life. The soft night stilled them all, young and old and middle-aged, in their kind, just as it held in soft shadow the Abbey, with all its grey pinnacles and immemorial towers. Nature cared nothing for the troubles of life; but life submitted to the gentle yoke of nature, which relieves the soul, while it binds the body, and makes a temporary truce and armistice with all the army of mortal cares.

Next morning Law lounged into the little drawing-room after breakfast with a big book in his hand. He had almost given up the pretence of reading for some time, so that it was all the more wonderful to see a book which was not a yellow railway novel in his hand. Lottie had been up early, awakened by the commotion in her mind, which did not allow her to rest—or rather which prevented her from going to sleep again when the early noises of the morning woke her up. Accordingly she had got through a great deal of her ordinary household work by this time, when Law, after a breakfast which was later than usual, lounged in upon her. He was very big, and filled up the little room; and his habit of doing as little as possible, and his want of money, which made some imperfections in his toilet inevitable, gave him a look of indolence and shabbiness such as was not natural to his age, or even to his disposition, for by nature Law was not lazy. He came sauntering in with one hand in his pocket, and with his book under the other arm; and he sat down in the only easy-chair the room contained, exasperating Lottie, to whom his very bigness seemed an offence. There were times when she was proud of Law's size, his somewhat heavy good-looks, his athletic powers; but this morning, as many times before, the very sight of those long limbs jarred upon her. What was the use of all that superfluous length and strength? He took the only easy-chair, and stretched out his long limbs half across the room, and Lottie at the height of her activity felt impatience rise and swell within her. She could not put up with Law that morning. His indolence was an offence to her.

"What do you want, Law?" she said, in a voice which was not so sweet as it had been at the Deanery. She gave a rapid glance up at him as she went on with her darning, and took in the whole picture, the easy-chair and the lounging attitude. If he had sat upright upon the little hard wickerwork chair, Lottie would have felt more merciful.

"Well, I want nothing in particular, except to talk to you a little," said Law. "You need not be so cross."

"I am not cross; but to see you in an easy chair, idling away all the morning——"

"How do you know I've been idling this morning? Look at my book: that's Virgil," said Law, looking at it with simple admiration. "I don't think a fellow could do much better than that."

"But have you *really* been reading?" Lottie's tone modified; she began to look at him with respect. "Oh, Law, if you only would work! it would make such a difference, it would make me quite happy. I was speaking to Mr. Ashford last night. You know Mr. Ashford, the minor canon. He is so clever with his pupils. If you could but go to him, if he would only take you, Law!"

"He would take me fast enough if we could afford the money. I say, Lottie, the governor was awfully late last night: did you hear him coming in? I want to tell you something about him—something I have heard."

"I think you were very late, too, Law."

"Oh! never mind about that; it does not matter about me. Lottie, listen. A friend—I mean somebody—was speaking to me about him. Did it ever come into your head that he was not an old man, and that such a thing was possible as that he might—it seems too ridiculous to say it—marry again?"

"Marry again? you are dreaming!" cried Lottie loudly, in her astonishment.

"Yes, while we knew nothing of it. After all, when you come to think of it, when you look at him, you know, he is not so awfully old. One thinks he must be, because he is one's father. But some of these old beggars are just as silly"—said Law in awestruck tones, "and you can't stop them doing things as you can a fellow that is young. It is an awful shame! a fellow that is under age, as they call it, you can pull him up, though there's no harm in him; but an old fellow of fifty, you can't stop him, whatever nonsense he may set his face to. That's what I heard last night."

"It is not true. I don't believe a single word of it," said Lottie. "You must have been in very strange company, Law," she added with severity, "to hear all this gossip about papa."

Lottie did not mean to pass such a tremendous sentence on her father; she spoke simply enough. To hear this gossip her brother must have been in haunts such as those that Captain Despard frequented. She did not know what they were, but she knew they were evil; therefore she made use of this weapon instinctively, which she found, as it were, lying by her, not meaning any censure upon her father, only a necessary reproof to Law.

"You may say what you please about bad company," he said, "but that's what I heard; that he wasn't so old after all; and what would become of us if he married again? It was not gossip. I believe really, though I was very angry at the time, that it was meant kindly; it was meant for a warning. You would have thought so yourself, if you had been there."

"I do not believe a word of it," said Lottie; but she had grown pale. She did not ask again who had told him or where he had been; she set herself seriously to prove the thing to be false, which showed that she was not so sure of not believing it as she pretended to be. "It is all a falsehood," she went on. "Is papa a man to do that sort of thing? Marry! he would have to give us a great many things if he married. He could not afford to spend his money as he does; he would not be allowed to be always out in the evenings as he is now. Why, even poor mamma, she did not give in to him as we are obliged to do; he had to pay a little attention to her—sometimes. And now he has got more used to do what he likes than ever, and has more money to spend; do you think he would give up that *for a wife*?" cried Lottie with disdain. "It only shows that you don't know papa."

"Ah! but you don't know——" said Law. He was about to say "Polly," but stopped in time. "You don't know what might be put into his head, Lottie. He might be made to believe that to get rid of us would put all right. If he got rid of us, don't you see? he would want a woman in the house; and if it was some one he liked himself, that would make herself agreeable to him, and flatter him, and coddle him—that would please him better," said Law, with precocious knowledge of a man's requirements, "than you, who are always trying to keep things straight but not to humour him, Lottie; or me—that am of no use at all."

Lottie grew paler and paler during this explanation. She had never humoured her father, it was true. She had made desperate exertions "to keep things straight," to recover the family credit, to pay the bills, to keep regular hours; but, with the hardihood of youth, she had not hesitated even to stint her father of a meal when it seemed to her impetuous determination to be necessary, and she had not flattered him, nor made his convenience the absolute rule of the household, as some girls would have been wise enough to do. Lottie had reflected that he kept the lion's share of the family income to himself, and was quite able to make up for any shortcomings in her bill of fare; and she had carried out her regulations with a high hand, feeling no compulsion upon her, no primary necessity to please her father. She perceived all this at a glance while Law spoke, and immediately felt herself confronting such a breach of all the ordinary usages of her life as made her shiver. What might he not do? turn them out suddenly from his doors, out upon the world, at any moment whenever he pleased. He had the power to do it whenever he pleased, whatever seemed to him good. She drew a long shivering breath, feeling as if all were over, as if already she heard the door clanging and barred behind her, and was looking out penniless and destitute upon the world, not knowing where to go. Was it possible that such a fate was reserved for her? She became as white as her dress with that sudden panic of the imagination which is more terrible than any reality. Law was very anxious and alarmed also, but he had got over the worst on the previous night, and it gave him a kind of half pleasure to see how he had frightened Lottie; though, at the same time, the effect of his communication upon her deepened his own conviction of the danger about to overtake them. He leaned back in his easy-chair with a certain solemn satisfaction, and stretched his long legs farther across the room than ever.

"You see, Lottie," he said, "it is what I have told you before; you never would humour him. I don't say that he's not unreasonable, but he might never perhaps have dropped among those sort of people if you had laid yourself out to——"

Lottie sprang to her feet in a sudden gust of passion. She took Law by the shoulders, and with the sudden surprise of her assault got the better of him and turned him out of the chair. "You sit there, lolling all over the room," she cried, "and tell me my duty, you lazy, idle, useless boy! If papa turns you out, it will serve you right. You have a hundred things open to you; you have the whole world open to you; but you will not so much as take the trouble to pass the door. You would like to be carried over all the ditches, to be set up on a throne, to have everything and to do nothing. It will serve you right! And where do you get all this gossip about papa?" she went on. "Who are the sort of people you are spending your time with? You thought I did not know how late you came in last night. Where were you, Law? where are you always, all these long evenings? You say you are going out, and you never mind that I am sitting in the house all alone. You go somewhere, but I never hear that you have been with anybody—anybody in our own class——"

"In our own class! I wonder what is our own class?" said Law, with a scornful sense of the weakness of the position. "Would you like me to take a hand in old O'Shaughnessy's rubber, or read the papers to old Dalrymple?

They are half as old again as the governor himself. I suppose that's what you call my own class."

Lottie felt that she had laid herself open to defeat, and the consciousness subdued her greatly. She sat down again on her little chair, and looked up at him as he stood leaning upon the door, red with indignation at her onslaught. Lottie herself was flushed with the exertion and the shame of having thus afforded him an opportunity for a scoff. She eluded the dilemma as he proposed it, however, and flung herself back into the larger question: "You are grown up," she said, indignantly; "a great big boy, looking like a man. It is a disgrace to you to be dependent on papa. It would be a good thing for you, a very good thing, if he were to—marry, as you say, and cast you off, and force you to work for yourself. What else have I been saying to you for years?"

"And what would it be for you?" said Law, taking, she thought, an unkind advantage of her; "there are two of us to be considered. What would it be for you, Lottie, I should like to know? What could you do any more than I?"

He stood up against the door, with a provoking smile on his face, and his big book under his arm, taunting her with her helplessness, even Lottie felt, with her high notions, which made her helplessness all the worse. He smiled, looking down upon her from that serene height. "If the worst came to the worst," said Law, "I could always carry a hod or 'list for a soldier. I don't stand upon our class as you do. I haven't got a class. I don't mind if I take the shilling to-morrow. I have always thought it would be a jolly life."

Lottie gave a scream of horror, and flew upon him, seizing his coat collar with one hand, while she threatened him with her small nervous fist, at which Law laughed. "Will you dare to speak of 'listing to me," she said, flaming like a little fury; "you, an officer's son, and a gentleman born!" Then she broke down, after so many varieties of excitement. "Oh, Law, for the sake of Heaven, go to Mr. Ashford! I will get the money somehow," she said, in a broken voice, melting into tears, through which her eyes shone doubly large and liquid. "Don't break my heart! I want you to be better than we are now, not worse. Climb up as far, as far as you please, above us; but don't fall lower. Don't forget you are a gentleman, unless you want to break my heart."

And then, in the overflow of feeling, she leaned her head upon his shoulder, which she had just gripped with fury, and cried. Law found this more embarrassing than her rage, at which he laughed. He was obliged to allow her to lean upon him, pushing his book out of the way, and his heart smote him for making Lottie unhappy. By this time it could not be said that he was unhappy himself. He had shuffled off his burden, such as it was, upon her shoulders. He shifted his book, and stood awkwardly enough, permitting her to lean upon him; but it cannot be said that he was much of a prop to his sister. He held himself so as to keep her off as far as possible. He was not unkind, but he was shy, and did not like to be placed in a position which savoured of the ridiculous. "I wish you wouldn't cry," he said, peevishly. "You girls always cry—and what's to be got by crying? I don't want to 'list if I can help it. I'd rather be an officer—but I can't be an officer, or get into something; but I never was bred up to anything; and what can I do?"

"You can go to Mr. Ashford," said Lottie, feeling herself repulsed, and withdrawing from him with a glimmer of indignation relighted in her eyes. "I met him last night, and I spoke to him about you. He seems very kind. If you go to him, he will at least tell us whether he thinks you have a chance for anything. Oh, Law, now that you do see the necessity——"

"But it's a great deal more serious for you," said the lad, mischievously. He was not unkind, but it seemed something like fun to him to treat Lottie as she had treated him so often, holding up before him the terrors and horrors of his idleness. Because she was a girl, did that make any difference? She had just as good a right to be bullied as he had, and to be made to see how little she could do for herself. Emma, who was younger than Lottie, worked for her living, and why should not Lottie do the same? why should she be exempted? Thus Law reasoned, whom Lottie, it must be allowed, had never spared. He watched, with mischievous curiosity, making an experiment, not knowing whether it would be successful or not. But the way in which Lottie took it after this did not give Law the amusement he expected. She sat down again in her chair, taking no further notice of him and relapsed into her own thoughts when he could not follow her. His own mind, however, had recovered its elasticity; for, after all, if the worst came to the worst, if the governor was such an ass as to marry Polly, it would not matter so very much to Law. Something, there was no doubt, would turn up; or he would 'list—that was an alternative not to be despised. He was tall enough for the Guards, among whom Law had often heard a great many gentlemen were to be found; and the life was a jolly life—no bother about books, and plenty of time for amusement. There was nothing really in the circumstances to appal him now he had considered them fully. But it was a great deal more serious for Lottie. After all the bullying he had endured at her hands, Law may perhaps be excused if, in sheer thoughtlessness, he rather enjoyed the prospect of this turning of the tables upon his sister. He wondered how she would like it when it came to her turn, she who was so ready to urge himself to the last limits of patience. He did not wish anything unpleasant to happen to her. He would not have had her actually brought into contact with Polly, or placed under her power. But that Lottie should "just see how she liked it herself" was pleasant to him. It would not do her any real harm, and perhaps it would teach her to feel for other people, and understand that they did not like it either. A slight tinge of remorse crossed Law's mind as he saw how pale and serious she looked, sitting there thinking; but he shifted his Virgil to his other arm, and went away, steeling his heart against it. It would make her feel for other people in future. To have it brought home to herself would do her no harm.

CHAPTER IX
VISITORS

And what a problem it was with which Lottie Despard was thus left alone! The house was still, no one moving in it—nothing to distract her thoughts. Now and then a swell of music from the Abbey, where service was going on, swept in, filling the silence for a moment; but most of the inhabitants of the Lodges were at matins, and all was very still in the sunshine, the Dean's Walk lying broad and quiet, with scarcely a shadow to break the light. Downstairs the little maid-of-all-work had closed the door of the kitchen, so that her proceedings were inaudible. And the Captain, as in duty bound, was in the Abbey, trolling forth the responses in a fine baritone, as he might have done had they been the chorus of a song. Lottie sat like a statue in the midst of this stillness, her eyes abstracted, her mind absorbed. What a problem to occupy her! Law, rustling over his books in his own room, grew frightened as he thought of her. She would break her heart; it would make her ill; it might almost kill her, he thought. She sat with her work dropped on her knee, her eyes fixed but not seeing anything; her mind—what could occupy it but one reflection? the sudden possibility of a breaking up of all her traditions, an end of her young life—a dismal sudden survey of the means of maintaining herself, and where she could go to in case this unthought-of catastrophe should occur at once. Poor desolate Lottie, motherless, friendless, with no one to consult in such an emergency, no one to fly to! What could be more terrible than to be brought face to face with such an appalling change, unwarned, unprepared? What was she to do? where was she to go? Worse than an orphan, penniless, homeless, what would become of her? No wonder if despair was paramount in the poor girl's thoughts.

Well—but then despair was not paramount in her thoughts. She made a stand for a moment with wild panic before the sudden danger. What was it that was going to happen? Lottie gave a momentary gasp as a swimmer might do making the first plunge; and then, like the swimmer, lo! struck off with one quick movement into the sunshine and the smoothest gentle current. Change! the air was full of it, the world was full of it, the sky was beautiful with it, and her heart sprang to meet it. Do you think a girl of twenty on the verge of love, once left free to silence and musing, was likely to forget her own dreams in order to plunge into dark reveries as to what would happen to her if her father married again? Not Lottie, at least. She launched herself indeed on this subject, the corners of her mouth dropping, a gleam of panic in her eyes; but something caught her midway. Ah! it was like the touch of a magician's wand. What did it matter to Lottie what might happen to other people; had not everything that was wonderful, everything that was beautiful, begun to happen to herself? She floated off insensibly into that delicious current of her own thoughts, losing herself in imaginary scenes and dialogues. She lost her look of terror without knowing it, a faint smile came upon her face, a faint colour, now heightening, now paling, went and came like breath. Sometimes she resumed her work, and her needle sped through her mending like the shuttle of the Fates; sometimes it dropped out of her hand altogether, and the work upon her knee. She lost count of time and of what she was doing. What was she doing? She was weaving a poem, a play, a romance, as she sat with her basket of stockings to darn. The *mise en scène* was varied, but the personages always the same; two personages—never any more; sometimes they only looked at each other, saying nothing; sometimes they talked for hours; and constantly in their talk they were approaching one subject, which something always occurred to postpone. This indefinite postponement of the explanation which, even in fiction, is a device which must be used sparingly, can be indulged in without stint in the private imagination, and Lottie in her romance took full advantage of this power. She approached the borders of her *éclaircissement* a hundred times, and evaded it with the most delicate skill, feeling by instinct the superior charm of the vague and undecided, and how love itself loses its variety, its infinite novelty, and delightfulness, when it has declared and acknowledged itself. Law, in his room with his big book, comforting himself under the confused and painful study to which the shock of last night's suggestion had driven him by the idea that Lottie too must be as uncomfortable as himself, was as much mistaken as it was possible to imagine. His compunction and his satisfaction were equally thrown away. Still the feeling that he had startled her, and the hope that it would "do her good," gave him a little consolation in his reading, such as it was. And how difficult it was to read with the sun shining outside, and little puffs of soft delicious air coming in at his open window, and laying hands upon him, who shall say? He was comforted to think that next door to him, Lottie, with her basket of clothes to mend, patching and darning, must be very much disturbed too; but it would have been hard upon Law had he known that she had escaped from all this, and was meanly and treacherously enjoying herself in private gardens of fancy. He had his Emma to be sure—but of her and the very well-known scenes that enclosed her, and all the matter-of-fact circumstances around, he felt no inclination to dream. He liked to have her by him, and for her sake submitted to the chatter of the workroom (which, on the whole, rather amused him in itself), and was quite willing to read the *Family Herald* aloud; but he did not dream of Emma as Lottie did of the incident which had happened in her career. It was true there was this fundamental difference between them, that Lottie's romance alone had any margin of the unknown and mysterious in it. About Emma there was nothing that was mysterious or unknown.

It was not likely, however, that these two young people in their two different rooms, Law gaping over his Virgil, and feeling his eyes wander after every fly that lighted on his book, and every bird that chirped in the deep foliage round the window; and Lottie with her needle and her scissors, thinking of everything in the world except what she was doing or what had just been told her, should be left undisturbed for long in these virtuous occupations. Very soon Law was stopped in the middle of a bigger yawn than usual by the sound of a step coming up the stairs, which distracted his not very seriously fixed attention—and Lottie woke up from the very middle of an imaginary conversation, to hear a mellow round voice calling her, as it came slowly panting upstairs. "Are you there then, Lottie, me honey? You'd never let me mount up to the top of the house, without telling me, if ye weren't there?" Mrs. O'Shaughnessy, like many of her country-folks, was half aware of the bull she was uttering, and there was a sound of laughter in her voice. Lottie, however, sat still, making no sign, holding her needle suspended in her fingers, reluctant to have her pleasant thoughts disturbed by any arrival. But while the brother and sister, each behind a closed door, thus paused and listened, the Captain (audibly) coming home from morning service, stepped in after Mrs. O'Shaughnessy, and addressed the new-comer. "Lottie is in the drawing-room," he said, "though she does not answer. I am just going out again when I've fetched something—but I must first see you upstairs;" and then there was an interval of talking on the stairs and the little landing-place. Lottie made no movement for her part. She sat amidst her darnings, and awaited what was coming, feeling that her time for dreams was over. Captain Despard came lightly up, three steps at a time, after Mrs. O'Shaughnessy had panted to the drawing-room door. He was jaunty and gay as ever, in his well-brushed coat with a rosebud in his button-hole. Few, very few, days were there on which Captain Despard appeared without a flower in his coat. He managed to get them even in winter, no one could tell how. Sometimes a flaming red leaf from the Virginia creeper, answered his purpose, but he was always jaunty, gay, decorated with something or other. He came in behind the large figure of their neighbour, holding out a glove with a hole in the finger reproachfully to Lottie. "See how my child neglects me," he said. He liked to display himself even to Mrs. O'Shaughnessy, and stood and talked to her while Lottie, with no very good grace, put down her darning and mended his glove.

"When I was a young fellow, my dear lady," he said, "I never wanted for somebody to mend my glove; but a man can't expect to be as interesting to his daughter as he was in another stage of life."

"Oh, Captain, take me word," said Mrs. O'Shaughnessy, "the likes of you will always be interesting to one or another. You won't make me believe that ye find nobody but your daughter to do whatever ye ask them. Tell that—to another branch of the service, Captain Despard, me dear friend."

"You do me a great deal too much honour," he said with the laugh of flattered vanity; for he was not difficult in the way of compliments. "Alas, Mrs. O'Shaughnessy, who would pay any attention to an old married man, the father of a grown-up son and daughter, like me?"

"Sure, and you're much to be pitied, so old as ye are, with one foot in the grave, Captain dear," the old Irishwoman said; and they both laughed, she enjoying at once her joke, and the pleasure of seeing her victim's pleased appreciation of the compliment; while he, conscious of being still irresistible, eyed himself in the little glass over the mantelpiece, and was quite unaware of the lurking demon of good-humoured malice and ridicule in her eyes.

"Not so bad as that perhaps," he said, "but bad enough. A man grows old fast in this kind of life. Matins every morning by cockcrow, to a man accustomed to take his ease, Mrs. O'Shaughnessy. The Major grumbles, I make no doubt, as well as I."

"Sure it's nothing half as bad as morning parade. That's what O'Shaughnessy says; and he never was used to his ease, Captain. I took better care of him than that. But, Lottie, me honey, here we're talking of ourselves, and it's you I've come to hear about. How many hearts did ye break? how many scalps have ye got, as we used to say in Canada? It wasn't for nothing ye put on your finery, and those roses in your hair. The Captain, he's the one for a flower in his coat; you're his own daughter, Miss Lottie dear."

"Were you out last night, my child?" said Captain Despard, taking his glove from Lottie's hand. "Ah, at the Deanery. I hope my friend the Dean is well, and my Lady Caroline? Lady Caroline was once a very fine woman, Mrs. O'Shaughnessy, though you would not think it. The Courtlands were neighbours of ours in our better days, and knew all our connections; and Lady Caroline has always been kind to Lottie. I do not think it necessary to provide any chaperon for her when she goes there. It is in society that a girl feels the want of a mother; but where Lady Caroline is, Lottie can feel at home."

"Fancy that now," said Mrs. O'Shaughnessy, "how a body may be deceived! I never knew ye were among old friends, Captain. What a comfort to you—till you find somebody that will be a nice chaperon for your dear girl!"

"Yes, Mrs. O'Shaughnessy, that would be a satisfaction; but where could I find one that would satisfy me after Lottie's dear mother, who was a pearl of a woman? Good-morning to you, my dear lady; I must be going," he said, kissing the fingers of the mended glove. And he went out of the room humming a tune, which, indeed, was as much a distinction of Captain Despard as the flower in his coat. He was always cheerful, whatever happened. His daughter looked up from her work, following him with her eyes, and Law, shut up in his room next door, stopped reading (which indeed he was very glad to do), and listened to the light carol of the Captain's favourite air and his jaunty step as he went downstairs. No lurch in that step now, but a happy confidence and cheerful ring upon the pavement when he got outside, keeping time surely not only to the tune, but to the Captain's genial and virtuous thoughts. Mrs. O'Shaughnessy looked after him without the cloud which was on his children's faces. She laughed. "Then, sure, it does one's heart good," she said, "to see a man as pleased with himself as me friend the Captain. And Lottie, me darlin', speaking of that, there's a word I have to say to you. Ye heard what I said and ye heard what he said about a chaperon—though, bless the child, it's not much use, so far as I can see, that you have for a chaperon——"

"No use at all," cried Lottie, "and don't say anything about it, please. Papa talks; but nobody pays any attention to him," she exclaimed, with a flush of shame.

"If he'd stop at talking! but Lottie, me dear, when a man at his age gets women in his head, there's no telling what is to come of it. I wouldn't vex ye, me dear, but there's gossip about—that the Captain has thoughts——"

"Oh, never mind what gossip there is about! there's gossip about everything——"

"And that's true, me honey. There's your own self. They tell me a dozen stories. It's married ye're going to be (and that's natural); and there's them that uphold it's not marriage at all, but music, or maybe the stage even, which is what I never would have thought likely——"

Lottie had risen to her feet, her eyes sparkling, her face crimson with excitement. "Wherever you hear it, please, *please* say it is a lie. I—on the stage! Oh, Mrs. O'Shaughnessy, could you believe such a thing? I would rather die!"

"Dying's a strong step to take, me dear. I wouldn't go that length, Lottie; but at your age, and with your pretty looks, and all the world before ye, it's not the thing I would advise. I don't say but there are chances for a pretty girl that's well conducted——"

"Mrs. O'Shaughnessy! do you dare to speak to me so?" said Lottie with crimson cheeks, her eyes blazing through indignant tears. Well conducted! the insult went to her very soul. But this was beyond the perception of her companion.

"Just so, me, dear," she said. "There was Miss O'Neil, that was a great star in my time, and another stage lady that married the Earl of— —, one of the English earls. I forget his title. Lords and baronets and that sort of people are thrown in their way, and sometimes a pretty girl that minds what she is about, or even a plain girl that is clever, comes in for something that would never— — Who is that, Lottie? Me dear, look out of the window, and tell me who it is."

Lottie did not say a word; she gasped with pain and indignation, standing erect in the middle of the room. How it made the blood boil in her veins to have the triumphs of the "stage-ladies" thus held up before her! She did not care who was coming. In her fantastical self-elevation, a sort of princess in her own sight, who was there here who would understand Lottie's "position" or her feelings? What was the use even of standing up for herself where everybody would laugh at her? There was no one in the Chevaliers' Lodges who could render her justice. They would all think that to "catch" an earl or a Sir William was enough to content any girl's ambition. So long as she was well conducted! To be well conducted, is not that the highest praise that can be given to anyone? Yet it made Lottie's blood boil in her veins.

While she stood thus flushed and angry, the door was suddenly pushed open by the untrained "girl," who was all that the household boasted in the shape of a servant. "She's here, sir," this homely usher said; and lo, suddenly, into the little room where sat Mrs. O'Shaughnessy taking up half the space, and where Lottie stood in all the excitement and glow of passion, there walked Rollo Ridsdale, like a hero of romance, more perfect in costume, appearance, and manner, more courteous and easy, more graceful and gracious, than anything that had ever appeared within that lower sphere. The Captain was jaunty and shabby-genteel, yet even he sometimes dazzled innocent people with his grand air; but Mr. Ridsdale was all that the Captain only pretended to be, and the very sight of him was a revelation. Mrs. O'Shaughnessy, sitting with her knees apart and her hands laid out upon her capacious lap, opened her mouth and gazed at him as if he had been an angel straight from the skies. Mrs. O'Shaughnessy knew him, as she knew every one who came within the Abbey precincts. She was aware of every visit he paid to his aunt, and saw him from her window every time he passed up and down the Dean's Walk, and she had the most intimate acquaintance with all his connections, and knew his exact place in the Courtland family, and even that there had been vicissitudes in his life more than generally fall to the lot of young men of exalted position. And, if it did her good even to see him from her window, and pleased her to be able to point him out as the Honourable Rollo Ridsdale, it may be imagined what her feelings were, when she found herself suddenly under the same roof with him, in the same room with him. Mrs. O'Shaughnessy sat and stared, devouring his honourable figure with her eyes, with a vague sensation of delight and grandeur taking possession of her soul.

"You must pardon my intrusion at such an early hour, Miss Despard," he said. "I wanted your maid to ask if I might come in, and I did not know she was ushering me into your very presence. But I have my credentials with me. I bear a note from Lady Caroline, which she charged me to support with my prayers."

The passion melted out of Lottie's countenance. Her eyes softened—the very lines of her figure, all proud and erect and vehement, melted too as if by a spell—the flush of anger on her cheek changed to a rose-red of gentler feeling. The transformation was exactly what the most accomplished actress would have desired to make, with the eye of an able manager inspecting her possibilities. "I beg your pardon," she said instinctively, with a sudden sense of guilt. It shocked her to be found so full of passion, so out of harmony with the melodious visitor who was in perfect tune and keeping with the sweet morning, and in whose presence all the vulgarities about seemed doubly vulgar. She felt humble, yet not humiliated. Here was at last one who would understand her, who would do her justice. She looked round to find a seat for him, confused, not knowing what to say.

"May I come here?" said Rollo, pushing forward for her the little chair from which she had evidently risen, and placing himself upon the narrow window-seat with his back to the light. "But let me give up my credentials first. My aunt is—what shall I say?—a little indolent, Miss Despard. Dear Aunt Caroline, it is an unkind word—shall I say she is not fond of action? Pardon if it is I who have acted as secretary. I do so constantly now that Augusta is away."

"Lottie," said Mrs. O'Shaughnessy, as Lottie, confused, took the note from his hand, and the chair he offered; "me dear!—you have not presented me to your friend."

Rollo got up instantly and bowed, as Lottie faltered forth his name ("A real bow," Mrs. O'Shaughnessy said after; "sure you never get the like but in the upper classes"), while she herself, not to be outdone, rose too, and extended a warm hand—("What does the woman expect me to do with her hand?" was Mr. Ridsdale's alarmed commentary on his side).

"I'm proud to make your acquaintance, sir," said Mrs. O'Shaughnessy. "Me husband the Major was once a great friend of an uncle of yours, Mr.

Ridsdale—or maybe it was a cousin; when we were out in Canada, in the Hundred and Fiftieth—the Honourable Mr. Green; they were together in musketry practice, and me Major had the pleasure of being of a great deal of use to the gentleman. Many a time he's told me of it; and when we came here, sure it was a pleasure to find out that me Lady Caroline was aunt—or maybe it was cousin to an old friend. I am very glad to make your acquaintance," Mrs. O'Shaughnessy continued, shaking him warmly by the hand, which she had held all this time. Mr. Ridsdale kept bowing at intervals, and had done all that he could, without positive rudeness, to get himself free.

"Oh, yes," he said, "I have cousins and uncles and that sort of thing scattered through the earth in every regiment under the sun; and very bad soldiers, I don't doubt, always wanting somebody to look after them. I am sure Major O'Shaughnessy was very kind. Won't you sit down?"

"It wasn't to make a brag of his kindness—not a bit of that—but he is a kind man and a good man, Mr. Ridsdale, though I say it that shouldn't. I have been married to me Major these forty years, and if anyone knows it I ought to be the one to know."

"Undoubtedly, Mrs. O'Shaughnessy. I for one am most ready to take the fact on your word."

"And you'd be in the right of it. A man's wife, that's the best judge of his character. Whatever another may say, she's the one that knows; and if she says too much, one way or the other, sure it's on herself it falls. But, maybe you're not interested, Mr. Ridsdale, in an old woman's opinions?"

"I am very much interested, I assure you," said Rollo, always polite. He kept an eye upon Lottie reading her note, but he listened to her friend (if this was her friend) with as much attention, Mrs. O'Shaughnessy always remembered, as if she had been a duchess at the least.

Meanwhile Lottie read the note, which purported to come from Lady Caroline, and had a wavering C. Huntington at the bottom of the page, which was her genuine autograph. The warmth of the appeal, however, to her dear Miss Despard, to take pity on the dulness of the Deanery and come in "quietly" that evening for a little music, was not in any way Lady Caroline's. She had consented indeed to permit herself to be sung to on Rollo's strenuous representation of the pleasure it had given her. "You know, Aunt Caroline, you enjoyed it," he had said; and "Yes, I know I enjoyed it," Lady Caroline, much wavering, had replied. It would not have been creditable not to have enjoyed what was evidently such very good singing; but it was not she who wrote of the dulness of the Deanery nor who used such arguments to induce her dear Miss Despard to come. Lottie's countenance bending over the note glowed with pleasure as Mrs.

O'Shaughnessy kept up the conversation. Even with those girls who think they believe that the admiration of men is all they care for, the approbation of a woman above their own rank is always a more touching and more thorough triumph than any admiration of men. And Lottie, though she was so proud, was all humility in this respect; that Lady Caroline should thus take her up, and encourage her, praise her, invite her, went to her very heart. She almost cried over the kind words. She raised her face all softened and glowing with happiness to the anxious messenger who was listening to Mrs. O'Shaughnessy, and as their eyes met a sudden smile of such responsive pleasure and satisfaction came to Rollo's face as translated Lottie back into the very paradise of her dreams.

"I can't say, me dear sir," said Mrs. O'Shaughnessy, "that things are just exactly as we wish here, or as we thought we had a right to look for. The Major and me, we've been used to a deal of fine company. Wherever we've gone, was it in Canada, was it the Channel Islands, was it at the depôt of the regiment, we've always been called upon by the best. But here, sure the position is not what we were led to expect. Money is all that most people are thinking of. There's the society in the town would jump at us. But that does not count, Mr. Ridsdale, you know, that does not count; for to us in Her Majesty's service, that have always been accustomed to the best— —"

"Surely, surely, I quite understand; and you have a right to the best. Miss Despard," said the ambassador, "I hope you are considering what Lady Caroline says, and will not disappoint our hopes. Last night was triumph, but this will be enjoyment. You, who must know what talent Miss Despard has—I appeal to you, Mrs. O'Shaughnessy—I am sure from your kind looks that we will have your aid."

"Is it to go and sing for them again, Lottie, me dear?" said the old lady in an undertone. "That's just what I don't like, Mr. Ridsdale—excuse me if I speak my mind free—me Lady Caroline and his reverence the Dean, they're ready enough to take an advantage, and make their own use of the Chevaliers'— —"

"Do I need to write a note?" said Lottie, interrupting hastily to prevent the completion of a speech which seemed to threaten the very foundations of her happiness. "Perhaps it would be more polite to write a note." She looked at him with a little anxiety, for the thought passed through her mind that she had no pretty paper like this, with a pretty monogram and "The Deanery, St. Michael's," printed on its creamy glaze, and even that she did not write a pretty hand that would do her credit; and, going further, that she would not know how to begin, whether she should be familiar, and venture upon saying, "Dear Lady Caroline," which seemed rather presumptuous, calling an old lady by her Christian name—or——

"I need not trouble you to write. I am sure you mean to say yes, Miss Despard, which is almost more than I dared hope. Yes is all we want, and I shall be so happy to carry it——"

"Yes is easy said," said Mrs. O'Shaughnessy; "a great deal easier than no. Oh, me dear, I don't object to your going; not a bit; only I take an interest in ye, and ye must not make yourself too cheap. Know her talent, Mr. Ridsdale? sure I can't say that I do. I know herself, and a better girl, saving for a bit of temper, don't exist. But a girl is the better of a spark of temper, and that's just what you've got, me dear Lottie. No; I don't know her talent. She has a voice for singing, that I know well; for to hear her and Rowley when she's having her lesson, sure it's enough to give a deaf person the ear-ache. But that's the most that I know."

"Then, Miss Despard," said Rollo, springing to his feet; "if your—friend is in this condition of doubt, it is impossible she can ever have heard you; will you not gratify me and convince her by singing something now? I know it is horrible impertinence on my part, so recent an acquaintance. But—no, Mrs. O'Shaughnessy, you never can have heard her. I have some songs here that I know you would sing to perfection. I deserve to be ordered out of the house for my presumption. I know it; but——" and he clasped his hands and fixed supplicating eyes upon Lottie, who, blushing, trembling, frightened, and happy, did not know how to meet those eyes.

"Sure he'll be down on his knees next," cried Mrs. O'Shaughnessy delighted; "and you wouldn't have the heart to deny the gentleman when he begs so pretty. I'll not say but what I've heard her, and heard her many a time, but maybe the change of the circumstances and the want of Rowley will make a difference. Come, Lottie, me darling, don't wait for pressing, but give us a song, and let us be done with it. If it was a good song you would sing, and not one of those sacred pieces that make me feel myself in the Abbey—where we all are, saving your presence, often enough——"

"I have a song here that will please you, I know," said Rollo. "We shall have you crying in two minutes. You don't know, my dear Mrs. O'Shaughnessy, what a glorious organ you are talking of."

"Organ! that's the Abbey all over; but, praised be Heaven, there's no organ here, only an old cracked piano——"

"Oh, indeed," cried Lottie. "It is not fit to play on, and I don't think I can sing at sight; and—I know I can't play an accompaniment."

"That shall be my happy office," he said, looking at her with those eyes that dazzled Lottie. They were not dazzling by nature, but he put a great deal of meaning into them, and Lottie, foolish Lottie, innocently deceived, put a great deal more. Her eyes sank beneath this look. She could scarcely keep the tears from coming into them, tears of confused pleasure and wonder and happiness; and she could not refuse him what he asked. He opened the wretched old piano, worn out and jingling, and out of tune as it was. And Mrs. O'Shaughnessy put her knees a little more apart, and threw her bonnet-strings over her shoulders, and spread out her warm hands in her lap. There was a little good-humoured cynicism in her face. She did not expect to enjoy the singing, but all her faculties were moved by the hint, the scent, of a flirtation; and that she was prepared to enjoy to the full.

CHAPTER X
THE MINOR CANON

Mr. Ashford had not said much to Miss Despard on the way home; it was but crossing the road, a brief progress which left little room for conversation, and the Signor was better acquainted with her than he was. Besides, the Minor Canon was not a man who could carry on a conversation with several people at a time, or open his heart to more listeners than one. He could sometimes be eloquent with a single interlocutor, but he was a silent man in society, with very little to say for himself, even when his companions were of the most congenial kind. He was an unsuccessful man, and carried in his soul, though without any bitterness, the burden of his own unsuccess. He was a man of "good connections," but none of his connections had done anything for him—and he had considerable talents, which had done nothing for him. He had got a scholarship, but no other distinction, at the University. Nobody was at all clear how this came about. He was not idle, he was not careless, but he did not succeed; his talents were not those that win success. At twenty he published a little volume of poetry, which was "full of promise." At thirty he brought out a learned treatise on some matter of classical erudition, which, as it is too high for us to understand, we will not venture to name. And nothing came of that; his poems were not sold, neither was his treatise. His fellow-scholars (for he was a true scholar, and a ripe and good one) occupied themselves with pulling holes in his coat, writing whole pages to show that he had taken a wrong view of a special passage. And there was something worse than this that he had done. He had put a wrong accent upon a Greek word! We tremble to mention such a crime, but it cannot be slurred over, for it was one of the heaviest troubles in Mr. Ashford's life. Whether it was his fault or the printer's fault will never be known till the day of judgment, and perhaps not even then: for it seems more than likely that a mistake in an accent, or even the absence of the accent altogether, will not affect the reckoning at that decisive moment; but this was what had been done. Not once—which might have been an accident, or carelessness in correcting the press, such a misfortune as might occur to any man—but a dozen times, if not more, had this crime been perpetrated. It disfigured at least the half of his book. It was a mistake which no properly conducted fourth-form boy would have been guilty of. So everybody said;—and it crushed the unlucky man. Even now, five years after, that incorrect accent coloured his life. He went in mourning for it all his days. He could not forget it himself, even if other people might have been willing to forget it. It seemed to justify and explain all the failures in his career. Everybody had wondered why he did not get a fellowship after he had taken his degree, but this explained everything. A man capable of making such a mistake! The buzz that arose in the University never died out of his ears. Robuster persons might laugh, but Ernest Ashford never got over it. It weighed him down for the rest of his days.

Nor was he a man to thrive much in his profession. He tried a curacy or two, but he was neither High Church enough for the High, nor Low Church enough for the Low. And he could not get on with the poor, his rectors said. Their misery appalled his gentle soul. He emptied his poor pockets in the first wretched house he went into, and retreated to his lodgings after he had done so, with a heart all aching and bleeding, and crying out against the pain he saw. He was not of the fibre which can take other people's sufferings placidly, though he had a fine nerve in bearing his own. This, no doubt, was weakness in him; and in all probability he got imposed upon on every side; but the fact was he could not support the wretchedness of others, and when he had given them every six-pence he had, and had entreated them to be comforted, he fled from them with anguish in his heart. He could not eat or drink for weeks after for thinking that there were people in the world near at hand who had little or nothing on their board. He suffered more from this than his fellow-curate did from neuralgia, or his rector from biliousness, and he did what neither of these martyrs felt themselves compelled to do—he fled from the trouble he could not cope with. They quoted Scripture to him, and proved, from the text "The poor ye have always with you," that nothing better was to be expected. But he answered with a passionate protestation that God could never mean that, and fled—which, indeed, was not a brave thing to do, and proved the weakness of his character. Thus the Church found him wanting, as well as the University. And when at last he settled down into a corner where at least he could get his living tranquilly, it was not by means of his talents or education, but because of a quality which was really accidental, the possession of a beautiful voice. This possession was so entirely adventitious that he was not even a learned musician, nor had he given much of his time to this study. But he had one of those voices, rich and tender and sweet, which go beyond science, which are delicious even when they are wrong, and please the hearers when they perplex the choir and drive the conductor out of his senses. Mr. Ashford did not do this, having an ear almost as delicate as his voice, but both of these were gifts of nature, and not improved by training to the degree which the Signor could have wished. He had been persuaded to try for the Minor Canonry of St. Michael's almost against his will; for to be a singing man, even in the highest grade, did not please his fancy. But no one had been able to stand before him. The Signor had strongly supported another competitor, a man with twice the science of Mr. Ashford; but even the Signor had been obliged to confess that his friend's voice was not to be compared with that of the successful candidate. And after knocking about the world for a dozen years without any real place or standing-ground, Ernest Ashford found himself at thirty-five suited with a life that was altogether harmonious to his nature, but which he felt half humiliated to have gained, not by his talents or his learning, or anything that was any credit to him, but by the mere natural accidental circumstance of his beautiful voice. He was half-ashamed and humbled to think that all his education, which had cost so much, went for nothing in comparison with this chance talent which had cost him nothing, and that all his hopes and ambitions, which had mounted high, had come to no loftier result. But as, by fair means or foul, for a good or bad reason, life had at last found a suitable career for him, where he could be independent, and do some sort of work, such as it was, he soon became content. The worst thing about it (he said) was that it could not be called work at all. To go twice a day and sing beautiful music in one of the most beautiful churches in the world, would have been the highest pleasure, if it had not been the business of his life. He had never even been troubled by religious doubts which might have introduced a complication, but was of a nature simply devout, and born to go twice a day to church. When, however, he found himself thus, as it were, exalted over the common lot, he made an effort to bring himself down to the level of common mortality by taking pupils, an experiment which succeeded perfectly, and brought him into hot water so speedily that he no longer felt himself elevated above the level of mankind.

This was the man whom Lottie had seized the opportunity of making acquaintance with, and speaking to, that evening at the Deanery. Mr. Ashford was not badly treated at the Deanery to be only a Minor Canon. He was often enough asked to dinner when there was not anybody of much consequence about: the Dean was very willing to have him, for he was a gentleman, and talked very pleasantly, and could be silent (which he always was when the company was large) in a very agreeable, gentlemanly sort of way; not the silence of mere dulness and having nothing to say. But when there was a large dinner-party, and people of consequence were there, Lady Caroline would often ask Mr. Ashford to come in the evening, and he had come to understand (without being offended) that on these occasions he would probably be asked to sing. He was not offended, but he was amused, and sometimes, with a little well-bred malice, such as he had never shown in any other emergency of his life, would have a cold, and be unable to sing. He had not strength of mind to carry out this little stratagem when there seemed to be much need of his services, but now and then he would wind himself up to do it, with much simple satisfaction in his own cleverness. Mr. Ashford was well treated in the Cloisters generally. The other Canons, those whom Mrs. O'Shaughnessy called "the real Canons," were all more or less attentive to him. He had nothing to complain of in his lot. He had at this moment two pupils in hand: one, the son of Canon Uxbridge, whom he was endeavouring to prepare for the simple ordeal of an army examination; and another, who was clever, the son of the clergyman in the town, and aspiring to a university scholarship. In consequence of the unfortunate failure of that Greek accent it was but few engagements of this more ambitious kind that Mr. Ashford had; his work was usually confined to the simplicity of the military tests of knowledge; but the rector of St. Michael's was a man who knew what he was about, and naturally, with a sharp young scholar for ever on his traces, the gentle Minor Canon, conscious of having once committed an inaccuracy, was kept very much upon his p's and q's.

On the same day on which Rollo Ridsdale wrote for Lady Caroline that invitation to Lottie, of the terms of which Lady Caroline was so little aware, the Dean gave a verbal invitation to the same effect to Mr. Ashford in the vestry. "Will you dine with us to-day, Ashford?" he said. "My nephew Ridsdale, who is mad about music, and especially about this girl's voice who sang last night, has persuaded Lady Caroline to ask her again. Yourself and the Signor; I believe nobody else is coming. Ridsdale has got something to do with a new opera company, and he is wild to find an English prima donna——"

"Is Miss Despard likely to become a professional singer?" said the Minor Canon in some surprise.

"I am sure I can't tell—why not? They are poor, I suppose, or they would not be here; and I don't see why she shouldn't sing. Anyhow, Rollo is most anxious to try. He thinks she has a wonderful voice. He is apt to think anything wonderful which he himself has anything to do with, you know."

"She has a wonderful voice," said Mr. Ashford, with more decision than usual.

"But—pardon me if I interrupt," cried the Signor, who had come in while they were talking, "no method; no science. She wants training—the most careful training. The more beautiful a voice is by nature, the more evident is the want of education in it," the musician added, with meaning. He did not look at Mr. Ashford, but the reference was very unmistakable. The Dean looked at them, and smiled as he took up his shovel hat.

"I leave you to fight it out, Science against Nature," he said; "as long as you don't forget that you are both expected this evening at the Deanery—and to sit in judgment as well as to dine."

"I know what my judgment will be beforehand," said the Signor; "absolute want of education—but plenty of material for a good teacher to work upon."

"And mine is all the other way," Mr. Ashford said, with some of the vehemence of intellectual opposition, besides a natural partisanship. "A lovely voice, full of nature, and freshness, and expression—which you will spoil, and render artificial, and like anybody else's voice, if you have your way."

"All excellence is the production of Art," said the Signor.

"Poeta nascitur," said the Canon; and though the words are as well known as any slang, they exercised a certain subduing influence upon the musician, who was painfully aware that he himself was not educated, except in a professional way. The two men went out together through the door into the Great Cloister, from which they passed by an arched passage to the Minor Cloister, where was Mr. Ashford's house. Nothing could be more unlike than the tall, stooping, short-sighted scholar, and the dark keen Italianism of the Anglicised foreigner—the one man full of perception, seeing everything within his range at a glance, the other living in a glimmer of vague impressions, which took form but slowly in his mind. On the subject of their present discussion, however, Ashford had taken as distinct a view as the Signor. He had put himself on Lottie's side instinctively, with what we have called a natural partisanship. She was like himself, she sang as the birds sing—and though his own education, after a few years of St. Michael's, had so far progressed musically that he was as well aware of her deficiencies as the Signor, still he felt himself bound to be her champion.

"I am not sure how far we have any right to discuss a young lady who has never done anything to provoke animadversion," he said, with an old-fashioned scrupulousness, as they threaded the shady passages. "I think it very unlikely that such a girl would ever consent to sing for the public."

"That is what she says," said the Signor, "but she can't understand what she is saying. Sing for the public! I suppose that means to her to appear before a crowd of people, to be stared at, criticised, brought down to the level of professional singers. The delight of raising a crowd to one'self, binding them into mutual sympathy, getting at the heart underneath the cold English exterior, that is what the foolish girl never thinks of and cannot understand."

"Ah!" said the Minor Canon. He was struck by this unexpected poetry in the Signor, who was not a poetical person. He said, "I don't think I thought of that either. I suppose, for my part, I am very old-fashioned. I don't like a woman to make an exhibition of herself."

"Do you suppose a real artist ever makes an exhibition of herself?" said the musician almost scornfully. "Do you suppose she thinks of herself? Oh, yes, of course there are varieties. Men will be men and women women; but anyone who has genius, who is above the common stock! However," he added, calming himself down, and giving a curious, alarmed glance at his companion, to see whether, perhaps, he was being laughed at for his enthusiasm, "there are other reasons, that you will allow to be solid reasons, for which I want to get hold of this Miss Despard. You know Purcell, my assistant, a young fellow of the greatest promise?"

"Purcell? oh, yes; you mean the son of— —"

"I mean my pupil," said the Signor, hurriedly, with a flush of offence.

"I beg your pardon. I did not mean anything unkind. It was only to make sure whom you meant. I know he is a good musician and everything that is good."

"He is a very fine fellow," said the Signor, still flushed and self-assertive. "There is nobody of whom I have a higher opinion. He is a better musician than I am, and full of promise. I expect him to reach the very top of his profession."

Mr. Ashford bowed. He had no objection to young Purcell's success: why should he be supposed to have any objection to it? but the conversation had wandered widely away from Miss Despard, in whom he was really interested, and his attention relaxed in a way which he could not disguise. This seemed to disturb the Signor still more. He faltered; he hesitated. At last he said with a sudden burst, "You think this has nothing to do with the subject we were discussing; but it has. Purcell, poor fellow! has a—romantic devotion; a passion which I can't as yet call anything but unhappy—for Miss Despard."

"For Miss Despard?"

The Minor Canon turned round at his own door with his key in his hand, lifting his eyes in wonder. "That is surely rather misplaced," he said the next moment, with much more sharpness than was usual to him, opening the door with a little extra energy and animation. He had no reason whatever for being annoyed, but he was annoyed, though he could not have told why.

"How misplaced?" said the Signor, following him up the little oak staircase, narrow and broken into short flights, which led to the rooms in which the Minor Canon lived. The landing at the top of the staircase was as large as any of the rooms to which it led, with that curious misappropriation of space, but admirable success in picturesque effect, peculiar to old houses. There was a window in it, with a window-seat, and such a view as was not to be had out of St. Michael's, and the walls were of dark wainscot, with bits of rich old carving here and there. The Canon's little library led off from this and had the same view. It was lighted by three small, deep-set windows set in the outer wall of the Abbey, and consequently half as thick as the room was large. They were more like three pictures hung on the dark wall than mere openings for light, which indeed they supplied but sparingly, the thickness of the wall casting deep shadows between. And the walls, wherever they were visible, were dark oak, here and there shining with gleams of reflection, but making a sombre background, broken only by the russet colour of old books and the chance ornaments of gilding which embellished them. Mr. Ashford's writing-table, covered with books and papers, stood in front of the centre window. There was room for a visitor on the inner side, between him and the bookcases on the further wall, and there was room for somebody in the deep recess of the window at his left hand; but that was all.

"How misplaced?" the Signor repeated, coming in and taking possession of the window-seat. "He is not perhaps what you call a gentleman by birth, but he is a great deal better. You and I know gentlemen by birth who—but don't let us talk blasphemy within the Precincts. I am a Tory. I take my stand upon birth and blood and primogeniture."

"And laugh at them?"

"Oh, not at all; on the contrary, I think they are very good for the country; but you and I have known gentlemen by birth—Well! my young Purcell is not one of these, but sprung from the soil. He is a capital musician; he is a rising young man. In what is he worse than the daughter of a commonplace old soldier, a needy, faded gentleman of a Chevalier?"

"Gently! gently! I cannot permit you to say anything against the Chevaliers. They are brave men, and men who have served their country— —"

"Better than a good musician serves his?" cried the Signor. "You will not assert as much. Better than we serve the country, who put a little tune and time into her, an idea of some thing better than fifes and drums?"

"My dear Rossinetti," said Mr. Ashford, with some heat, "England had music in her before a single maestro had ever come from the South, and will have after— —"

"No tragedy," said the Signor, with a low laugh, putting up his hand. "I am not a maestro, nor do I come from the South. I serve my country when I teach these knavish boys, that would rather be playing in the streets, to lengthen their snipped vowels. But suppose they do better who fight—I say nothing against that. I am not speaking of all the Chevaliers, but of one, and one who is very unlike the rest—the only person who has anything to do with the argument—a wretched frequenter of taverns, admirer of milliners' girls, who is said to be going to marry some young woman of that class. Why should not Purcell, the best fellow in the world, be as good as he?"

"I don't know the father—and it is not the father Purcell has a romantic devotion for. But don't you see, Rossinetti, we are allowing ourselves to discuss the affairs of people we know nothing of, people we have no right to talk about. In short, we are *gossiping*, which is not a very appropriate occupation."

"Oh, there is a great deal of it done by other persons quite as dignified as we are," said the Signor, with a smile; but he accepted the reproof and changed the subject. They sat together and talked, looking over the great width of the silent country, the trees and the winding river, the scattered villages, and the illuminated sky. How beautiful it was! fair enough of itself to make life sweeter to those who had it before their eyes. But the two men talked and took no notice. They might have been in a street in London for any difference it made.

When, however, the Signor was gone, Mr. Ashford, having closed the door upon his visitor, came straying back to the window in which Rossinetti had been seated, and stood there gazing out vaguely. In all likelihood he saw nothing at all, for he was short-sighted, as has been said; but yet it is natural to seek the relief of the window and look out when there is something within of a confused and vaguely melancholy character to occupy one's thoughts. Twenty-four hours before, Mr. Ashford had not known who Lottie Despard was. He had seen her in the Abbey, and perhaps had found, without knowing it, that sympathy in her face which establishes sometimes a kind of tacit friendship long before words. He thought now that this must have been the case; but he knew very little about her still—nothing except that she had a beautiful voice, a face that interested him, and something she wanted to talk to him about. What was it she wanted to talk to him about? He could not imagine what it could be, but he recollected very well how pleasant a thing it was when this beautiful young lady, lifting the long fringes which veiled them, turned upon him those beautiful blue eyes which (he thought) were capable of expressing more feeling than eyes of any other colour. Probably had Lottie's eyes been brown or grey, Mr. Ashford would have been of exactly the same opinion. And to think of this creature as the beloved of Purcell gave him a shock. Purcell! it was not possible. No doubt he was a respectable fellow, very much to be applauded and encouraged:—but Mr. Ashford himself had nothing to do with Miss Despard; he was pleased to think that he should meet her again and hear her sing again, and he must try, he said to himself, to find an opportunity to ask her what it was about which she wanted to speak to him. Otherwise he had no hand, and wanted to have no hand, in this little conspiracy of which she seemed the unconscious object. On the contrary, his whole sympathies were with Lottie against the men who wanted to entrap her and make her a public singer whether she would or not. He was glad she did not want it herself, and felt a warm sympathy with her in those natural prejudices against "making an exhibition of herself" which the Signor scorned so much. The Signor might scorn those shrinkings and shyness; they were altogether out of his way; he might not understand them. But Mr. Ashford understood them perfectly. He liked Lottie for having them, comprehended her, and felt for her. Anything rather than *that*, he thought, with a little tremulous warmth, as if she had been his sister. If there should be any discussion on this subject to-night at the Deanery, and she was in need of support, he would stand by her. Having made this resolution he went back to his writing-table and sat down in his usual place, and put this intrusive business, which did not in the least concern him, out of his mind.

The most intrusive subject! What had he to do with it? And yet it was not at all easy to get it out of his mind. He had not read three lines when he felt himself beginning to wonder why Rollo Ridsdale had chosen Miss Despard as his prima donna above everybody else, and why the Signor concerned himself so much about it. She had certainly a beautiful voice, but still voices as beautiful had been heard before. It could not be supposed that there was no one else equal to her. Why should they make so determined a set at this girl, who was a lady, and who had not expressed any wish or intention of being a singer? To be sure, she was very handsome as well, and her face was full of expression. And Rollo was a kind of enthusiast when he took anything in his head. Then there was the other imbroglio with the Signor and Purcell. What was Purcell to the Signor that he should take up his cause so warmly? But, then, still more mysterious, what was it all to him, Ernest Ashford, that it should come between him and the book he was reading? Nothing could be more absurd. He got up after awhile, and went to the window again, where he finally settled himself with a volume of Shelley, to which he managed to fix the thoughts which had been so absurdly disturbed by this stranger, and this question with which he had nothing to do. It was a very idle way of spending the afternoon, to recline in a deep window looking out upon miles of air and distance and read Shelley; but it was better than getting involved in the mere gossip of St. Michael's and turning over in his head against his will the private affairs of people whom he scarcely knew. This was the disadvantage of living in a small circle with so few interests, he said to himself. But he got delivered from the gossip by means of the poetry, and so lay there while the brilliant sunshine slanted from the west, now sending his thoughts abroad over the leafy English plain, now feeding his fancy with the poet among the Euganean hills.

CHAPTER XI
ANOTHER EVENING AT THE DEANERY

Mr. Ridsdale had perhaps never touched, and rarely heard, anything so bad as the old cracked piano which Lottie had inherited from her mother, and which was of the square form now obsolete, of a kind which brokers (the only dealers in the article) consider very convenient, as combining the character of a piano and a sideboard. Very often had Lottie's piano served the purpose of a sideboard, but it was too far gone to be injured—nothing could make it worse. Nevertheless Mr. Ridsdale played the accompaniments upon it, without a word, to Lottie's admiration and wonder, for he seemed to be able to draw forth at his fingers' ends a volume of sound which she did not suppose to be within the power of the old instrument. He had brought several songs with him, being fully minded to hear her that morning, whatever obstacles might be in the way. But it so happened that there were no obstacles whatever in the way; and Mrs. O'Shaughnessy was of the greatest service as audience. With the true talent of a manager, Mr. Ridsdale addressed himself to the subjugation of his public. He placed before Lottie the song from "Marta," to which, hearing it thus named, Mrs. O'Shaughnessy prepared herself to listen with a certain amiable scorn. "Ah, we shall have you crying in five minutes," he said. "Is it me you're meaning?" she cried in high scorn. But the fact was that when the melting notes of "The Last Rose of Summer" came forth from Lottie's lips, Mrs. O'Shaughnessy was altogether taken by surprise, and carried out Rollo's prophecy to the letter by weeping abundantly. There was much of Mr. Ridsdale's music which Lottie could not sing—indeed, it would have been wonderful if she had been able to do so, as he had brought with him the finest *morceaux* of a dozen operas, and Lottie's musical education had been of the slightest. But he so praised, and flattered, and encouraged her, that she went on from song to song at his bidding, making the best attempt at them that was possible, while Mrs. O'Shaughnessy sat by and listened. Her presence there was of the utmost consequence to them. It at once converted Rollo's visit into something allowable and natural, and it gave him a pretence for beginning what was really an examination into Lottie's powers and compass, at once of voice and of intelligence. Lottie, innocent of any scheme, or of any motive he could have, save simple pleasure in her singing, exerted herself to please him with the same mixture of gratitude and happy prepossession with which she had thought of him for so long. If she could give a little pleasure to him who had given her his love and his heart (for what less could it be that he had given her?), it was her part, she thought, to do so. She felt that she owed him everything she could do for him, to recompense him for that gift which he had given her unawares. So she stood by him in a soft humility, not careful that she was showing her own ignorance, thinking only of pleasing him. What did it matter, if he were pleased, whether she attained the highest excellence? She said sweetly, "I know I cannot do it, but if you wish it I will try," and attempted feats which in other circumstances would have appalled her. And the fact was, that thus forgetting herself, and thinking only of pleasing him, Lottie sang better than she had ever done in her life, better even than she had done in the Deanery on the previous night. She committed a thousand faults, but these faults were as nothing in comparison with the melody of her voice and the purity of her taste. Rollo became like one inspired. All the enthusiasm of an amateur, and all the zeal of an enterprising manager, were in him. The old piano rolled out notes of which in its own self it was quite incapable under his rapid fingers. He seemed to see her with all London before her, at her feet, and he (so to speak) at once the discoverer and the possessor of this new star. No wonder the old piano grew ecstatic under his touch; he who had gone through so many vicissitudes, who had made so many failures; at last it seemed evident to him that his fortune was made. Unfortunately (though that he forgot for the moment) he had felt his fortune to be made on several occasions before.

Mrs. O'Shaughnessy gave a great many nods and smiles when at last he went away. "I say nothing, me dear, but I have my eyesight," she said, "and a blind man could see what's in the wind. So that is how it is, Lottie, me darling? Well, well! I always said you were the prettiest girl that had been in the Lodges this many a year. I don't envy ye, me love, your rise in the world. And I hope, Lottie, when ye're me lady, ye'll not forget your old friends."

"How should I ever be my lady?" said Lottie; "indeed, Mrs. O'Shaughnessy, I don't know what you mean."

"No, me honey, the likes of you never do, till the right moment comes," said the old lady, going down the narrow stairs. She kissed her hand to Lottie, who looked after her from the window as she appeared on the pavement outside, and, with her bonnet-strings flying loose, turned in at her own door. Her face was covered with smiles and her mind full of a new interest. She could not refrain from going into the Major's little den, and telling him. "Nonsense!" the Major said, incredulously; "one of your mare's-nests." "Sure it was a great deal better than a mare, it was turtle-doves made the nest I'm thinking of," said Mrs. O'Shaughnessy; and she took off her bonnet and seated herself at her window, from which she became evident to Lottie that to speak was a necessity, to break the spell which might otherwise stupefy her senses too.

"It is a beautiful night," was all she managed to say; could anything be more feeble? but Lady Caroline gave no reply. She made the usual little movement of her eyelids, which meant an assent; indeed it was not a remark which required reply. And the silence fell on them again as bad as ever. The night air blew in, the moths whirled about the candles, dashed against the globe of the lamp, dropped on the floor with fatal infinitesimal booms of tragic downfall; and Lady Caroline lay on the sofa, with eyes directed to vacancy, looking at nothing. Lottie, with the roses in her hair, and so much life tingling in her, could not endure it. She wanted to go and shake the vision on the sofa, she wanted to cry out and make some noise or other to save herself from the spell. At last, when she could keep silence no longer, she jumped up, throwing over a small screen which stood near in her vehemence of action. "Shall I sing you something, Lady Caroline?" she said.

Lady Caroline was startled by the fall of the screen. She watched till it was picked up, actually looking at Lottie, which was some advance; then she said, "If you please, Miss Despard," in her calm tones. And Lottie, half out of herself, made a dash at the grand piano, though she knew she could not play. She struck a chord or two, trembling all over, and began to sing. This time she did not feel the neglect or unkindness of the way in which she was treated. It was a totally different sensation. A touch of panic, a touch of amusement was in it. She was afraid that she might be petrified too if she did nothing to break the spell. But as she began to sing, with a quaver in her voice, and a little shiver of nervous chilliness in her person, the door opened, and voices, half discerned figures of men, life and movement, came pouring in. Lottie came to an abrupt stop in the middle of a bar.

"This will never do," said the suave Dean: "you make too much noise, Rollo. You have frightened Miss Despard in the middle of her song."

Then Rollo came forward into the light spot round the piano, looking very pale; he was a good deal more frightened than Lottie was. Could it be possible that she had made a false note? He was in an agony of horror and alarm. "I—make a noise!" he said; "my dear uncle!" He looked at her with appealing eyes full of anguish. "You were not—singing, Miss Despard? I am sure you were not singing, only trying the piano."

"I thought it would perhaps—amuse Lady Caroline." Lottie did no know what she had done that was wrong. The Signor wore an air of troubl too. Only Mr. Ashford's face, looking at her, as one followed another int the light, reassured her. She turned to him with a little anxiety. "I canno play; it is quite true; perhaps I ought not to have touched the piano," sh said.

inspected the world with a new warmth of interest, determined not to lose a single incident in this new fairy tale.

Law came out of his room, where he had been "reading," when Mrs. O'Shaughnessy went away. "What has all this shrieking been about," said Law, "and thumping on that old beast of a piano? You are always at a fellow about reading, and when he does read you disturb him with your noise. How do you think I could get on with all that miauling going on? Who has been here?"

"Mr. Ridsdale has been here," said Lottie demurely. "He brought me a note from Lady Caroline, and I am going again to the Deanery to-night."

Law whistled a long whew—ew! "Again, to-night! she'd better ask you to go and live there," said the astounded boy; and he said no more about his interrupted reading, but put his big book philosophically away; for who could begin to read again after all the disturbances of the morning, and after such a piece of news as this?

Lottie dressed herself with more care than ever that evening. She began to wish for ornaments, and to realise how few her decorations were; the little pearl locket was so small, and her arms seemed so bare without any bracelets. However, she made herself little bands of black velvet, and got the maid to fasten them on. She had never cared much for ornaments before. And she spent a much longer time than usual over the arrangement of her hair. Above all she wanted to look like a lady, to show that, though their choice of her was above what could have been expected, it was not above the level of what she was used to. *Their* choice of her—that was how it seemed to Lottie. The young lover had chosen, as it is fit the lover should do; but Lady Caroline had ratified his selection, and Lottie, proud yet entirely humble in the tender humility born of gratitude, wanted to show that she could do credit to their choice. She read the note which purported to be Lady Caroline's over and over again; how kind it was! Lady Caroline's manner perhaps was not quite so kind. People could not control their manner. The kindest heart was often belied, Lottie was aware, by a stiffness, an awkwardness, perhaps only a shyness, which disguised their best intentions. But the very idea of asking her was kind, and the letter was so kind that she made up her mind never again to mistake Lady Caroline. She had a difficulty in expressing herself, no doubt. She was indolent perhaps. At her age and in her position it was not wonderful if one got indolent; but in her heart she was kind. This Lottie repeated to herself as she put the roses in her hair. In her heart Lady Caroline was kind; the girl felt sure that she could never mistake her, never be disappointed in her again. And in this spirit she tripped across the Dean's Walk, Mrs. O'Shaughnessy watching from her window. It was almost dark, but it was not one of the Signer's nights for practice, and only a few of the inhabitants of the Abbey Precincts were enjoying the air on the Terrace pavement. They all saw her as she came out in the twilight with her uncovered head. Law had gone out, and there was nobody to go with her this time to the Deanery door. But Lottie had no difficulty in finding an escort: as she came out, looking round her shyly to watch for a quiet moment when no one was about, Captain Temple came forward, who lived two doors off, and was passing as she came to the little garden gate. He was the preux chevalier of all the Chevaliers. He came forward with a fatherly smile upon his kind face. "You are looking for some one to go with you," he said; "your father has gone out. I saw him. Let me take his place."

"Oh, thanks! I am going to the Deanery. I thought Law would have waited for me."

"Law, like others of his age, has his own concerns to think of," said Captain Temple, "but I am used to this kind of work. You have heard of my girl, Miss Despard?"

"Yes, Captain Temple— —." Lottie, touched suddenly in the sympathetic sentiment of her own beginning life, looked up at him with wistful eyes.

"She was a pretty creature, like yourself, my dear. My wife and I often talk of you, and think you like her. She was lost to us before she went out of the world, and I think it broke her heart—as well as ours. Take care of the damp grass with your little white shoes."

"Oh, Captain Temple, do not come with me," said Lottie, with tears in her eyes. "I can go very well alone. It is too hard upon you."

"No—I like it, my dear. My wife cannot talk of it, but I like to talk of it. You must take care not to marry anyone that will carry you quite away from your father's house."

"As if that would matter! as if papa would care!" Lottie said in her heart, with a half pity, half envy, of Captain Temple's lost daughter; but this was but a superficial feeling in comparison with the great compassion she had for him. The old Chevalier took her across the road as tenderly and carefully as if even her little white shoes were worth caring for. There was a moist brightness about his eyes as he looked at her pretty figure. "The roses are just what you ought to wear," he said. "And whenever you want anyone to take care of you in this way, send for me; I shall like to do it. Shall I come back for you in case your father should be late?"

"Oh, Captain Temple, papa never minds! but it is quite easy to get back," she said, thinking that perhaps this time *he*— —

"I think it is always best that a young lady should have her own attendant, and not depend on anyone to see her home," said the old Captain. And he rang the bell at the Deanery door, and took off his hat,

with a smile which almost made Lottie forget Lady Caroline. She went into the drawing-room accordingly much less timidly than she had ever done before, and no longer felt any fear of Mr. Jeremie, who admitted her, though he was a much more imposing person than Captain Temple. This shade of another life which had come over her seemed to protect Lottie, and strengthen her mind. The drawing-room was vaguely lighted with clusters of candles here and there, and at first she saw nobody, nor was there any indication held out to her that the mistress of the house was in the room, except the solemn tone of Jeremie's voice announcing her. Lottie thought Lady Caroline had not come in from the dining-room, and strayed about looking at the books and ornaments on the tables. She even began to hum an air quietly to herself, by way of keeping up her own courage, and it was not till she had almost taken her seat unawares on Lady Caroline's dress, extended on the sofa, that she became aware that she was not alone. "Oh, I beg your pardon," she cried out in a sudden panic. "I thought there was no one in the room." Lady Caroline made no remark at all, except to say "How do you do, Miss Despard?" That was what she had made up her mind to say, feeling it to be quite enough for the occasion—and Lady Caroline did not easily change her mind when it was once made up. She thought it very impertinent of the girl to come in and look at the photographs on the tables, and even to take the liberty of singing, but there was no calculating what these sort of people might do. She had nearly sat down on Lady Caroline's feet! "This is what I put up with for Rollo," the poor lady said to herself; and it seemed to her that a great deal of gratitude from Rollo was certainly her due. She did not move, nor did she ask Miss Despard to sit down; but Lottie, half in fright, dropped into a chair very near the strange piece of still life on the sofa. The girl had been very much frightened to see her, and for a moment was speechless with the horror of it. Nearly to sit down upon Lady Caroline! and a moment of silence ensued. Lady Caroline did not feel in the least inclined to begin a conversation. She had permitted the young woman to be invited, and she had said "How do you do, Miss Despard?" and she did not know what more could be expected from her. So they sat close together in the large, half-visible, dimly-illuminated room, with the large window open to the night, and said nothing to each other. Lottie, who was the visitor, was embarrassed, but Lady Caroline was not embarrassed. She felt no more need to speak than did the table with the photographs upon i which Lottie had stopped to look at. As for Lottie, she bore it as long as sh could, the stillness of the room, the flicker of the candles, the dash and fall o a moth now and then flying across the lights, and the immovable figure o the sofa with its feet tucked up, and floods of beautiful rich silk envelopin them. A strange sense that Lady Caroline was not living at all, that it wa only the picture of a woman that was laid out on the sofa came over her. her nervousness she began to tremble, then felt inclined to laugh. At last

"You were startled," said the Minor Canon, kindly. "Your voice fluttered like those candles in the draught." The others still looked terribly serious, and did not speak.

"And I sang false," said Lottie; "I heard myself. It was terrible; but I thought I was stiffening into stone," she said, in an undertone, and she gave an alarmed look at Lady Caroline on the sofa. This restored the spirits of the others spectators, who looked at each other relieved.

"Thank Heaven, she knew it," Rollo whispered to the Signor; "it was fright, pure fright—and my aunt——"

"What else did you suppose it was?" answered in the same tone, but with some scorn, the Signor.

"Miss Despard, don't think you are to be permitted to accompany yourself," said Rollo. "Here are two of us waiting your pleasure. Signor, I will not pretend to interfere when you are there. May we have again that song you were so good——?"

"Ah, pardon me," he cried coming close to her to get the music. "I do not want to lose a minute. I have been on thorns this half-hour. I ought to have been here waiting ready to receive you, as you ought to be received."

"Oh, it did not matter," said Lottie, confused. "I am sorry I cannot play. I wanted—to try—to amuse Lady Caroline."

By this time the Signor had arranged the music on the piano and began to play. The Dean had gone off to the other end of the room, where the evening paper, the last edition, had been laid awaiting him on a little table on which stood a reading-lamp. The green shade of the lamp concentrated the light upon the paper, and the white hands of the reader, and his long limbs and his little table, making a new picture in the large dim room. On the opposite side sat Lady Caroline, who had withdrawn her feet hastily from the sofa, and sat bolt upright as a tribute to the presence of "the gentlemen." These two pieces of still life appeared to Lottie vaguely through the partial gloom. The master and mistress of the house were paying no attention to the visitors. Such visitors as these were not of sufficient importance to be company, or to disturb their entertainers in the usual habits of their evening. Lady Caroline, indeed, seldom allowed herself to be disturbed by anyone. She put down her feet for the sake of her own dignity, but she did not feel called upon to make any further sacrifice. And as for Lottie, she was not happy among these three men. She shrank from Rollo, who was eyeing her with an anxiety which she could not understand, and longed for Mrs. O'Shaughnessy, or, indeed, any woman to stand by her. Her heart sank, and she shivered again with that chill which is of the nerves and fancy. The Dean with his rustling paper, and Lady Caroline with her vacant eyes, were at the other end of the room, and Lottie felt isolated, separated, cast upon the tender mercies of the three connoisseurs, a girl with no woman near to stand by her. It seemed to her for the moment as if she must sink into the floor altogether, or else turn and fly.

It was Mr. Ashford again who came to Lottie's aid. "Play something else first," he said softly to the Signor, disregarding the anxious looks of Rollo, who had placed himself on a chair at a little distance, so that he might be able to see the singer and stop any false note that might be coming before it appeared. The others were both kind and clever, kinder than the man whom Lottie thought her lover, and whose anxiety for the moment took all thought from him, and more clever too. The Signor began to play Handel, the serious noble music with which Lottie had grown familiar in the Abbey, and soon Mr. Ashford stepped in and sang in his beautiful melodious voice. Then the strain changed, preluding a song which the most angelic of the choristers had sung that morning. The Minor Canon put the music into Lottie's hands. "Begin here," he whispered. She knew it by ear and by heart, and the paper trembled in her hands; but they made her forget herself, and she began, her voice thrilling and trembling, awe and wonder taking possession of her. She had heard it often, but she had never realised what it was till, all human, womanish, shivering with excitement and emotion, she began to sing. It did not seem her own doing at all. The dim drawing-room, with the Dean reading the paper, the men in their evening coats, the glimmering reflection of herself which she caught in the long mirror, in her simple decorations, the roses trembling in her hair, all seemed horribly inappropriate, almost profane, to Lottie. And the music shook in her hands, and the notes, instead of remaining steadily before her eyes, where she could read them, took wings to themselves and floated about, now here, now there, sometimes gleaming upon her, sometimes eluding her. Yet she sang, she could not tell how, forgetting everything, though she saw and felt everything, in a passion, in an inspiration, penetrated through and through by the music and the poetry, and the sacredness, above her and all of them. "I know that my Redeemer liveth." Oh, how did she dare to sing it, how could those commonplace walls enclose it, those men stand and listen as if it was *her* they were listening to? By and by the Dean laid down his paper. Rollo, in the background, gazing on her at first in pale anxiety, then with vexed disapproval (for what did he want with Handel?), came nearer and nearer, his face catching some reflection of hers as she went on. And when Lottie ended, in a rapture she could not explain or understand, they all came pressing round her, dim and blurred figures in her confused eyes. But the girl was too greatly strained to bear their approach or hear what they said. She broke away from them, and rushed, scarcely knowing what she did, to Lady Caroline's side. Lady Caroline herself was roused. She made room for the trembling creature, and Lottie threw herself into the corner of the capacious sofa and covered her face with her hands.

But when she came to herself she would not sing any more. A mixture of guilt and exultation was in her mind. "I ought not to have sung it. I am not good enough to sing it. I never thought what it meant till now," she said trembling. "Oh, I hope you will forgive me. I never knew what it meant before."

"Forgive you!" said the Dean. "We don't know how to thank you, Miss Despard." He was the person who ought to know what it meant if anybody did. And when he had thus spoken he went back to his paper, a trifle displeased by the fuss she made; as if *she* could have any new revelation of the meaning of a thing which, if not absolutely written for St. Michael's, as good as belonged to the choir, which belonged to the Dean and Chapter! There was a certain presumption involved in Lottie's humility. He went back to his reading-lamp, and finished the article which had been interrupted by her really beautiful rendering of a very fine solo. It was really beautiful; he would not for a moment deny that. But if Miss Despard turned out to be excitable, and gave herself airs, like a real prima donna! Heaven be praised, the little chorister boys never had any nerves, but sang whatever was set before them, without thinking what was meant, the Dean said to himself. And it would be difficult to describe Rollo Ridsdale's disappointment. He sat down in a low chair by the side of the sofa, and talked to her in a whisper. "I understand you," he said; "it is like coming down from the heaven of heavens, where you have carried us. But the other spheres are celestial too. Miss Despard, I shall drop down into sheer earth to-morrow. I am going away. I shall lose the happiness of hearing you altogether. Will you not have pity upon me, and lead me a little way into the earthly paradise?" But even these prayers did not move Lottie. She was too much shaken and disturbed out of the unconscious calm of her being for anything more.

CHAPTER XII
BROTHER AND SISTER

Lottie ran out while Rollo Ridsdale was getting his hat to accompany her home. She caught up her shawl over her arm without pausing to put it on, and ran through the dark Cloister and across the Dean's Walk to her own door, before he knew she was ready. "The young—lady is gone, sir," Mr. Jeremie said, who was rather indignant at having to open the door to such sort of people. He would have said young woman had he dared. Rollo, much piqued already in that she had refused to sing for him further, and half irritated, half attracted by this escapade now, hurried after her; but when he emerged from the gloom of the Cloister to the fresh dewy air of the night, and the breadth of the Dean's Walk, lying half visible in summer darkness in the soft indistinct radiance of the stars, there was no one visible, far or near. She had already gone in before he came in sight of the door. He looked up and down the silent way, on which not a creature was visible, and listened to the sound of the door closing behind her. The flight and the sound awoke a new sentiment in his mind. Ladies were not apt to avoid Rollo.

> Not his the form nor his the eye
> That youthful maidens wont to fly.

He was piqued and he was roused. Heretofore, honestly, there had been little but music in his thoughts. The girl was very handsome, which was so much the better—very much the better, for his purpose; but this sparkle of resistance in her roused something else in his mind. Lottie had been like an inspired creature as she sang, this evening. He had never seen on the stage or elsewhere so wonderful an exhibition of absorbed impassioned feeling. If he could secure her for his prima donna, nowhere would such a prima donna be seen. It was not that she had thrown herself into the music, but that the music had possessed her, and transported her out of herself. This was not a common human creature. She was no longer merely handsome, but beautiful in the fervour of her feeling. And for the first time Lottie as Lottie, not merely as a singer, touched a well-worn but still sensitive chord in his breast. He stood looking at the door, which still seemed to echo in the stillness with the jar of closing. What did her flight mean? He was provoked, tantalised, stimulated. Whatever happened, he must see more of this girl.

Why should she fly from him? He did not choose to return and tell the story of her flight, which was such an incident as always makes the man who is baulked present a more or less ridiculous aspect to the spectators; but he stood outside and waited till the steps of the Minor Canon and the Signor had become audible turning each towards their habitation, and even the turning of Mr. Ashford's latchkey in his door. Everything was very still in the evening at St. Michael's. The respectable and solemn Canons in their great houses, and the old Chevaliers in their little lodges, went early to bed. Rollo saw no light anywhere except a dim glow in the window of the little drawing-room where he had spent the morning, and where no doubt the fugitive was seated breathless. His curiosity was raised, and his interest, supplanting that professional eagerness about her voice which he had expressed so largely. Why did she run away from him? Why did she refuse to sing for him? These questions suddenly sprang into his mind, and demanded, if not reply, yet a great deal of consideration. He could not make up his mind what the cause could be.

As for Lottie, she could not have given any reasonable answer to these questions, though she was the only living creature who could know why she ran away. As a matter of fact, she did not know. The music had been more than she could bear in the state of excitement in which she was. Excited about things she would have been ashamed to confess any special interest in—about her relations with the Deanery, about Lady Caroline, and, above all, about Rollo—the wonderful strain to which she had all unconsciously and unthinkingly, at first, given utterance, had caught at Lottie like a hand from heaven. She had been drawn upward into the fervour of religious ecstasy, she who was so ignorant; and when she dropped again to earth, and was conscious once more of Rollo and of Lady Caroline, there had come upon her a sudden sense of shame and of her own pettiness and inability to disentangle herself from the links that drew her to earth which was as passionate as the sudden fervour. How dare she sing *that* one moment, and the next be caught down to vulgar life, to Lady Caroline and Rollo Ridsdale? Lottie would sing no more, and could not speak, so strong was the conflict within her. She could not even encounter the momentary *tête-à-tête* which before she had almost wished for. She was roused and stirred in all her being as she had never been before, able to encounter death or grief, she thought vaguely, or anything that was solemn and grand, but not ordinary talk, not compliments, not the little tender devices of courtship. She flew from the possible touch of sentiment, the half-mock, half-real flatteries that he would be ready to say to her. Love real, and great, and solemn, the Love of which the Italian poet speaks as twin sister of Death, was what Lottie's mind was prepared for; but from anything lower she fled, with the instinct of a nature highly strained and unaccustomed to though capable of, passion. Everything was seething in her mind, her heart beating, the blood coursing through her veins. She felt that she could not bear the inevitable downfall of ordinary talk. She ran out into the soft coolness of the night, the great quiet and calm of the sleeping place, a fugitive driven by this new wind of strange emotion. The shadow of the Abbey was grateful to her, lying dimly half-way across the broad silent road—and the dim lamp in her own window seemed to point out a refuge from her thoughts. She rushed across the empty road, like a ghost flitting, white and noiseless, and swift as an arrow, from the gate of the Cloister, wondering whether the maid would hear her knock at once, or if she would have to wait there at the door till Mr. Ridsdale appeared. But the door was opened at her first touch, to Lottie's great surprise, by Law, who seemed to have been watching for her arrival. He wore a very discontented aspect, but this Lottie did not at first see, in her grateful sense of safety.

"How early you are!" he said. "I did not expect you for an hour yet. It was scarcely worth while going out at all, if you were to come back so soon."

Lottie made no reply. She went upstairs to the little drawing-room, where the lamp had been screwed as low as possible to keep alight for her when she should return. The room was still more dim than Lady Caroline's, and looked so small and insignificant in comparison. On the table was a tray with some bread and butter and a cup of milk, which was Lottie's simple supper after her dissipation; for Lady Caroline's cup of tea was scarcely enough for a girl who had eaten a not too luxurious dinner at two o'clock. She had no mind, however, for her supper now; but sat down on the little sofa and covered her eyes with her hand, and went back into her thoughts, half to prolong the excitement into which she had plunged, half to still herself and get rid of this sudden transport. It would be difficult to say which she wished most; to calm herself down or to continue that state of exaltation which proved to her new capabilities in her own being. She thought it was the former desire that moved her, and that to be quiet was all she wanted; but yet that strong tide running in her veins, that hot beating of her heart, that expansion and elevation of everything in her, was full of an incomprehensible agony of sweetness and exquisite sensation. She did not know what it was. She covered her eyes to shut out the immediate scene around her. The little shabby room, the bread and butter, and Law's slouching figure manipulating the lamp—these, at least, were accessories which she had no desire to see.

"Bother the thing!" said Law, "I can't get it to burn. Here, Lottie! you can manage them. Oh! if you like to sit in the dark, I don't mind. Were your fine people disagreeable? I always told you they wanted nothing but that you should sing for them and amuse them. They don't care a rap for *you*!"

Lottie took no notice of this speech. She withdrew her hand from her face, but still kept her eyes half-closed, unwilling to be roused out of her dream.

"They're all as selfish as old bears," said Law; "most people are, for that matter. They never think of you; you've got to look after yourself; it's their own pleasure they're thinking of. What can you expect from strangers when a man that pretends to be one's own father— —?"

"What are you talking about?" asked Lottie, slowly waking, with a feeling of disgust and impatience, out of her finer fancies. She could not keep some shade of scorn and annoyance from her face.

"You needn't put on those supercilious looks; you'll suffer as much from it as I shall, or perhaps more, for a man can always do for himself," said Law; "but you—you'll find the difference. Lottie," he continued, forgetting resentment in this common evil, and sinking his voice, "he's down there at the old place again."

"What old place?"

As soon as his complaining voice became familiar, Lottie closed her eyes again, longing to resume her own thoughts.

"Oh! the old place. Why, down there; you know—the place where— — I say!" cried Law, suddenly growing red, and perceiving the betrayal of himself as well as of his father which was imminent. "Never mind where it is; it's where that sharp one, Polly Featherstone, works."

Lottie was completely awakened now; she looked up, half-bewildered, from the dispersing mists. "Of whom are you talking?" she cried. "Law, what people have you got among—who are they? You frighten me! Who is it you are talking of?"

"There's no harm in them," cried Law, colouring more and more. "What do you mean? Do you think they're— — I don't know what you mean; they're as good as we are," he added sullenly, walking away with his hands in his pockets out of the revelations of the lamp. Dim and low as it was, it disclosed, he was aware, an uncomfortable glow of colour on his face.

"I don't know who *they* may be," said Lottie, severe, yet blushing too; "I don't want to know! But, oh, Law! you that are so young, my only brother, why should you know people I couldn't know? Why should you be ashamed of anyone you go to see?"

"I was not talking of people *I* go to see; I wish you wouldn't be so absurd; I'm talking of the governor," said Law, speaking very fast; "he's there, I tell you, a man of his time of life, sitting among a lot of girls, talking away fifteen to the dozen. He might find some other way of meeting her if he must meet her!" cried Law, his own grievance breaking out in spite of him. "What has he got to do there among a pack of girls? it's disgraceful at his age!"

Law was very sore, angry, and disappointed. He had gone to his usual resort in the evening, and had seen his father there before him, and had been obliged to retire discomfited, with a jibe from Emma to intensify his trouble. "The Captain's twice the man you are!" the little dressmaker had said; "he ain't afraid of nobody." Poor Law had gone away after this, and strolled despondently along the river-side. He did not know what to do with himself. Lottie was at the Deanery; he was shut out of his usual refuge, and he had nowhere to go. Though he had no money, he jumped into a boat and rowed himself dismally about the river, dropping down below the bridge to where he could see the lighted windows of the workroom. There he lingered about, nobody seeing or taking any notice of him. When he approached the bank, he could even hear the sound of their voices, the laughter with which they received the Captain's witticisms. A little wit went a long way in that complaisant circle. He could make out Captain Despard's shadow against the window, never still for a moment, moving up and down, amusing the girls with songs, jokes, pieces of buffoonery. Law despised these devices; but, oh! how he envied the skill of the actor. He hung about the river in his boat till it got quite dark, almost run into sometimes by other boats, indifferent to everything but this lighted interior, which he could see, though nobody in it could see him. And when he was tired of this forlorn amusement he came home, finding the house very empty and desolate. He tried to work, but how was it possible to work under the sting of such a recollection? The only thing he could do was to wait for Lottie, to pour forth his complaint to her, to hope that she might perhaps find some remedy for this intolerable wrong. It did not occur to him that to betray his father was also to betray himself, and that Lottie might feel as little sympathy for him as he did for Captain Despard. This fact flashed upon him now when it was too late.

Lottie had not risen from her seat, but as she sat there, everything round seemed to waver about her, then settle down again in a sudden revelation of mean, and small, and paltry life, such as she had scarcely ever realised before. Not only the lofty heaven into which the music had carried her rolled away like a scroll, but the other world, which was beautiful also of its kind, from which she had fled, which had seemed too poor to remain in, after the preceding ecstasy, departed as with a glimmer of wings; and she found herself awaking in a life where everything was squalid and poor, where she alone, with despairing efforts, tried to prop up the house that it might not fall into dishonoured dust. She had borne with a kind of contemptuous equanimity Law's first story about her father. Let him marry again! she had said; if he could secure the thing he called his happiness in such a way, let him do it. The idea had filled her with a high scorn. She had not thought of herself nor of the effect it might have upon her, but had risen superior to it with lofty contempt, and put it from her mind. But this was different. With all her high notions of gentility, and all her longings after a more splendid sphere, this sudden revelation of a sphere meaner, lower still, struck Lottie with a sudden pang. A pack of girls! what kind of girls could those be of whom Law spoke? Her blood rushed to her face scorching her with shame. She who scorned the Chevaliers and their belongings! She who had "kept her distance" from her own class, was it possible that she was to be dragged down lower, lower, to shame itself? Her voice was choked in her throat. She did not feel able to speak. She could only cry out to him, clasping her hands, "Don't tell me any more—oh, don't tell me any more——"

"Hillo!" said the lad, "what is the matter with you? Don't tell you any more? You will soon know a great deal more if you don't do something to put a stop to it. There ought to be a law against it. A man's children ought to be able to put a stop to it. I told you before, Lottie, if you don't exert yourself and do something——"

"Oh," she said, rising to her feet, "what can I do? Can I put honour into you, and goodness, and make you what I want you to be? Oh, if I could, Law! I would give you my blood out of my veins if I could. But I can't put me into you," she said, wringing her hands—"and you expect me to listen to stories—about people I ought not to hear of—about women—Oh, Law, Law, how dare you speak so to me?"

"Hold hard!" said Law, "you don't know what you are speaking of. The girls are as good girls as you are—" his own cheeks flushed with indignant shame as he spoke. "You are just like what they say of women. You are always thinking of something bad. What are you after all, Lottie Despard? A poor shabby Captain's daughter! You make your own gowns and they make other people's. I don't see such a dreadful difference in that."

Lottie was overpowered by all the different sensations that succeeded each other in her. She felt herself swept by what felt like repeated waves of trouble—shame to hear of these people among whom both her father and brother found their pleasure, shame to have thought more badly of them than they deserved, shame to have betrayed to Law her knowledge that there were women existing of whom to speak was a shame. She sank down upon the sofa again trembling and agitated, relieved yet not relieved. "Law," she said faintly, "we are poor enough ourselves, I know. But even if we don't do much credit to our birth, is it not dreadful to be content with that, to go down lower, to make ourselves nothing at all?"

"It is not my fault," said Law, a little moved, "nor yours neither. I am very sorry for you, Lottie; for you've got such a high mind—it will go hardest with you. As for me, I've got no dignity to stand on, and if he drives me to it, I shall simply 'list—that's what I shall do."

"'List!" Lottie gazed at him pathetically. She was no longer angry, as she had been when he spoke of this before. "You are out of your senses, Law! You, a *gentleman*!"

"A gentleman!" he said bitterly, "much good it does me. It might, perhaps, be of some use if we were rich, if we belonged to some great family which nobody could mistake; but the kind of gentlefolks we are!—nobody knowing anything about us, except through what *he* pleases to do and say. I tell you, if the worst comes to the worst, I will go straight off to the first sergeant I see, and take the shilling. In the Guards there's many a better gentleman than I am, and I'm tall enough for the Guards," he said, looking down with a little complacence on his own long limbs. The look struck Lottie with a thrill of terror and pain. There were soldiers enough about St. Michael's to make her keenly and instantly aware how perfectly their life, as it appeared to her, would chime in with Law's habits. They seemed to Lottie to be always lounging about the streets stretching their long limbs, expanding their broad chests in the sight of all the serving maidens, visible in their red coats wherever the idle congregated, wherever there was any commotion going on. She perceived in a moment, as by a flash of lightning, that nothing could be more congenial to Law. What work might lie behind, what difficulties of subordination, tyrannies of hours and places, distasteful occupations—Lottie knew nothing about. She saw in her brother's complacent glance, a something of kin to the swagger of the tall fellows in their red jackets, spreading themselves out before admiring nursemaids. Law would do that too. She could not persuade herself that there was anything in him above the swagger, superior to the admiration of the maids. A keen sense of humiliation, and the sharp impatience of a proud spirit, unable to inspire those most near to it with anything of its own pride and energy, came into her mind. "You do not mind being a gentleman—you do not care," she cried. "Oh, I know you are not like me! But how will you like being under orders, Law, never having your freedom, never able to do what you please, or to go anywhere without leave? That is how soldiers live. They are slaves; they have to obey, always to obey. You could not do anything because you wanted to do it—you could not spend an evening at home—Oh," she cried with a sudden stamp of her foot in impatience with herself, "that is not what I mean to say; for what would you care for coming home? But you could not go to that place—that delightful place—that you and papa prefer to home. I know you don't care for home," said Lottie. "Oh, it is a compliment, a great compliment to me!"

And, being overwrought and worn out with agitation, she suddenly broke down and fell a-crying, not so much that she felt the slight and the pang of being neglected, but because all these agitations had been too much for her, and she felt for the moment that she could bear no more.

At the sight of her tears sudden remorse came over Law. He went to her side and stood over her, touching her shoulder with his hand. "Don't cry, Lottie," he said, with compunction. And then, after a moment, "It isn't for you; you're always jolly and kind. I don't mind what I say to you; you might know everything I do if you liked. But home, you know, home's not what a fellow cares for. Oh, yes! I care for it in a way—I care for you; but except you, what is there, Lottie? And I can't always be talking to you, can I? A fellow wants a little more than that. So do you; you want more than me. If I had come into the drawing-room this morning and strummed on the piano, what would you have done? Sent me off or boxed my ears if I'd have let you. But that fellow Ridsdale comes and you like it. You needn't say no; I am certain you liked it. But brother and sister, you know that's not so amusing! Come, Lottie, you know that as well as I."

"I don't know it, it is not true!" Lottie cried, with a haste and emphasis which she herself felt to be unnecessary. "But what has that to do with the matter? Allow that you do not care for your home, Law; but is it necessary to go off and separate yourself from your family, to give up your position, everything? I will tell you what we will do. We will go to Mr. Ashford, and he will let us know honestly what he thinks—what you are fit for. All examinations are not so hard; there must be something that you could do."

Law made a wry face, but he did not contradict his sister. "I wish he would cut me out with a pair of scissors and make me fit somewhere," he said, with a shrug of his shoulders. Then he added, almost caressingly, "Take your supper, Lottie; you're tired, and you want something; I have had mine. And you have not told me a word about to-night. Why did you come in so early? How are you and Ridsdale getting on? Oh! what's the good of making a fuss about it? Do you think I can't see as plain as porridge what *that* means?"

"What what means?" cried Lottie, springing from her seat with such passionate energy as half frightened the lad. "How dare you, Law? Do you think I am one of the girls you are used to? How dare you speak to me so?"

"Why should you make such a fuss about it?" cried Law, laughing, yet retreating. "If there is nothing between you and Ridsdale, what does the fellow want loafing about here? Lottie! I say, mind what you're doing. I don't mind taking your advice sometimes, but I won't be bullied by you."

"You had better go to bed, Law!" said Lottie, with dignified contempt. After all the agitations of the evening it was hard to be brought down again to the merest vulgarities of gossip like this. She paid no more attention to her brother, but gathered together her shawl, her gloves, the shabby little fan which had been her mother's, and put out the lamp, leaving him to find his way to his room as he could. She was too indignant for words. He thought her no better than the dressmaker-girls he had spoken of, to be addressed with vulgar stupid raillery such as no doubt they liked. This was the best Lottie had to look for in her own home. She swept out, throwing the train of her long white skirt from her hand with a movement which would have delighted Rollo, and went away to the darkness and stillness of her own little chamber, with scarcely an answer to the "Good-night" which Law flung at her as he shuffled away. She sat down on her little bed in the dark without lighting her candle; it was her self-imposed duty to watch there till she heard her father's entrance. And there, notwithstanding her stately withdrawal, poor Lottie, overcome, sobbed and cried. She had nobody to turn to, nor anything to console her, except the silence and pitying darkness which hid her girlish weakness even from herself.

CHAPTER XIII
CAPTAIN DESPARD

Morning service at the Abbey was more business-like than the severe ritual in the afternoon. The evening prayers were more pleasurable. Strangers came to them, new faces, all the visitors about, and there could be no doubt that the Signor chose his anthems with a view to the new people who were always coming and going. Sometimes representatives from every quarter of England, from the Continent—members of "the other church" even, which Anglicanism venerates and yearns after: and people from America, pilgrims to the shrine of the past, would gather within the Abbey, and carry away the fame of the music and the beautiful church to all the winds. The staff of the Abbey was pleasantly excited, the service was short, the whole ritual was pleasurable. It was the dull hour in the afternoon when it is good for people to be occupied in such an elevating way, and when, coming in with the fresh air hanging about you in the summer, out of the sunshine, to feel the house so shady and cool—or in winter from the chill and cold out of doors to a blazing fire, and lamps, and candles, and tea—you had just time for a little lounge before dressing for dinner, and so cheated away the heaviest hour of the day. But in the morning it was business. The Minor Canons felt it, getting up from their breakfast to sing their way steadily through litany and versicles. And nobody felt it more than the old Chevaliers as they gathered in their stalls, many of them white-headed, tottering, one foot in the grave. It was the chief occupation of their lives—all that they were now obliged to do. Their whole days were shaped for this. When the bells began the doors would open, the veterans come out, one by one, some of them battered enough, with medals on their coats. Captain Despard was the most jaunty of the brotherhood. Indeed he was about the youngest of all, and it had been thought a bad thing for the institution when a man not much over fifty was elected. He was generally the last to take his place, hurrying in fresh and debonair, with his flower in his coat, singing with the choir whenever the music pleased him, and even now and then softly accompanying the Minor Canon, with a cheerful sense that his adhesion to what was being said must always be appreciated. His responses were given with a grand air, as if he felt himself to be paying a compliment to the Divine Hearer. And indeed, though it was the great drawback of his existence to be compelled to be present there every morning of his life, still when he was there he enjoyed it. He was part of the show. The beautiful church, the fine music, and Captain Despard, had all, he thought, a share in the silent enthusiasm of the general congregation. And Captain Despard was so far right that many of the congregation, especially those who came on Sundays and holidays, the townsfolk, the tobacconists, and tradespeople, and the girls from the workroom, looked upon him with the greatest admiration, and pointed out to each other, sometimes awed and respectful, sometimes tittering behind their prayer-books, where "the Captain" sat in state. The Captain was a "fine man" everybody allowed—well proportioned, well preserved—a young man of his age; and his age was mere boyhood in comparison with many of his peers and brethren. It was ridiculous to see him there among all those old fellows, the girls said; and as for Polly, as she slipped humbly into a free seat, the sight of him sitting there in his stall quite overpowered her. If all went well, she herself would have a place there by-and-by—not in the stalls indeed, but in the humble yet dignified places provided for the families of the Chevaliers. It must not be supposed that even the Chevaliers' stalls were equal to those provided for the hierarchy of the Abbey. They were a lower range, and on a different level altogether, but still they were places of dignity. Captain Despard put his arms upon the carved supports of his official seat, and looked around him like a benevolent monarch. When anyone asked him a question as he went or came he was quite affable, and called to the verger with a condescending readiness to oblige.

"You must find a place for this gentleman, Wykeham," he would say; "this gentleman is a friend of mine." Wykeham only growled at these recommendations, but Captain Despard passed on to his stall with the air of having secured half a dozen places at least; and his *protégés* felt a vague belief in him, even when they did not find themselves much advanced by it. And there he sat, feeling that every change in his position was noted, and that he himself was an essential part of the show—that show which was so good for keeping up all the traditions of English society, making the Church respected, and enforcing attention to religion—indeed, a very handsome compliment to the Almighty himself.

Captain Despard, however, though he admired himself so much, was not, as has been already hinted, proportionately admired by his brother Chevaliers, and it was something like a surprise to him when he found himself sought by two of them at once, as they came out of the Abbey. One of these was Captain Temple, who had encountered Lottie on the evening before, going alone to the Deanery. None of all the Chevaliers of St. Michael's was so much respected as this old gentleman. He was a little man, with white hair, not remarkable in personal appearance, poor, and old; but he was all that a Chevalier ought to be, *sans reproche*. The story of his early days was the ordinary one of a poor officer without friends or interest; but in his later life there had happened to him something which everybody knew. His only daughter had married a man greatly above her in station, a member of a noble family, to the great admiration and envy of all beholders. She was a beautiful girl, very delicate and sensitive; but no one thought of her qualities in comparison with the wonderful good fortune that had befallen her. A girl that had been changed at a stroke from poor little Mary Temple, the poor Chevalier's daughter, into the Honourable Mrs. Dropmore, with a chance of a Viscountess's coronet! was ever such good luck heard of? Her father and mother were congratulated on all sides with malign exuberance. Mrs. Temple got credit for being the cleverest of mothers, that applause, which in England means insult, being largely showered upon her. Whether she deserved it, poor soul! is nothing to this history; but if so, she soon had her reward. The girl who had been so lucky was carried off summarily from the father and mother who had nothing else to care for in the world. They were not allowed to see her, or even to communicate with her but in the most limited way. They bore everything, these poor people, for their child's sake, encouraging each other not to complain, to wait until her sweetness had gained the victory, as sweetness and submission are always said to do—and encouraging *her* to think only of her husband, to wait and be patient until the prejudices of his family were dispelled. But this happy moment never came for poor Mary. She died after a year's marriage—wailing for her mother, who was not allowed to come near her, and did not even know of her illness. This had almost killed the old people too—and it had pointed many a moral all the country round; and now this incident, which had nothing to do with her, came in to influence the career of Lottie Despard. It was Captain Temple who first came up to his brother Chevalier as he strolled through the nave of St. Michael's, on his way out from the service. A great many people always lingered in the nave to get every note of the Signor's voluntary, and it was Captain Despard's practice to take a turn up and down to exhibit himself in this last act of the show before it was over. The sun shone in from the high line of south windows, throwing a thousand varieties of colour on the lofty clustered pillars, and the pavement all storied with engraved stones and brasses. The Captain sauntered up and down, throwing out his chest, and conscious of admiration round him, while the music rolled forth through the splendid space, with a voice proportioned to it, and groups of the early worshippers stood about listening, specks in the vastness of the Abbey. Just as it ended, with an echoing thunder of sweet sound, the old Captain, putting on his hat at the door, encountered the younger warrior for whom he had been lying in wait.

"May I speak a word to you, Captain Despard?" he said.

"Certainly, my dear sir; if I can be of use to you in any way, command me," said Captain Despard, with the most amiable flourish of his hat. But he was surprised; for Captain Temple was a man who "kept his distance," and had never shown any symptom of admiration for the other Chevalier.

"You will forgive me speaking," said the old man. "But I know that your evenings are often engaged. You have many occupations; you are seldom at home in the evening?"

"My friends are very kind," said Captain Despard, with another flourish. "As a matter of fact, I—dine out a great deal. I am very often engaged."

"I thought so. And your son—very often dines out too. May I ask as a favour that you will allow me to constitute myself the escort of Miss Despard when she is going anywhere in the evening? I had that pleasure last night," said the old man. "I am a very safe person, I need not say: and fond of—young people. It would be a great pleasure to me."

Captain Despard listened with some surprise. Perhaps he saw the reproach intended, but was too gaily superior to take any notice of it. When the other had ended, he took off his hat again, and made him a still more beautiful bow. "How glad I am," he said, "to be able to give you a great pleasure so easily! Certainly, Captain Temple, if my little girl's society is agreeable to you."

"She is at an age when she wants—someone to watch over her," said the old Captain. "She is very sweet—and very handsome, Captain Despard."

"Is she?" said the other, indifferently. "A child, my dear sir, nothing more than a child; but good looks belong to her mother's family—without thinking of my own side of the house."

"She is very handsome. A mother is a great loss to a girl at that age."

"You think it is a want that ought to be supplied," said Captain Despard, with a laugh, stroking his moustache. "Perhaps you are right—perhaps you are right. Such an idea, I allow, has several times crossed my own mind."

"Despard," said another voice, behind him, "I've got something to say to ye. When ye're at leisure, me dear fellow, step into my place."

"Don't let me detain you," said the other old man, hurrying away. His kind stratagem had not succeeded. He was half sorry—and yet, as he had already prophesied its failure to his wife, he was not so much displeased after all. Major O'Shaughnessy, who was a heavy personage, hobbled round to the other side.

"Despard," he said, "me dear friend! I've got something to say to you. It's about Lottie, me boy."

"About Lottie?—more communications about Lottie. I've had about enough of her, O'Shaughnessy. There is that solemn old idiot asking if he may escort her when she goes anywhere. Is he going to give his wife poison, and offer himself to me as a son-in-law?" said the Captain, with a laugh.

"I'll go bail he didn't tell you what I'm going to tell you. Listen, Despard. My pretty Lottie—she's but a child, and she's as pretty a one as you'd wish to see: well, it's a lover she's gone and got for herself. What d'ye think of that? Bless my soul, a lover! What do you make of that, me fine fellow?" cried the Major, rubbing his fat hands. He was large of bulk, like his wife, and round and shining, with a bald head, and large hands that looked bald too.

"Is this a joke?" said the Captain, drawing himself up; "by George I'll have no jokes about my child."

"Joke? it is my wife told me, that is as fond of the girl as if she were her own. 'Mark my words,' says Mrs. O'Shaughnessy, 'she'll be the Honourable Mrs. Ridsdale before we know where we are.' And Temple's been at ye, Despard; I know it. The man is off his head with his own bad luck, and can't abide the name of an Honourable. But, from all I hear, there's little to be said against this one except that he's poor."

"The Honourable——" said Captain Despard, with a bewildered look. Then, as the good Major talked, he recovered himself. "Well!" he said, when that speech came to an end, "you may think that it's very fine, O'Shaughnessy, and I'm sure I am much obliged to you for telling me, but you don't suppose an Honourable is anything out of the way to me? With her family and her beauty, I would grudge the child to a man without a title anyhow, even if he weren't poor."

The Major had his mouth open to speak, but he was so bewildered by this grandeur that he stopped and closed it again, and uttered only a murmur in his throat. "Well!" he said, when he came to himself, "you know your own affairs best; but now that your girl is taken out, and into society, and with her prospects, you'll be standing by her and giving her more of your company, Despard? Lottie's the best of girls: but it might make all the difference to her, having her father at home, and always ready to stand up for her—not meaning any offence."

"Nor is any taken, O'Shaughnessy; make your mind quite easy," said the Captain, looking extremely stately though his coat was shabby. Then he added, "I've got some business down town, and an appointment at twelve o'clock. I'm sorry to hurry off, but business goes before all. Good-morning to you, Major!" he said, kissing the ends of his fingers; then turning back after he had gone a few steps. "My respects to your wife, and thanks for finding it all out; but I've known it these three weeks at least, though I'm obliged to her all the same." And so saying, Captain Despard resumed the humming of his favourite tune, and went swinging his arm down the Dean's Walk, the rosebud in his coat showing like a decoration, and the whole man jaunty and gay as nobody else was at St. Michael's. It was a sight to see him as he marched along, keeping time to the air he was humming; a fine figure of a man! The good Major stood and looked after him dum-foundered; he was almost too much taken by surprise to be offended. "Manage your own affairs as you please, my fine fellow!" he said to himself, and went home in a state of suppressed fury. But he relented when he saw Lottie, in her print frock, at the window; and he did not give his wife that insolent message. "What is the use of making mischief?" the Major said.

Captain Despard was not, however, so entirely unmoved as he looked. The news bewildered him first, and then elated him. Where had the girl picked up the Honourable Mr.——, what was his name? He knew so little of Lottie and was so little aware of her proceedings, that he had only heard accidentally of her visits at the Deanery at all, and knew nothing whatever of Rollo. He must inquire, he said to himself; but in the meantime did not this free him from all the hesitations with which, to do him justice, he had been struggling? For if, instead of "presiding over his establishment"—which was how Captain Despard put it—Lottie was to be the mistress of a house of her own and ascend into heaven, as it were, as the Honourable Mrs. Something-or-other, there would be no doubt that Captain Despard would be left free as the day to do what pleased himself. This wonderful piece of news seemed to get into his veins and send the blood coursing more quickly there, and into his head, and made that whirl with an elation which was perfectly vague and indefinite. With Lottie as the Honourable Mrs. So-and-so, all obstacles were removed out of his own way. Law did not count; the Captain was afraid more or less of his daughter, but he was not at all afraid of his son. The Honourable Something-or-other! Captain Despard did not even know his name or anything about him, but already various privileges seemed to gleam upon him through this noble relation. No doubt such a son-in-law would be likely to lend a gentleman, who was not over-rich and connected with him by close family ties, a small sum now and then; or probably he might think it necessary for his own dignity to make an allowance to his wife's father to enable him to appear as a gentleman ought; and in the shooting season he would naturally, certainly, give so near a relation a standing invitation to the shooting-box which, by right of his rank, he must inevitably possess somewhere or other, either his own or belonging to his noble father. Probably he would have it in his power to point out to Her Majesty or Commander-in-Chief that to keep a man who was an honour to his profession, like Captain Henry Despard, in the position of a Chevalier of St. Michael's, was equally a disgrace and a danger to the country. Captain Despard seemed to hear the very tone in which this best of friends would certify to his merits. "Speak of failures in arms! What can you expect when General So-and-so is gazetted to the command of an expedition, and Henry Despard is left in a Chevalier's lodge?" he seemed to hear the unknown say indignantly. Nothing could be more generous than his behaviour; he did nothing but go about the world sounding the Captain's praises: "I have the honour to be his son-in-law," this right-thinking young man would say. Captain Despard went down the hill with his head buzzing full of this new personage who had suddenly stepped into his life. His engagement was no more important than to play a game at billiards with one of his town acquaintances, but even there he could not keep from throwing out mysterious hints about some great good fortune which was about to come to him. "What! are you going away, Captain? Are you to have promotion? or is it you they have chosen for the new warden of the Chevaliers?" his associates asked him, half in curiosity, half in sarcasm. "I am not in circumstances," said the Captain solemnly, "to say what are the improved prospects that are dawning upon my house; but of this you may rest assured—that my friends in adversity will remain my friends in prosperity." "Bravo, Captain!" cried all his friends. Some of them laughed, but some of them put their faith in Captain Despard. They said to themselves, "He's fond of talking a bit big, but he's got a good heart, has the Captain!" and they, too, dreamed of little loans and treats. And, indeed, the Captain got an immediate advantage out of it; for one of the billiard-players, who was a well-to-do tradesman with habits not altogether satisfactory to his friends, gave him a luncheon at the "Black Boar," not because he expected to profit by the supposed promotion, but to see how many lies the old humbug would tell in half-an-hour, as he himself said; for there are practical democrats to whom it is very sweet to see the pretended aristocrat cover himself with films of lying. The shopkeeper roared with laughter as the Captain gave forth his oracular sayings. "Go it, old boy!" he said. They all believed, however, more or less, in some good luck that was coming, whatever it might be; and the sensation of faith around him strengthened Captain Despard in his conviction. He resolved to go home and question Lottie after this luncheon; but that was of itself a prolonged feast, and the immediate consequence of it was a disinclination to move, and a sense that it would be just as well for him not to show himself for some little time, "till it had gone off"—for the Captain in some things was a wise man, and prudent as he was wise.

CHAPTER XIV
THE WORKROOM

There were two factions in the workroom by the side of the river where Mrs. Wilting's daughters worked, with Polly Featherston for their forewoman. One of these, though very small and consisting, indeed, only of Ellen Wilting, the eldest girl—who was "serious"—and a little apprentice who was in her class at the Sunday School—was greatly against the intrusion of "the gentlemen" into the workroom, and thought it highly improper and a thing likely to bring all the young ladies who worked there into trouble. Ellen was, contrary to the usual opinion which would have selected the plainest sister for this *rôle,* the prettiest of the girls. She was fair-haired, but not frizzy like the rest; and her face was pale, with a serious expression which made her very lady-like, many persons thought, and gave her, the others felt not without envy, a distinction which did not belong to their own pinkness and whiteness. There were four sisters, of whom Emma—who was the object of Law's admiration—was the youngest. Kate and 'Liza came between these two, and they were both of Polly's faction, though without any reason for being so. They thought Ellen was a great deal too particular. What was the harm if a gentleman came and sat a bit when they were not too busy, and talked and made them laugh? The object of life to these young women was to get as much laughing and talking as possible made consistent with the greatest amount of work done, of gowns and bonnets made; and anyone who made the long evening appear a little shorter, and "passed the time" with a little merriment, was a real benefactor to them. Ellen, for her part, took more serious views of life. She would have liked to go to morning service every day had that been practicable, and called it matins as the ladies themselves did, which was very uncommon in the River Lane; and she was a member of the Choral Society, and had a pretty voice, and had sung in a chorus along with Miss Despard, and even with Miss Huntington before she married. All this made her feel that it was not "nice" to encourage the gentlemen who were of a different condition in life, and whose visits could not be for any good. And she would much rather have heard stories read out of the *Monthly Packet,* or something in which instruction was joined with amusement, than from the *Family Herald;* except, indeed, when she got interested in the trials, continued from number to number, of some virtuous young heroine like the Lady Araminta. Ellen wore a black gown like the young ladies in the shops, with her pretty fair hair quite simply dressed, without any of the padding and frizzing which were popular at the time; and fondly hoped some time or other to wear a little black bonnet like those of the sisters who had an establishment near. Her mother sternly forbade this indulgence now, but it was one of the things to which the young woman looked forward. And it must be allowed that Ellen rather prided herself on her total unlikeness in every way to Polly Featherston, who considered herself the head of the workroom, and who was certainly the ringleader in all its follies. Kate and 'Liza and Emma and the other apprentice, though they by no means gave their entire adhesion to Polly, and had many remarks to make upon her in private, yet were generally led by her as a person who knew the world and was "much admired," and always had somebody after her. That this somebody should be for the moment "a gentleman," gave Polly an additional advantage. It must not be supposed that her reputation was anyhow in danger, though she was known to "keep company" with the Captain; for Polly, though not "particular," and ready to talk and laugh with anyone, was known to be very well able to take care of herself, and much too experienced to be taken in by any of the admirers whom she was supposed to be able to wind round her little finger. For this, and for her powers of attracting admiration, and for her fluent and ready speech, and the dauntless disposition which made her afraid of nobody and ready to "speak up," if need were, even to the very Dean himself, the girls admired her; and they would not be persuaded by Ellen that Polly ought to be subdued out of her loud and cheerful talk, and the doors of the workroom closed on the gentlemen. Little Emma, indeed, the youngest of the girls, was vehement against this idea, as was easily understood by all the rest.

"What is the harm?" she cried, with tears in her eyes, tears of vexation and irritation and alarmed perception of the change it would make if Law should be shut out; a terrible change, reducing herself, who now enjoyed some visionary superiority as "keeping company" in her own small person with a gentleman, into something even lower than 'Liza and Kate, who had their butchers and bakers, at least, to walk out with on Sunday—a privilege which Emma seldom dared enjoy with Law. "What is the use," Emma said, "of making a fuss? What harm do they do? They make the time pass. It's long enough anyhow from eight o'clock in the morning till nine at night, or sometimes later, and so little time as mother allows for meals. I am sure I am that tired," Emma declared, and with reason, "I often can't see how to thread my needle; and to have somebody to talk to passes the time."

"We have always plenty of talk even when we are by ourselves," said Ellen; "and I am sure we might make better use of our time and have much more improving conversation if these men would not be always coming here."

"Oh! if you are so fond of improvement," cried Polly, "I daresay you would like to have Mr. Sterndale the Scripture Reader come and read to us; or we might ask Mr. Langton upstairs, who is a clergyman. I shouldn't mind having *him*; he is so shy and frightened, and he wouldn't know what to say."

"Lord!" cried Kate; "fancy being frightened for us!"

"Oh!" said the better-informed Polly, "there's heaps as are frightened for us; and the gooder they are the more frightened they would be; a curate is always frightened for us girls. He knows he daren't talk free in a friendly way, and that makes him as stiff as two sticks. As sure as fate, if he was pleasant, somebody would say he had a wrong meaning, and that's how it's always in their mind."

"A clergyman," said Ellen authoritatively, "would come to do us good. But it wouldn't be his place to come here visiting. It's our duty to go to him to relieve our consciences. As for Mr. Sterndale, the Scripture Reader, I don't call him a Churchman at all; he might just as well be a Dissenter. What good can he do anybody? The thing that really does you good is to go to church. In some places there are always prayers going on, and then there is half an hour for meditation, and then you go to work again till the bell rings. And in the afternoon there is even-song and self-examination, and that passes the time," cried Ellen, clasping her hands. "What with matins, and meditation, and something new for every hour, the days go. They're gone before you know where you are."

The young women were silenced by this enthusiastic statement. For after all, what could be more desirable than a system which made the days fly? Polly was the only one who could hold up her head against such an argument. She did her best to be scornful. "I daresay!" she cried, "but I should just like to know if the work went as fast! Praying and meditating are very fine, but if the work wasn't done, what would your mother say?"

"Mother would find it answer, bless you," said Ellen, her pale face lighted with enthusiasm; "you do double the work when you can feel you're doing your duty, and could die cheerful any moment."

"Oh! and to think how few sees their duty, and how most folks turns their backs upon it!" replied the little apprentice, who was on Ellen's side.

Polly saw that something must be done to turn the tide. The girls were awed. They could not hold up their commonplace little heads against this grand ideal. There were little flings of half-alarmed impatience indeed among them, as when Kate whispered to 'Liza that "one serious one was enough in a house," and little Emma ventured a faltering assertion "that going to church made a day feel like Sunday, and it didn't seem right to do any more work." Polly boldly burst in, and threw forth her standard to the wind.

"Week days is week days," she said oracularly. "We've got them to work in and to have a bit of fun as long as we're young. Sundays I say nothing against church—as much as anyone pleases; and it's a great thing to have the Abbey to go to, where you see everybody, if Wykeham the verger wasn't such a brute. But, if I'm not to have my bit of fun, I'd rather be out of the world altogether. Now I just wish Mr. Law were passing this way, for there's the end of Lady Araminta in the *Family 'Erald*, and it is very exciting, and she won't hear of marrying the Earl, let alone the Duke, but gives all her money and everything she has to the man of her heart."

"The baronet!" cried Kate and 'Liza in one breath. "I always knew that was how it was going to be." Even Ellen, wise as she was, changed colour, and looked up eagerly.

It was Polly who took in that representative of all that the world calls letters and cultivation, to these girls. Ellen looked wistfully at the drawer in which the treasure was hidden. "I will read it out if you like," she said somewhat timidly. "I can't get on with this till the trimming is ready." Thus even the Church party was vanquished by the charms of Art.

That evening the Captain again paid them a visit. It was not often that he came two days in succession, and Emma, who was the least important of all, was very impatient of his appearance, notwithstanding the saucy speech she had made to Law. In her heart she thought there was no comparison between the father and son. The Captain was an old man. He had no business to come at all, chatting and making his jokes; it was a shame to see him turning up night after night. She wondered how Miss Despard liked to have him always out. Emma regarded Miss Despard with great interest and awe. She wondered when she met her in the street, as happened sometimes, what she would say *if she knew*. And Emma wondered, with a less warm thrill of personal feeling, but yet with much heat and sympathetic indignation, what Miss Despard would think if she knew of Polly. She would hate her, and that would be quite natural. Fancy having Polly brought in over your head in the shape of a stepmother! and if Emma herself felt indignant at such an idea, what must Miss Despard do who was a lady, and used to be the mistress? It made the girl's heart ache to think that she would have to close the door upon Law again, for it would never do to have the father and son together. Polly, on the contrary, bore a look of triumph on her countenance. She pushed her chair aside a little as Emma had done for Law, thus making room for him beside her, and she said, with a delighted yet nervous toss of her mountain of hair, "Ah, Captain, back again! Haven't you got anything better to do than to come after a lot of girls that don't want you? Do we want him, Kate?" to which playful question Kate replied in good faith, No, she did not want him; but, with a friendly sense of what was expected of her, giggled and added that the Captain didn't mind much what *she* thought. The Captain, nothing daunted, drew in a stool close to Polly, and whispered that, by George, the girl was right; it didn't matter much to him what *she* thought; that it was someone else he would consult on that subject; upon which Polly tossed her head higher than ever, and laughed and desired him to Get along! The Captain's coming was not nearly so good for the work as Law's, who was not half so funny, and whom they all received in a brotherly sort of indifferent, good-humoured way. The Captain, on the contrary, fixed their attention as at a play. It was as good as a play to watch him whispering to Polly, and she arching her neck, and tossing her head, and bidding him Get along! Sometimes, indeed, he kept them all laughing with his jokes and his mimicries, himself enjoying the enthusiasm of his audience. But though on these occasions he was very entertaining, the girls perhaps were still more entertained when he sat and whispered to Polly, giving them the gratification of an actual romance, such as it was, enacted before their eyes. A gentleman, an officer, with such a command of fine language, and such an air! They gave each other significant glances and little nudges to call each other's attention, and wondered what Miss Despard would think, and what would happen if really, really, some fine day Polly Featherston were made into a lady, a Chevalier's wife, and Mr. Law's stepmother—what *would* everybody say? and Miss Despard, would she put up with it? Even the idea of so exciting an event made the blood move more quickly in their veins.

The Captain was not in his jocular mood to-night. He was magnificent, a thing which occurred now and then. In this state of mind he was in the habit of telling them splendid incidents of his early days—the things he said to the Duke of Blank, and what the Duke of Blank replied to him, and the money he gave for his horses, and how he thought nothing of presenting any young lady he might be paying attention to (for he was a sad flirt in those days, the Captain allowed) with a diamond spray worth a thousand pounds, or a sapphire ring equally valuable, or some pretty trifle of that description. But he was altogether serious to-night. "I intended to have come earlier," he said, "for I have family business that calls me home soon; but I was detained. It is very tiresome to be continually called upon for advice and help as I am, especially when in one's own affairs something important has occurred."

"La, Captain, what has happened?" said Polly. "You ought to tell us. We just want something to wake us up. You've had some money left you; or I shouldn't wonder a bit if the Commander-in-Chief— —"

Here she stopped short with sudden excitement, and looked at him. Captain Despard was fond of intimating to his humbler friends that he knew the Commander-in-Chief would send for him some day, indignant with those whose machinations had made him shelve so valuable an officer for so long. It seemed possible to Polly that this moment had arrived, and the idea made her black eyes blaze. She seemed to see him at the head of an expedition, leading an army, and herself the general's lady. It did not occur to Polly that there was no war going on at the moment; that was a matter of detail; and how should she know anything about war or peace, a young woman whose knowledge of public manners was limited to murders and police cases? She let her work fall upon her knee, and there even ran through her mind a rapid calculation, if he was starting off directly, how long it would take to get the wedding things ready, or if she could trust the Wiltings to have them packed and sent after her in case there should not be time enough to wait.

"No," the Captain said, with that curl of his lip which expressed his contempt of the authorities who had so foolishly passed him over. "It is nothing about the Commander-in-Chief—at least not yet. There will soon be a means of explaining matters to his Royal Highness which may lead to——. But we will say nothing on that point for the moment," he added grandly, with a wave of his hand. Then he leaned over Polly, and whispered something which the others tried vainly to hear.

"Oh!" cried Polly, listening intently. At first her interest failed a little; then she evidently rose to the occasion, put on a fictitious excitement, clasped her hands, and cried, "Oh, Captain, *that* at last!"

"Yes—that is what has happened. You may not see all its importance at the first glance. But it is very important," said the Captain with solemnity. "In a domestic point of view—and otherwise. People tell you interest does not matter now-a-days. Ha! ha!" (Captain Despard laughed the kind of stage-laugh which may be represented by these monosyllables.) "Trust one who has been behind the scenes. Interest is everything—always has been, and always will be. This will probably have the effect of setting me right at the Horse Guards, which is all that is necessary. And in the meantime," he added, with a thoughtful air, "it will make a great difference in a domestic point of view; it will change my position in many ways, indeed in every way."

Polly had been gazing at him during this speech, watching every movement of his face, and as she watched her own countenance altered. She did not even pretend to take up her work again, but leaned forward nervously fingering the thread and the scissors on the table, and beginning to realise the importance of the crisis. To Captain Despard it was a delightful opportunity of displaying his importance, and there was just enough of misty possibility in the castle of cards he was building up to endow him with a majestic consciousness of something about to happen. But to Polly it was a great deal more than this. It was the crisis of something that was at least melodrama, if not tragedy, in her life. All her hopes were suddenly quickened into almost reality, and the change in her fortunes, which had been a distant and doubtful if exciting chance, seemed suddenly in a moment to become real and near.

The spectacle that this afforded to the other young women in the workroom it is almost beyond the power of words to describe. Their bosoms throbbed. A play! plays were nothing to it. They pulled each other's gowns under the table. They gave each other little nods, and looks under their eyebrows. Their elbows met in emphatic commentary. He, absorbed in his own all-important thoughts, she looking up at him with that rapt and pale suspense—never was anything more exciting to the imagination of the beholders. "He won't look at her," one whispered; "she's all of a tremble," said another; and "Lord, what *are* they making such a fuss about?" breathed Kate.

"Yes, it will alter our position in every way," the Captain said, stroking his moustache, and fixing his eyes on vacancy. Then Polly touched his arm softly, her cheek, which had been pale, glowing crimson. *Our* position! the word gave her inspiration. She touched him shyly at first to call his attention; then, with some vehemence, "Captain! that will make— —a deal easier," she said; but what words were between these broken bits of the sentence, or if any words came between, the excited listeners could not make out.

"Yes," he said with dignity. But he did not look at her. He maintained his abstracted look, which was so very impressive. They all hung upon, not only his lips, but every movement. As for Polly, the suspense was more than she could bear. She was not a patient young woman, nor had she been trained to deny herself like Ellen, or control her feelings as women in a different sphere are obliged to do. She resumed her work for a moment with hurried hands, trying to control her anxiety; then suddenly threw it in a heap on the table, without even taking the trouble to fold it tidily. She did not seem to know what she was doing, they all thought.

"I am going home," she said, with a hoarseness in her voice. "There is nothing very pressing, so it won't matter. I've got such a headache I don't know what to do with myself."

"Oh, Polly, a headache! that's not like you—yes, there's Mrs. Arrowsmith's dress that was promised."

"I don't care—and she's not a regular customer. And it's only a bit of an alpaca with no trimmings—you can finish it yourselves. Captain, if you're coming my way, you can come—if you like; unless," said Polly, with feverish bravado, "you've got something to say to the girls more than you seem to have to me—I'm going home."

The Captain woke up from his abstraction, and looked round him, elevating his eyebrows. "Bless my heart, what is the matter?" he said. And then he made a grimace, which tempted the girls to laugh notwithstanding Polly's tragic seriousness. "I had hoped to have contributed a little to the entertainment of the evening, my dear young ladies. I had hoped to have helped you to 'pass the time,' as you say. But when a lady bids me go— —"

"Oh, you needn't unless you like," cried Polly; "don't mind me! I don't want nobody to go home with me. I can take care of myself—only leave me alone if you please. I won't be made fun of, or taken off. Let me out into the fresh air, or I think I shall faint." The Captain took an unfair advantage of the excited creature. He turned round upon them all when Polly rushed out to get her jacket and hat, which hung in the hall, and "took her off" on the spot, making himself so like her, that it was all they could do to keep from betraying him by their laughter. When she had put on her "things," she put her head into the room she had just left. "Good-night, I'm going," she said, with a look of impassioned anxiety and trouble. She was too much absorbed in her own feelings to see through the mist in which their faces shone to her, the laughter that was in them. She only saw the Captain standing up in the midst of them. Was he coming after her? or was he going to fall off from her at this crisis of his affairs? Perhaps it was foolish of her to rush off like this, and leave him with all these girls about him. But Polly had never been used to restrain her feelings, and she could not help it she vowed to herself. Everything in the future seemed to depend upon whether he came after her or not. Oh, why could not she have had a little more patience! oh, why should not he come with her, say something to her after all that had passed! As great a conflict was in her mind as if she had been a heroine of romance. The Captain and she had been "keeping company" for a long time. He had "kept off" others that would not have shilly-shallyed as he had done. A man's "intentions" are rarely inquired into in Polly's sphere. But if he cared for her the least bit, if he had any honour in him, she felt that he would follow her now. Polly knew that she might have been Mrs. Despard long ago if she had consented to be married privately as the Captain wished. But she was for none of those clandestine proceedings. She would be married in her parish church, with white favours and a couple of flys, and something that might be supposed to be a wedding breakfast. She had held by her notions of decorum stoutly, and would hear of no hole-and-corner proceedings. And now when fortune was smiling upon them, when his daughter had got hold of someone (this was Polly's elegant way of putting it), and when the way would be clear, what if he failed her? The workroom with its blaze of light and its curious spectators had been intolerable to her, but a cold shudder crossed her when she got out of doors into the darkness of the lane. Perhaps she ought to have stayed at any cost, not to have left him in the midst of so many temptations. Her heart seemed to sink into her shoes. Oh, why had she been so silly! Her hopes seemed all dropping, disappearing from her. To sink into simple Polly Featherston, with no dazzling prospect of future elevation, would be death to her, she felt, now.

Polly was half way up the lane before the Captain, coming along at his leisure, made up to her; and, what with passion and fright, she had scarcely any voice left. "Oh, you have come after all!" was all she could manage to say. And she hurried on, so rapidly that he protested. "If you want to talk, how can we talk if we race like this?" he said. "Who wants to talk?" cried Polly breathless; but nevertheless she paused in her headlong career. They went up the hill together, on the steep side next the Abbey, where there never was anybody, and there the Captain discoursed to Polly about his new hopes. She would have liked it better had he decided how the old ones were to be realised. But still, as he was confidential and opened everything to her as to his natural confidant, her excitement gradually subsided, and her trust in him returned. She listened patiently while he recounted to her all the results that would be sure to follow, when an influential son-in-law, a member of a noble family, brought him to the recollection of the Commander-in-Chief.

"They think I'm shelved and superannuated," he said; "but let me but have an opening—all I want is an opening; and then you can go and select the handsomest phaeton and the prettiest pair of ponies, my lady—"

Polly laughed and reddened with pleasure at this address, but she said prudently, "A bird in the hand is worth two in the bush. I wouldn't give up being a Chevalier. It's a nice little house and a nice little income too."

"Pooh! a nothing," cried the Captain. This was very fine and gave a sense of superiority and exaltation. Polly could not but allow a vision to float before her eyes of the phaeton and the ponies, nay more, of the march of a regiment with the flags and the music. She even seemed to see the sentry at her own door, and all the men presenting arms as she passed (what less could they do to the wife of their commander?). But, on the other hand, to live here at Michael's where she was born, and be seen in her high estate by all the people who had known her as a poor dressmaker, that was a happiness which she did not like to give up, even for the glories of a high command far away.

CHAPTER XV
ROMANCE AND REALITY

Lottie was entirely unconscious of the intimation that had been made to her father, and of the excitement which had risen among her neighbours about Mr. Ridsdale. It did not occur to her that anyone but herself knew anything about him. The delighted curiosity of the O'Shaughnessys and the anxious concern of Captain Temple were equally unknown to her. Her mind was still moved by an echo of the sentiment of their last meeting—a thrill of emotion half from the music, half from the awakening feelings, the curiosity, the commotion of her developing nature. Of all Law's communications which had excited himself so powerfully, and which had also to some extent excited her, she remembered little in comparison. The large dim room at the Deanery, the faint night air breathing about, blowing the flames of the candles, the moths that circled about the lights and did themselves to death against every flame, seemed to glimmer before her eyes continually—everything else, even the danger of her father's marriage, the danger of Law's imprudence, fell into the background and became distant; everything receded before the perpetual attraction of this shadowy scene.

Mr. Ridsdale made a second call upon her in the morning after service, just at the moment when Captain Temple and Major O'Shaughnessy were talking to her father. This time he brought no note, and had no excuse ready to explain his visit. "I came to say good-by," he said, holding out his hand and looking rather wistfully into her face. Lottie offered him her hand demurely. She scarcely met his eyes. Her heart began to beat as soon as she heard his voice asking for her at the door. It brought back all the terrors of the previous night. She did not however ask him to sit down, but stood faltering opposite to him, embarrassed, not knowing what to do.

"You would not accept my escort last night," he said; "I was dreadfully disappointed when I came out and found you gone. I had been waiting, not wishing to hurry you. I hope you did not think I was a laggard?"

"Oh no, it was my fault," said Lottie, not raising her eyes. "There was no need for anyone to come with me. It is but two steps, and at that hour there is no one about. There was no need—for any escort."

"May I sit down for a few minutes, Miss Despard? My train is not till one o'clock."

Lottie blushed crimson at this implied reproach. It might be right to be shy of him, but not to be rude to him. "Oh, I beg your pardon," she said, pointing to a chair.

"You took us all by surprise last night," he said, carefully placing hers for her. "I think it was a revelation to everybody. We hear that music in the Abbey, and we suppose we understand it; till someone like you suddenly interprets it to us, and we wake up and feel that we never heard it before."

"I never knew what it was—to sing anything like that before," said Lottie. It disturbed her even to think about it; "and it had all been so different—so——"

"Commonplace? from the ridiculous to the sublime; from poor dear Aunt Caroline on her sofa to Handel fluting among the angels. It *was* a step indeed."

"I did not mean that. It was myself I was thinking of—I had been so full of silly fancies of my own."

"But all at once the inspiration came? I should like to be capable of anything like that; but I am not. I can only listen, and worship," said Rollo. There was fervour in his voice—a real something which was not mere fanaticism about music. And the two young people sat for a few moments in silence, a most dangerous thing to do, looking at each other—nay, not looking at each other—for Lottie did not feel either able or disposed to raise her eyes. She was the first to speak, in order to break the silence, which alarmed her, though she did not know why.

"It is wonderful how the Signor plays. I never understood it in the Abbey. He seems to place you up somewhere above yourself—and make your voice come independent of you."

"Never in his life, I am sure, did he have such a beautiful compliment paid to him," said Rollo; "but, Miss Despard, you do him too much credit. You permitted even me to accompany you—and sang just as divinely——"

"Oh no," said Lottie. Then she blushed and recollected herself. "You play very well, Mr. Ridsdale; but we could not compare those trumpery songs with——"

"Trumpery songs! only Mozart and Bellini, and a few more," he cried, with a gasp. "Ah, I know what you mean; you meant the 'Marta' song, which made your good friend, that good woman, cry——"

"I like the 'Last Rose of Summer' very much. I have always liked it. I used to hear an old fiddler play it in the street when I was a child, when I was lying in the dark, trying to go to sleep. It was like a friend keeping me company; but a friend that had a breaking heart, that cried and took all my thoughts off myself—I shall never forget it," said Lottie, the tears coming to her eyes at the recollection. "I like it better than all the rest."

"Miss Despard, do not drive me to despair. Not better than 'Casta Diva,' or Margaret's song, or— —"

"You forget I don't know where they come, nor the meaning of them," said Lottie, calmly. "I never heard an opera. I think these things are beautiful, but they only sing to my ear, they don't come in to *me*."

Rollo shook his head. He was half touched, half shocked. It was her ignorance; but then a woman destined for a prima donna, a woman with musical genius, *ought* to know the best by intuition, he thought. All the same, he was more interested than if she had raved as the commonplace, half educated amateur raves. "But Handel does," he said.

"Ah!" Lottie cried, her face lighting up. But she added, after a moment, "I am too ignorant to be worth talking to; you will be disgusted. I never thought much about Handel. It was not Handel, it was *that*." A flush of colour came over her face with the recollection. She was too uninstructed (notwithstanding the neighbourhood of the Abbey) to have fully woke up to Handel or anyone. "I suppose I have heard it and did not pay much attention to it," she said; "it was singing it. One does not understand at first—till suddenly one hears one's self, and you say, 'What is this that is speaking; what is this? it cannot be *me*!'"

"I think I understand—a little," said Rollo doubtfully; "though it is simply *you* that makes a something quite familiar, a piece of music we have all heard a hundred times, become a new revelation to us all in a moment. I am going away, Miss Despard, and it may be some time before I return. Would you do me such a great favour—which I have no right to ask—as to sing me something now before I go?"

But Lottie would not sing. She said, "Oh no, no," with a half terror which he did not understand, and which she did not understand herself. The tone was one which forbade the repetition of the request. He begged her pardon anxiously, and there was a little languid conversation about other subjects, and then he rose. He put out his hand again, looking into her eyes, which she raised shyly, almost for the first time. Rollo had a way of looking into the eyes of women to whom he wished to make himself agreeable. It is sometimes very impertinent, and always daring, but, especially when the woman's imagination is on the side of the gazer, it is very efficacious. Lottie was entirely inexperienced, and she trembled under this look, but felt it penetrate to her very heart.

"Till we meet again," he said, with a smile, holding her hand for that necessary moment while he said his good-by. "It will not be very long; and I hope that you will be kind to me, Miss Despard, and let me hear you— —"

"Good-by," said Lottie. She could not bear it any longer. She blamed herself afterwards for being rude, as she sat down and went over the incident again and again. She seemed to herself to have dismissed him quite rudely, pulling her hand away, cutting short what he was saying. But Rollo, for his part, did not feel that it was rude. He went down the narrow stairs with his heart beating a little quicker than usual, and a sense that here was something quite fresh and novel, something not like the little flirtations with which he was so familiar, and which amused him a great deal in general. This he had just touched, floated over with his usual easy sentiment, was something quite out of the common. It startled him with the throb in it. He went away quite thoughtful, his heart in a most unusual commotion, and forgot until he was miles away from St. Michael's that Lottie Despard was to be the English prima donna, who was to make his fortune, if properly managed. "Ah, to be sure, that was it!" he said to himself suddenly in the railway carriage, as he was going to town. He really had forgotten what it was that took him to town at this unsuitable moment of the year.

The rest of the morning glided dreamily away after an incident like this; and it was not till late in the afternoon that Lottie suddenly awoke to the necessity of making an effort, and shaking off the empire of dreams: and this was how she became convinced of the necessity for doing so. She had been sitting, as on the former occasion, with a basket of mending by her when Rollo came in. She had all the clothes of the household to keep in order, and naturally they were not done in one day. After Mr. Ridsdale was gone, she took up her work languidly, keeping it on her knee while she went over all that had happened, again and again, as has been recorded. When, at last startled by a sound outside, she began to work in earnest, then and there a revelation of a character totally distinct from that made by Handel burst upon her. It was not a revelation of the same kind, but it was very startling. Lottie found—*that she had not yet finished the hole in the sock which she had begun to mend before Mr. Ridsdale's first visit*! She was still in the middle of that one hole. She remembered exactly where she stuck her needle, in the middle of a woolly hillock, as she heard him coming upstairs; and there it was still, in precisely the same place. This discovery made her heart jump almost as much as Mr. Ridsdale's visit had done. What an evidence of wicked idling, of the most foolish dreaming and unprofitable thought was in it! Lottie blushed, though she was alone, to the roots of her hair, and seizing the sock with an impassioned glow of energy, never took breath till the stern evidence of that hole was done away with. And then she could not give herself any rest. She felt her dreams floating about her with folded pinions, ready to descend upon her and envelope her in their shadow if she gave them the chance; but she was determined that she would not give them the chance. As soon as she had finished the pair of socks, and folded them carefully up, she went to look for Law to suggest that they should go immediately to Mr. Ashford. Law had only just come in from a furtive expedition out of doors, and had scarcely time to spread his books open before him when she entered his room. But he would not go to Mr. Ashford. It was time enough for that, and he meant in the meantime to "work up" by himself, he declared. Lottie became more energetic than ever in the revulsion of feeling, and determination not to yield further to any vanity. She pleaded with him, stormed at him, but in vain. "At the worst I can always 'list," he said, half in dogged resistance to her, half in boyish mischief to vex her. But he would not yield to her desire to consult Mr. Ashford, though he had assented at first. He did not refuse to go "some time," but nothing that she could say would induce him to go now. This brought in again all the contradictions and cares of her life to make her heart sore when she turned back out of the enchanted land in which for a little while she had been delivered from these cares. They all came back upon her open-mouthed, like wild beasts, she thought. Law resisting everything that was good for him, and her father——. But Lottie could not realise the change that threatened to come upon her through her father. It seemed like the suggestion of a dream. Law must be deceived, it must be all a delusion, it was not possible, it was not credible. The Captain came in early that night, and he came upstairs into the little drawing-room, to which he had no habit of coming. He told his daughter in a stately way that he heard her singing had given great satisfaction at the Deanery. "More than one person has mentioned it to me," he said; "that is of course a satisfaction. And—who is the gentleman you have been having here so much?"

"There has been no one here very much," said Lottie; then she blushed in spite of herself, though she did not suppose that was what he alluded to. "You do not mean Mr. Ridsdale?" she said.

"How many visitors have you got?" he said, in high good humour. "Perhaps it is Mr. Ridsdale—Lady Caroline's nephew? Ah, I like the family. It was he you sang to? Well, no harm; you've got a very pretty voice—and so had your mother before you," the Captain added, with a carefully prepared sigh.

"It was only once," said Lottie, confused. "Mrs. O'Shaughnessy was here; it was after we had been singing at the Deanery; it was——"

"My child," said the Captain, "I am not finding fault. No harm in putting your best foot foremost. I wish you'd do it a little more. At your age you ought to be thinking about getting married. And, to tell the truth, it would be a great convenience to me, and suit my plans beautifully, if you would get married. You mustn't stand shilly-shallying; let him come to the point: or, if he won't, my dear, refer him to me."

"I don't know what you mean," cried Lottie. Fortunately for her, he had thought her a child up to the time of their migration to St. Michael's, and she had been subjected to very little advice of this description. But, though she gazed at him with wondering eyes, she knew very well by the instinct of horror and repulsion in her mind what he meant. It gave her a shock of pain and shame which ran like electricity to her very finger points. "I think you must be making a mistake," she said. "I scarcely know Mr. Ridsdale at all. He has called here twice—on business—for Lady Caroline—and now he has gone away."

"Gone away!" the Captain said, his face lengthening with disappointment and dismay; "gone away! then you're a fool—a greater fool than I thought you. What's to become of you, do you ever ask yourself? Good lord, what a chance to throw away! One of the Courtland family—a fellow with a turn for music—that you could have turned round your little finger! And to let him go away! By George," said the Captain, making a stride towards her, and clenching his fist in the energy of his disapproval, "I don't believe you're any child of mine. Clever—you think you're clever? and so did your mother, poor woman! but you're an idiot, that is what you are—an idiot! to let such a chance slip through your fingers. Good lord! to think such a fool should be a child of mine!"

Lottie stood her ground firmly. She was not afraid of the clenched fist, nor even of the angry voice and eyes, which were more genuine. If there was a slight tremor in her, it was of her own excited nerves. She made no reply; if she had spoken, what could she have done but express her own passionate loathing for his advice, and for his disapproval, and perhaps even for himself? for she had not been brought up to reverence the faulty father, whose evil qualities her mother had discussed in Lottie's presence as long as she could remember. There had not been any illusion in his children's eyes after their babyhood, in respect to Captain Despard, and perhaps in the present emergency this was well. She stood and met his fury, pale, but more disdainful than desperate. It was no more than she would have expected of him had she ever thought of the emergency at all.

Law had heard the sound of the battle from afar; he heard his father's voice raised, and the sound of the stroke upon the table with which he had emphasised one of his sentences. It was a god-send to the unenthusiastic student to be disturbed by anything, and he came in sauntering with his hands in his pockets, partly with the intention of taking Lottie's part, partly for the sake of "the fun," whatever it might be. "What's the row?" he asked. He had slippers on, and shuffled along heavily, and his coat was very old and smelt of tobacco, though that was a luxury in which Law could indulge but sparingly. He had his hands in his pockets, and his hair was well rubbed in all directions by the efforts he had made over his unbeloved books. Thus it was but a slovenly angel that came to Lottie's aid. He stopped the yawn which his "reading" had brought on, and looked at the belligerents with some hope of amusement. "I say, don't bully Lottie," he exclaimed, but not with any fervour. He would not have allowed anyone to lay a finger upon her, but a little bullying, such as she administered to him daily, that perhaps would do Lottie no harm. However, he was there in her defence if things should come to any extremity. She was of his faction, and he of hers; but yet he thought a little bullying of the kind she gave so liberally might do Lottie no harm.

"Go away, Law; it is no matter; it is nothing. Papa was only communicating some of his ideas—forcibly," said Lottie, with a smile of defiance; but as there was always a fear in her mind lest these two should get into collision, she added hastily, "Law, I don't want you—go away."

"He can stay," said the Captain. "I have something to say to you both. Look here. I thought in the first place that she had hit off something for herself," he said, turning half round to his son. "I thought she had caught that fellow, that Ridsdale; from what I had heard, I thought that was certain—that there would be no difficulty on that side."

The Captain had left his original ground. Instead of reproaching Lottie, in which he was strong, he was in the act of disclosing his own intentions, and this was much less certain ground. He looked at Law, and he wavered. Big lout! he knew a great deal too much already. Captain Despard looked at Law as at a possible rival, a being who had been thrust into his way. The workroom had no secrets from Law.

"I think the governor's right there," said Law confidentially; "he's a big fish, but he's all right if you give him time."

A gleam of sudden fury blazed over Lottie's face. She, too, clenched her hands passionately. She stamped her foot upon the floor. "How dare you?" she said, "how dare you insult me in my own home, you two men? Oh, yes, I know who you are—my father and my brother, my father and my brother! the two who ought to protect a girl and take care of her! Oh! is it not enough to make one hate, and loathe and despise—!" said Lottie, dashing her white clenched hand into the air. Tears that seemed to burn her came rushing from her eyes. She looked at them with wild indignation and rage, in which there was still a certain appeal. How could they, how could they shame a girl so? They looked at her for a moment in this rage, which was so impotent and so pitiful, and then they gave a simultaneous laugh. When an exhibition of passionate feeling does not overawe, it amuses. It is so ludicrous to see a creature crying out, weeping, suffering for some trifle which would not in the least affect ourselves. Lottie was struck dumb by this laugh. She gave a startled look up at them through those hot seas of salt scalding tears that were in her eyes.

"What a fool you are making of yourself!" said the Captain. "Women are the greatest fools there are on this earth, always with some high-flown rubbish or other in their stupid heads. Your own home! and who made it your home, I should like to know? I don't say you hadn't a right to shelter when you were a little thing; but that's long out of the question. A girl of twenty ought to be thinking about getting herself a real home of her own. How are you going to do it? that's the question. You are not going to stay here to be a burden upon me all your life; and what do you mean to do?"

"I will go to-morrow!" cried Lottie, wildly; "I would go to-night if it were not dark. I will go—and free you of the burden!" Here she stopped; all the angry colour went out of her face. She looked at them with great wide eyes, appalled; and clasped her hands together with a lamentable cry. "Oh! but I never thought of it before, I never thought of it!" she cried; "where am I to go?"

Law's heart smote him; he drew a step nearer to her. To agree with his father (however much in his heart he agreed with his father) was abandoning his sister—and his own side. "He doesn't mean it," he said soothingly in an undertone; "he only wants to bully you, Lottie. Never mind him, we'll talk it over after," and he put his big hand upon her shoulder to console her. Lottie turned upon him, half furious, half appealing. She could not see him till two big tears fell out of her eyes, and cleared her sight a little. She clutched at the hand upon her shoulder in her distraction and despair.

"Come with me, Law. Two of us together, we can go anywhere; two can go anywhere. Oh! how can you tell me never to mind? Do you hear me?" she cried, seizing his arm with both her hands, half shaking him, half clinging to him; "say you will come with me, Law!"

"Stop this stuff!" said the Captain. "I am not telling you to go; I am telling you what is your plain duty, the only thing a woman is fit for. Besides, this young fellow would be of great use to me; it's your duty to get hold of him for the good of the family. He might say a good word for me at the Horse Guards; he might get Law something. I never expected you would have such a chance. Do you think I want you to go away just when there's a chance that you might be of some use? Am I a fool, do you think? You'll stay where you are, Lottie Despard! you'll not go disgracing your family, governessing, or anything of that sort."

"Ah!" said Law suddenly, "she'll wish she had listened to the Signor now."

"To the Signor? what of the Signor? is he after her too?" cried the Captain eagerly. A bird in the hand is worth two in the bush; and though the Signor had no interest with the Horse Guards, he had money, and might be of use in many ways. Captain Despard's eyes lighted up. "Whew!" he whistled. "Lottie! so, my child, you've got two strings to your bow?"

Lottie turned upon her brother, whose arm she had been holding with both her hands. She pushed him, flung him from her with an energy of which she had not appeared capable, and throwing her head high, looked her father in the face and walked out of the room. Law, confounded by the force with which she threw him from her, caught at her angrily as she passed; but she pulled her dress from his hand, and walked past him with a contempt that stung him—callous as he was. As for the Captain, he made no effort to detain her, partly because of his surprise, partly that he was anxious to have more information about (as he supposed) this second suitor. She went straight to her own room, while they stood listening till she had shut the door upon herself and her passion. Then the Captain ventured to laugh again, but low, not to be heard; for the look of any creature driven to bay is alarming, and Lottie's sudden withdrawal was a relief.

"Whoever gets her will catch a Tartar! eh, Law?" he said. "But now that she's gone, let's hear all about the Signor."

There was no light in Lottie's room; nothing but the faint starlight outside, and as much of the familiar glimmer of the few feeble lamps in the Dean's Walk as could get in through her small window. How is it that so small a bit of space, such four straight walls, should hold in such a throbbing, palpitating, agitated being, with projects wide enough and fury hot enough to burst them like a child's toy? It was in her to have torn her hair or anything that came in the way of her fevered hands; to have filled the air with cries; to have filled the whole world with her protest against the intolerable shame and wretchedness which they were trying to force upon her thoughts! But she only threw herself on her bed in the dark and silence, letting no sound or movement betray her. She was not prostrated as by unkindness, or stung by reproach; but wounded, shamed, desecrated—the very sanctity of her dreams turned into a horror to her. And Law gone against her—Law gone over to the other side!

CHAPTER XVI
THE SIGNOR'S HOUSEHOLD

The Despard family became a great centre of interest to many people both within and without the Abbey precincts at this period of their history. Without any doing, so to speak, of theirs, Fate mixed them up both with the great and the small, so that their proceedings moved a great many circles of thought and feeling beyond that in which they themselves stood. We have said without any doing of theirs—but this, perhaps, is true only in respect to Lottie, who took no steps consciously to produce the *rapprochement* which had taken place so strangely between the heaven of the Deanery and the earth of the Lodges. She had not done anything to recommend herself to Lady Caroline or Lady Caroline's nephew. And yet with both she had become an important "factor," to use a fashionable term, in the immediate concerns of life. The Captain was not so innocent of purpose in the commotion he had begun to make. But still he had not calculated upon the interest that would be excited by his proceedings. The community at St. Michael's was quiet and had little to rouse its interest. Sometimes a Canon would be translated to a higher and a better stall—sometimes an old Chevalier would die and be replaced by another veteran not much less old than he—sometimes a son would "go wrong" and create a great deal of whispered communication and shaking of heads. At the present time there were no daughters to marry except Lottie, so that the pleasanter strain of possibility was little thought of. All this made it very inspiring, very agitating to the dwellers round the Abbey, when a family within the precincts gave them so much to think about. A girl likely to make a very good match in a romantic way: a man likely to make a very bad one, in a way which might have been quite as romantic had it not been on the wrong side, such as would debase, not exalt his class; these two probabilities coming together had a great effect upon the popular mind. In the Chevaliers' Lodges there was very little else talked about. Captain Temple, the most respected of all the Chevaliers, could not keep still, so excited was he. He had spoken to "the father," he told his wife, to put him on his guard, and to show him how necessary it was to take proper care of his child. That was all he could do: but he could not content himself with thus doing what he could. He paced about his little sitting-room, disturbing Mrs. Temple at her wool-work. She was not like her husband. She was a still, composed, almost stern woman, with a passionate heart, to which she gave very little expression. She could not talk of her daughter as Captain Temple could. The remembrance of the years during which her child was separated from her was terrible to her. When her husband talked as he was accustomed to do of this great grief of theirs, she never stopped him, but she herself was dumb. She closed all her windows, as it were, and retired into a fortress of silent anguish, out of which no cry came; but she listened to him all the same. This was what she did now, though it pained her to hear of this other girl who stood between life and death, between good and evil, as once her child had stood. She would have helped Lottie with all her heart, but she could not bear to hear her talked of—though this was precisely what she had to bear.

"I told him it was his duty to look after his daughter," said Captain Temple, pacing—three steps one way, four the other—about the room. "But he won't—you will see he won't. A beautiful girl, far too good for him, a girl who deserves a better fate. She puts me in mind of our own dear girl, Lucy. I have told you so before."

To this Mrs. Temple made no reply. He had told her so a great many times before. She selected a new shade of her Berlin wool, and set her elbow rigidly against the arm of her chair, that she might thread her needle without trembling, but she made no reply.

"She puts me constantly in mind of her. The way she holds her head, and her walk, and—— I beg your pardon, my dear. I know you don't like this kind of talk; but if you knew how I seem to see her wherever I go—wherever I go! I wonder if she is permitted to come and walk by her old father's side, God bless her. Ah! well, it was Despard's daughter we were talking of. To think *he* should have this girl who takes no care of her—and we to whom ours was everything!"

The poor woman made a spasmodic movement, and turned her eyes upon him dumbly. She could not bear it. The needle fell out of her hands, and she stooped to hunt for it on the carpet. She would not stop him to whom it was so great a relief to talk; but it was death to her.

"But I told him," said Captain Temple. "I showed him his duty, Lucy. I told him he ought to be thankful he had such a daughter to watch over. And what more could I do? I set the whole thing before him. There was nothing more that I could do?"

"Then you must be satisfied, William, and perhaps it will have some effect; we must wait and see," said Mrs. Temple, coming to the surface again with her needle, which she had found, in her hand. She managed to get it threaded this time with great exertion, while her husband set off again upon his restricted promenade, shaking his white head. Captain Temple, it may be recollected, had not said so much to Captain Despard as he thought he had said—but if he had said everything that man could say it is not probable that it would have made much difference. The kind old Chevalier shook his white head. His eyes were full of moisture and his heart of tenderness. He did not feel willing to wait and see, as his wife suggested. He wanted to do something there and then for Lottie, to go to her and warn her, to keep watch at her door, and prevent the entrance of the wolf—anything, he did not mind what it was so long as he could secure her safety.

The other subject was discussed that same evening in another and very different scene, when Mrs. Purcell, the Signor's housekeeper, asked her old fellow-servant, Pickering, what news there was in the precincts, and if anything was stirring. It was the most delicious moment for a gossip, when tea was over in the kitchen, and dinner upstairs, and twilight was beginning to drop over the country, bringing quiet and coolness after the blaze of the day. Mrs. Purcell sat by the open window, which was cut in the very boundary wall of the Abbey precincts, as in the side of a precipice. It was not safe for anyone of uncertain nerves to look straight down upon the slope of St. Michael's Hill, on which the walls were founded, and on the steep street winding below. But Mrs. Purcell had her nerves in the most steady and well-regulated condition. She was not afraid to sit at the head of the precipice, and even to look out and look down when the shop windows began to be lighted. She liked to see the lights coming out below. It was cheerful and felt like "company" when she sat alone. Old Pickering had just come in after an errand into the town. He was the man-servant, while she was the housekeeper, but the work of the establishment was chiefly done by a sturdy young woman who was under the orders of both.

"News—I don't know much about news," said old Pick. "It wants young folks to make news; and there ain't many of that sort about here."

"Dear!" said Mrs. Purcell (but it must not be supposed that this exclamation meant any special expression of affection to old Pickering). "There's heaps of young folks! There's the Signor, and there's my John——"

"Master? you may call him young, if it don't go again your conscience—my notion is as he never was no younger than he is now. So you may put what name to it you please. But you don't ask me for news of master, nor Mr. John neither—him, oh ah, there'll be news of him one of these days. He'll get a cathedral, or he'll be had up to London. We'll see him, with his baton in his hand, afore the biggest chorus as can be got together; and won't he lead 'em grand!" said old Pick. "When he was but a little thing in his white surplice I seen it in his eye."

"You were always one that did my John justice," said the housekeeper, warmly. "Just to think of it, Pick—one day a bit of a mite in his surplice, and the next, as you may say, with his baton, leading the chief in the land! We bring children into the world, but we can't tell what's to come of them," she added, with pious melancholy. "Them as is fortunate shouldn't be proud. The young men as I've seen go to the bad since I've been here!"

"That should be a real comfort to you," said Pickering, and they paused both, to take full advantage of this consolation. Then, drawing a long breath, Mrs. Purcell resumed—

"And so it should, Pick—when I see my boy that respectable, and as good as any gentleman's son, and reflect on what I've seen! But pride's not for the like of us—seeing the Lord can bring us low as fast as He's set us up." The good woman dropped her voice, with that curious dread lest envious fate should take her satisfaction amiss, which seems inherent in humanity. As for old Pick, sentiment was not in his way. He took up a little old-fashioned silver salver which stood on the table with some notes upon it, waiting the sound of the Signer's bell, and began to polish it with his handkerchief. "Them girls," he said, "there's no trust to be put in them. The times I've told her to be careful with my plate. She says she haven't the time, but you and me knows better than that. What is there to do in this house? We gives no trouble, and as for master, he's dining out half his time."

"She'll find the difference," said Mrs. Purcell, "when she's under a lady. There's many a thing I does myself. Instead of calling Maryanne till I'm hoarse, I takes and does it myself; but a lady will never do that. Ah, Pick, it's experience as teaches. They don't put any faith in what we tell them; and her head full of soldiers, and I don't know what—as if a soldier ever brought anything but harm to a servant girl."

"They are all alike," said old Pick. "There's them Despards in the Lodges—all the Abbey's talking of them. The Captain—you know the Captain? the one as sings out as if it all belonged to him—though he's neither tenor, nor alto, nor bass, but a kind of a jumble, and as often as not sings the air!" said the old chorister, with contempt which was beyond words. Mrs. Purcell looked upon the Captain from another point of view.

"He's a fine handsome man," she said. "He looks like a lord when he comes marching up the aisle, not an old Methusaleh, like most of 'em."

"Ah!" cried Pickering, with a groan, "that's the way the women are led away. He's a fine fellow, he is! oh, yes, he's like a lord, with bills in every shop in the town, and not a penny to pay 'em."

"Them shops!" said Mrs. Purcell. "I don't wonder, if a gentleman's of a yielding disposition. They offer you this, and they offer you that, and won't take an answer. It's their own fault. They didn't ought to put their temptations in folk's way. It's like dodging a bait about a poor fish's nose; and then swearing it will make up lovely, and be far more becoming than what you've got on. I think it's scandalous, for my part. They deserve to lose their money now and again."

"They say he's going to be married," said old Pick, stolidly.

"Married! You're dreaming, Pick! Lord bless us," said Mrs. Purcell, "that's news, that is! Married? I don't believe a word of it; at his age!"

"You said just now he wasn't a Methusaleh, and no more he is; he's a fine handsome man. He thinks a deal of himself, and that's what makes other folks think a deal of him. The women's as bad as the shops," said old Pick; "they bring it on themselves. Here's a man as is never out of mischief. I've seen him regularly coming home—well—none the better for his liquor; and gamblin' day and night, playing billiards, betting, I don't know what. We all know what that comes to; and a grown-up family besides— —"

"Dear!" said Mrs. Purcell, in great concern. She knew a good deal about Miss Despard, and her feelings were very mingled in respect to her. In the first place, to know that her John was in love with *a lady* flattered and excited her, and had made her very curious about Lottie, every detail of whose looks, and appearance generally, she had studied. A Chevalier's daughter might not be any very great thing; but it was a wonderful rise in the world for Mrs. Purcell's son to be able to permit himself to fall in love with such a person. On the other hand, Miss Despard was poor, and might interfere with John's chance of rising in the world. But anyhow, everything about her was deeply interesting to John's mother. She paused to think what effect such a change would have upon her son before she asked any further questions. What would Miss Despard do? It was not likely she would care for a stepmother after being used to be mistress of the house—would she be ready to accept anyone that asked her, in order to get "a home of her own"? And would John insist upon marrying her? and would he be able to keep a wife? These questions all hurried through Mrs. Purcell's mind on receipt of this startling news. "Dear! dear!" she said—and for a long time it was all she could say. The interests were so mixed that she did not know what to desire. Now or never, perhaps, was the time for John to secure the wife he wanted; but even in that case, would it be right for him to marry? Mrs. Purcell did not know what to think. "Did you hear who the lady was?" she asked, in a faint voice.

"Lady?—no lady at all—a girl that works for her living. I know her well enough by sight. One of the dressmaker's girls in the River Lane. Ladies is silly enough, but not so silly as that; though I don't know neither," said old Pick, "what women-folks will do for a husband is wonderful. They'll face the world for a husband. It don't matter what sort he is, nor if he's worth having— —"

"They haven't took that trouble for you, anyhow," said Mrs. Purcell faintly, standing up amid her preoccupations for her own side.

"I've never given 'em the chance," said Pick, with a chuckle. "Lord bless you! they've tried a plenty, but I've never given 'em the chance. Many's the story I could tell you. They've done their best, poor things. Some has been that enterprising, I never could keep in the same room with 'em. But I've kep' single, and I'll keep single till my dying day. So will master, if I can judge. There's some has the way of it, and some hasn't. It would be a clever one," said old Pickering, caressing his chin with an astute smile, "to get the better of me."

The housekeeper threw at him a glance of mingled indignation and derision. She gave her head a toss. It was not possible for feminine flesh and blood to hear this unmoved. "You're so tempting," she said, with angry energy. "'Andsome and well to do, and worth a woman's while."

"Bless you, they don't stick at that," said the old man with a grin. "I could tell you of things as has happened—some to myself—some to other folks— —"

"Dear!" cried Mrs. Purcell, "and me to think you were an old stick of an old bachelor, because nobody would have you, Pick! There's some, as a body reads it in their face—as dry as an east wind, and cutting like an east wind does, that is never happy but when it's blighting up something. I daresay it's all a story about Captain Despard—just like the rest."

"None of 'em likes it, when you speak free," said old Pick, chuckling to himself. "Some pretends, just to please a man; but women does hang together, whoever says different, and they none of them likes to hear the truth. About Captain Despard, it's a story if you please, but it's true. The girl she makes no secret, she tells everybody as she'll soon make a difference in the house. She'll pack off the son to do for himself, and the daughter— —"

"What of the daughter, Pick? Oh, the shameless hussy, to talk like that of a poor motherless young girl— —"

"If she wasn't motherless, what would Polly have to do with her? It can't be expected as a second wife should cry her eyes out because the first's gone."

"Polly!" said Mrs. Purcell, with bated breath; "and she says she'll pack the son about his business; and the daughter?—What is she going to do about the daughter, when she's got the poor misfortunate man under her thumb? And who's Polly, that you know so much about her? She's a pretty kind of acquaintance, so far as I can see, for a man as considers himself respectable, and comes out of a gentleman's house."

"That's the other side," said Pick, still chuckling to himself. "I said women hangs together. So they do, till you come to speak of one in particular, and then they fly at her. I don't know nothing against Polly. If the Captain's in love with her, it ain't her fault; if she wants to better herself, it's no more than you or me would do in her place. She's as respectable as most of the folks I know. To work for your living ain't a disgrace."

"It's no disgrace; but a stepmother that is a dressmaking girl will be something new to Miss Despard. Oh, I can't smile! A dressmaker as— — And young, I suppose, like herself? Oh, trust a man for that; she's sure to be young. Poor thing, poor thing! I'm that sorry for her, I can't tell what to do. A lady, Pick; they may be poor, but I've always heard there was no better gentlefolks anywhere to be found. And a woman that the likes of you calls Polly. Oh, that's enough, that's enough for me! A nice, good, respectable girl, that knows what's her due—you don't call *her* Polly. Polly—there's a deal in a name."

"Aha!" said old Pick, rubbing his hands, "I knew as soon as I named one in particular what you would say. Fly at her, that's what all you women do. A name is neither here nor there. I've known as good women called Polly as was ever christened Mary; eh? ain't they the same name? I had a sister Polly; I had a— —"

"Dear, dear!" said Mrs. Purcell, softly. She was paying no attention to him; her mind was much disturbed. She turned away instinctively from the gathering gloom of evening in which her old companion stood, and cast her anxious eyes upon the wide landscape outside—the sky between grey and blue, the lights beginning to twinkle far down in the steep street. There was something in the great space and opening which seemed to give counsel and support in her perturbation. For she did not know what to do for the best. At such a moment would not John have a better chance than he might ever have? And yet, if he got his heart's desire, was it quite certain that it would be good for John? The Signor's housekeeper was just as anxious about her boy as if she had been a great lady. Twinges of maternal jealousy, no doubt, went through her mind. If John married, he would be separated from his mother, and his wife would look down upon her and teach him to despise her—a mother who was in service. What could she expect if her son married a lady? All these thoughts went through her mind as she looked out with anxiety, which drew deep lines upon her forehead. But, on the whole, she was not selfish, and considered it all anxiously, ready to make any sacrifice for that which in the long run would be most good for John.

In the meantime old Pickering talked on. When he was set a-going it was difficult to bring him to a stop. He was quite aware that at the present moment he ought not to stay there talking; he knew he ought to be lighting the lamps, and kept listening with expectant ear for a sharp tinkle of the Signor's bell, which should warn him of his retarded duties. But for all that he talked on. Dinner was over for some time, and Pick knew very well that he ought to carry in the notes which he had piled again upon the salver after giving it that polish with his handkerchief. However, though he knew his duty, he took no steps towards performing it, but moved leisurely about, and put various articles back into the old polished cupboard with glass doors, which showed all the best china, and was the pride of Mrs. Purcell's heart. When Maryanne came in, he emptied the salver again and showed her how imperfectly she had cleaned it. "I can't think how folks can be so stupid," Pickering said. "How do you think you are ever to better yourself if you don't take a lesson when it's giv' you? and proud you should be that anyone would take the trouble. If I see it like this again I'll—I don't know what I shan't do." He knew very well that it was what ought to have been his own work that he was thus criticising, and, as it happened, so did Maryanne, whose spirit was working up to a determination not to be longer put upon. But for all that he found fault, (always waiting to hear the bell ringing sharply, with a quaver of impatience in it,) and she submitted, though she was aware that she was being put upon. Mrs. Purcell, in the window, paid no attention to them. She kept gazing out upon the wide world of grey-blue clouds, and asking herself what would be best for John.

They were disturbed in all these occupations by a step which came briskly downstairs, perhaps betokening, Pickering thought, that the Signor was going out again, and that his own delay about the lamps had been a wise instinct. But, after all, it was not the Signor's step; it was young Purcell, who came along the little winding passage full of corners, and entered the housekeeper's room, scattering the little party assembled there. Maryanne fled as a visitor from the outer world flies from the chamber of a servant of the court, at the advent of the queen. Though she would assure herself sometimes that Mrs. Purcell's son was "no better nor me," yet in his presence Maryanne recognised the difference. He was "the young master" even in Pick's eyes, who stopped talking, and put the notes back once more upon the salver with a great air of business, as if in the act of hastening with them to the Signor. Mrs. Purcell was the only one who received her son with tranquillity. She turned her eyes upon him quietly, with a smile, with a serene pride which would not have misbecome an empress. No one in the house, not the Signor himself, had ascended to such a height of being as the housekeeper; no one else had produced such a son.

"Go and light the candles in the study, Pick," said young Purcell. "The Signor is in the dark, and he's composing. Quick and carry him the lights. Don't bother him with those letters now. He is doing something beautiful," he said, turning to his mother. "There's a phrase in it I never heard equalled. He has been sitting out on the terrace getting inspiration. I must run back and keep old Pick from disturbing him, making a noise——"

"Stay a moment, Johnny, my own dear——"

"What's the matter, mother? Oh, I know; you've heard of this last offer. But if I take any I'll take St. Ermengilde's, where I could still go on living at home, the Signor says. It's less money, but so long as I can help him and see *her* now and again, and please you— —"

"Ah, John, your mother's last; but that's natural," said Mrs. Purcell, shaking her head, "quite natural. I don't complain. Is it another organ you've got the offer of? Well, to be sure! and there are folks that say merit isn't done justice to! John, I've been hearing something," said the housekeeper, putting out her hand to draw him to her; "something as perhaps you ought to know."

The young man looked at her eagerly. In this place he bore a very different aspect from that under which he had appeared to Lottie. Here it was he who was master of the situation, the centre of a great many hopes and wishes. He looked at her closely in the dusk, which made it hard to see what was in her face. He was a good son, but he was his mother's social superior, and there was a touch of authority, even in the kindness of his voice.

"Something I ought to know? I know it already: that Mr. Ridsdale has been visiting at the Lodges. That is nothing so extraordinary. If you think a little attention from a fashionable fop will outweigh the devotion of years!" said the young man, with a flush of high-flown feeling. He had a great deal of sentiment and not very much education, and naturally he was high-flown. "People may say what they like," he went on in an agitated voice, "but merit does carry the day. They've offered me St. Ermengilde over the heads of half-a-dozen. Is it possible, can you suppose, that she should be so blind!"

"That wasn't it," said Mrs. Purcell quietly; "it's something quite different, my dear. Shut the door, that we mayn't have old Pick coming in again (it was he that told me), and you shall hear."